D0348600

The Sun Witch

"Entertaining and imaginative, with a wonderful blend of worlds and technology and magic. The characters are different and engrossing; the villain is fascinating."
—*New York Times* bestselling author Linda Howard

"Charming . . . winsome . . . The perfect choice when you want a lighthearted and fun, yet sensual romance . . . with all the magic of a fairy tale." —*Bookbug on the Web*

"Fabulous . . . the story is spectacular and this author is unforgettable." —*Road to Romance*

"Let the fireworks begin! This whimsical, entrancing tale will satisfy the romance fan demanding something unusual and wonderful. With a skillful blend of the fanciful and the mundane, author Linda Winstead Jones weaves a marvelous tale of love and happy-ever-after, with a twist. Remarkable in imagination." —*Word Weaving*

"Amazing adventures unfold . . . Marvelously captivating, sensuous, fast-paced." —*Booklist* (starred review)

"Hot." —*Affaire de Coeur*

Prince of Swords

LINDA WINSTEAD JONES

BERKLEY SENSATION BOOKS, NEW YORK

THE BERKLEY PUBLISHING GROUP
Published by the Penguin Group
Penguin Group (USA) Inc.
375 Hudson Street, New York, New York 10014, USA
Penguin Group (Canada), 90 Eglinton Avenue East, Suite 700, Toronto, Ontario M4P 2Y3, Canada
(a division of Pearson Penguin Canada Inc.)
Penguin Books Ltd., 80 Strand, London WC2R 0RL, England
Penguin Group Ireland, 25 St. Stephen's Green, Dublin 2, Ireland (a division of Penguin Books Ltd.)
Penguin Group (Australia), 250 Camberwell Road, Camberwell, Victoria 3124, Australia
(a division of Pearson Australia Group Pty. Ltd.)
Penguin Books India Pvt. Ltd., 11 Community Centre, Panchsheel Park, New Delhi—110 017, India
Penguin Group (NZ), 67 Apollo Drive, Mairangi Bay, Auckland 1311, New Zealand
(a division of Pearson New Zealand Ltd.)
Penguin Books (South Africa) (Pty.) Ltd., 24 Sturdee Avenue, Rosebank, Johannesburg 2196,
South Africa

Penguin Books Ltd., Registered Offices: 80 Strand, London WC2R 0RL, England

This is a work of fiction. Names, characters, places, and incidents either are the product of the author's imagination or are used fictitiously, and any resemblance to actual persons, living or dead, business establishments, events, or locales is entirely coincidental. The publisher does not have any control over and does not assume any responsibility for author or third-party websites or their content.

PRINCE OF SWORDS

A Berkley Sensation Book/published by arrangement with the author

PRINTING HISTORY
Berkley Sensation mass-market edition/May 2007

Copyright © 2007 by Linda Winstead Jones.
Cover art by Danny O'Leary.
Cover design by Lesley Worrell.
Interior text design by Stacy Irwin.

ISBN: 978-0-425-21574-6

BERKLEY SENSATION®
Berkley Sensation Books are published by The Berkley Publishing Group,
a division of Penguin Group (USA) Inc.,
375 Hudson Street, New York, New York 10014.
BERKLEY SENSATION is a registered trademark of Penguin Group (USA) Inc.
The "B" design is a trademark belonging to Penguin Group (USA) Inc.

PRINTED IN THE UNITED STATES OF AMERICA

10 9 8 7 6 5 4 3 2 1

To the absolute joys of grandchildren.

Prologue

THE FIRST TWO OF THE PROPHESIED WARRIORS WHO WERE *called to the fight against darkness—the healer Ariana and the psychic Queen Keelia—have fulfilled their destinies, but they have not given up the battle against Prince Ciro and the demon that possesses his body. All that is left is for Lyr Hern, Prince of Swords, to wield the crystal dagger. When contemplating on the dagger and the questions of where and why, the answers did not come easily, not even to a psychic as powerful as Keelia. So she allowed Joryn to take her through the fire once more, to the land in-between where spirits spoke the truth and no dark interference clouded her mind. There she discovered the secrets of the dagger. She saw the weapon's location and its purpose.*

The crystal dagger was the only weapon in this world or any other which was powerful enough to take the life of the monster Ciro had become.

❊ The Prophesy of the Firstborn ❊

A darkness creeps beneath Columbyana and the lands beyond. This darkness grows stronger each and every day, infecting those who have an affinity for evil. As it grows stronger, it will also begin to affect those who are of weak mind, and eventually it will grow so strong no one among us will be able to defeat it. If this darkness is allowed to grow to this point, the world is doomed to eternal shadows, where evil will reign.

*

Only the firstborn children of three fine women *[later translated as Fyne]* have the power to stop the darkness and restore the world to light. These firstborn will be the warriors who lead the fight. Our fate rests in their hands, and in the hands of the armies they will call to them.

*

Of the three fine *[Fyne]* warriors who are called to this battle, one will find and wield the crystal dagger. One will betray love in the name of victory. And one, the eldest, will die at the hands of a monster who will hurtle a weary soul into the Land of the Dead.

*

Many monsters will rise from among us in this unholy war, soulless monsters such as the world has never seen. Heroes will be born and heroes will die. Death and darkness will threaten all those who choose to fight for the light.

*

Scribbled in the lefthand margin, in an almost illegible hand:

Beware Serrazone,

and beside it,

He who walks through fire may show the way.

Scribbled in the righthand margin:

Those who are called must choose between love and death, between heart and intellect, between victory of the sword and victory of the soul.

The remainder of the prophesy is illegible scribbling and indecipherable sketches. A scraggly tree; a bird with wings too large; a flower; a heart; a dagger *[The crystal dagger, perhaps?]*. Do they have meaning or are they simply a dying old man's insignificant doodles?

I

RAYNE HADN'T ATTEMPTED TO ESCAPE FROM HER PRISON for several weeks. In months past she'd tried everything from pleading with the old man who was on constant guard to attempting to physically yank the chains that bound her from the wall. Her jailer was deaf to her pleas, and she didn't even make the mortar rattle with her physical attempts.

She was doomed. Doomed to wait here in the dank cellar of her home until Prince Ciro returned to make her his bride. Doomed to helplessness. Doomed to rely on people who despised her for food, water, implements for the occasional attempt at bathing.

Rayne hadn't even known her father's odd guest was a prince until after his departure. The servant whom Ciro had left in charge of her care referred to him as "prince" often, and when Rayne had challenged the ridiculous notion, it had been explained that Ciro was indeed the only son of the Emperor Arik and next in line for the throne.

The man in question did not fulfill any of Rayne's notions of what a prince should be. From a distance, he had the outward appearance of a finely bred prince, she supposed, but his eyes were alternately dead or heart-stoppingly wicked, and his actions were not at all what she considered to be majestic.

Sitting on her cot, as she had all morning, Rayne stole a glance at the guard who kept constant watch over her. Jiri was an elderly man who had worked for her father for many years. A simple and quiet man, he'd always been pleasant enough in the past as he'd gone about his odd jobs on the grounds and in the house. She'd certainly never thought of him as threatening in any way.

The thin old man still didn't strike her as being at all fearsome, but he was mightily afraid of Prince Ciro. Jiri would not help her in any way, not if he thought the man who commanded him might be displeased. When Ciro had left this servant in charge of her care, he'd promised to drink his blood and eat his soul if he failed. That wasn't possible, she was sure of it, but Jiri seemed to think that the threat was a real one.

Jiri wasn't frightening, but there were others . . . others who remained above stairs, others who were devoted to the prince. She heard them often, their boots pounding and their laughter grating. There were many loud arguments, and daily noises which sounded as if they were literally tearing her home apart. These others never ventured into the cellar where she was imprisoned. For that, Rayne was grateful. Their distant laughter caused a chill which danced in her blood and down her spine.

Even though she was a prisoner, Ciro had gone to great pains to see that she was relatively comfortable. Her bonds were not too tight, though the shackles rubbed her wrists raw when she fought against them. There was a fairly comfortable if smallish bed, a few books, candles which were replenished as necessary, and plenty of food. In the early days of Rayne's imprisonment, a few of the maids who'd worked in this house before Ciro had incarcerated her had remained. These female servants were always skittish, and Rayne could understand why. They'd constantly sported bruises and small cuts on their hands and faces, injuries they refused to speak of when she asked. They'd brought food, and they'd helped her with her awkward baths, but there was none of the easy banter she remembered from the days before all had changed. Like her, they were helpless. The frightened girls followed orders, and were too afraid to so much as speak to the woman who'd been their mistress for many years. They didn't even dare to whisper.

The maids hadn't lasted very long, in spite of their devotion to their duties. In those early days, when Rayne still had hopes of escape, she'd sometimes heard screams from above. For many weeks past she'd heard only the soldiers. The women no longer came to her. It was now Jiri who fetched her food and water, and she saw to her own bathing with the inadequate rags and water he provided. She tried not to think of what had happened to the maids who'd done nothing to deserve their fate, but she knew in her heart that there was no one left to scream. No one but her. She was afraid her screams would bring the men from above down into the basement, so she remained quiet. Quiet and doomed.

Rayne's view through the one high, narrow window of the basement signaled the time that had passed. Summer was gone. She'd spent an entire season chained to the wall of her own cellar. Autumn, with its cooler winds and changing leaves, was upon them. What had become of her garden? She could not imagine that any of the coarse men above stairs would've bothered to tend it. Without watering and weeding and loving attention, her garden had likely perished long ago, the flowers wilting and the vegetables drying on the vine. Such a shame.

Perhaps it was silly to think of something so meaningless as her plants, but it soothed her to think of her garden. Rayne had always loved her time outdoors. She relished digging her hands into the dirt and watching things grow. Her mother had introduced her to gardening at a very early age, and in truth Rayne could not remember a time when she had not tended a garden or two. If she cared enough, she could urge things to grow even here, where the ground was often rocky and unfriendly.

Perhaps she'd loved her time outdoors because this house, her father's house, had always been oppressive in a way she could not explain. It was as if the air were heavier here, as if someone were always watching, as if something was always wrong. It was a fine house with many comforts, and still . . . she had never cared for her home much, especially not after her mother's death had taken all the light out of it.

Even now she remembered vividly the hours she and her mother had spent outdoors; she remembered the flowers they had grown, the vegetables they had nurtured, and the hours of freedom away from this house.

Being of agreeable spirit, Rayne had bided her time, taking comfort in her hours out of doors and dreaming of the day when her father would arrange a suitable marriage for her. When she had her own home, she would fill it with love and light, as her mother had tried to do here. Even if it was much smaller and plainer than this home where she'd been born and raised, she would make it agreeable.

That simple dream had begun to fade long before she'd been imprisoned. Rayne was almost twenty years old, and her father had never mentioned marriage. In the weeks before she'd been trapped here in this cellar, she'd begun to fear that her father intended for her to marry Ciro. Those two had spent much time together, locked in her father's study. Her father was a talented wizard who had always openly mourned the fact that his daughter, his only child, possessed no magic. Perhaps Ciro was a wizard as well as a prince, and when her father and the man who called her "beloved" were alone, they honed and practiced their magic.

The wizard Fynnian, who grieved because his daughter had no magical gifts, might've been planning to demand that she produce gifted grandchildren who would follow in his footsteps.

Rayne wanted no magic in her life. She wanted a simple marriage with an ordinary man, but that was likely a foolish desire. Her father would never allow her to marry anyone ordinary or simple.

Since the age of fifteen, she'd more than once thought of running away, but when faced with reality, she'd always been too afraid to confront what might await her beyond the walls of this home. In all her life she'd never been forced to fend for herself, and her father had always painted a bleak picture of what existed beyond these walls. She'd been spoiled horribly. Did her father realize that making her dependent upon him and his servants would keep her tied to him? Or was she simply weak of character? Her skittish nature had never before seemed to her to be egregious, but now, trapped as she was, she wished she'd been braver. She wished a thousand times that she'd followed her instincts and taken her chances in facing whatever awaited beyond the walls of this house.

Rayne looked again at haggard, elderly Jiri. Though he had worked in this household for many years, he was now Ciro's servant in a way she could not explain. She remembered the last time she'd seen Ciro, and she wished with all her heart that she'd run away from this place when she'd had the opportunity, that she'd taken a chance at discovering what lay beyond these walls.

As if her father would've allowed that to happen.

Ciro, who was young and handsome, well dressed and well spoken, had no life in his eyes. At first glance he was every young girl's dream, with long fair hair and lovely blue eyes, but when one looked into those eyes and saw only darkness, that dream became a nightmare. She could not think of anything else but those dead eyes when she remembered him and his last words to her, words that had followed a cold kiss and a terrifying grab at her breasts.

"We will be married," he'd said with confidence. *"There will be a priest of my choosing in attendance, and we will have a few witnesses as our guests. And if you do not happily agree in front of them all to be my wife, I will kill them one at a time until you do. I'll start with your father, if he lives that long."*

Her father had left this house with Prince Ciro at summer's outset, and she could not help but wonder if he had survived. There was no goodness in the man who claimed to love her. There was nothing even remotely human in the eyes of the man who called her "beloved." Rayne could very well imagine Ciro taking her father's life without a moment's regret. Perhaps if she and her father had been closer, she'd know somehow if he lived or not. More than eight years past her mother's death, there were times when Rayne was sure she felt her mother's spirit near her. She did not think she would sense her father's spirit in the same way, if indeed he were dead. A daughter should know, shouldn't she?

The sounds from above changed. A distant shout spoke of fear, but it was not of the type she had heard in the past.

Rayne glanced up, even though all she could see was a plain wooden ceiling reinforced in many places with sturdy rafters. As she watched, the ceiling shook slightly and dust drifted down.

Metal met metal, clanging even though the conflict was far away. Sword fight! This was unlike the brief skirmishes she had heard from above in months past, when those men fought among themselves. This was more intense, and it spread and continued long after a burst of temper would've ended. She was not the only one who realized that something had changed. Jiri drew a short sword of his own, but he did not run up the stairs to join the battle. Instead he placed himself before Rayne and adopted a defensive pose, ready to take on any who tried to rescue her.

Rescue. This was the first moment she'd dared to think of such a possibility. The house her father had built long before her birth was isolated and high in the mountains, no one knew that she was being held prisoner, and Jiri had told her that the men above were fearsome fighters sworn to do as their prince commanded. Even if anyone did attempt to rescue her, it was unlikely that they would succeed.

Did she dare to hope?

"Jiri, there is no reason for you to stand guard as you do." Rayne spoke in a calm voice, even though her heart pounded hard and she had not known *calm* in many months. "If the men above are defeated, then you do not stand a chance of winning against the intruders. You are a gardener and a carpenter, not a swordsman. If someone you do not recognize comes down those stairs, step aside. Surrender."

"I cannot," he said evenly. "You are to remain pure for Prince Ciro. No man is to come near his beloved before he returns to collect you."

Pure? Ciro himself was anything but pure, so why did Jiri seem so adamant that he was to protect that attribute in his intended? "I'm sure he would not want you to sacrifice your life. There are other women in the world, and I can be easily replaced."

The old man turned to look at her, and she saw the depths of fear in his eyes. "No, it must be you. The prince told me so, you see, before he left. You are pure of soul and heart and body, and you must remain so until he gives you a child on your wedding night. Why do you think the men above have not come down here in all this time? Why do you think Prince Ciro has allowed me to keep my soul thus far? He does not trust his Own to guard you. He's afraid of what they might do to you in a moment of rage or lust."

Rayne shuddered. She hugged herself with trembling arms, and the chains which bound her to the stone wall clanked gently. "What has Ciro promised you in return for this betrayal? What does my sacrifice gain for you?"

"Everything," Jiri whispered. "When you are wed to the prince, my wife and child will be returned to me, whole and alive after all these years in the Land of the Dead. There will be eternal life for all of us, and we will live together in a place so beautiful it would take your breath away were you allowed to see it."

"You know what kind of man he is," Rayne whispered.

"Yes."

"And yet you would sacrifice me for a promise that is impossible. The dead do not come back! There is no eternal life on this earth!"

"Ciro said . . ."

"He lied!" Rayne insisted. "Do you really believe that a man who threatens you as your prince did would reward you in such a way?" She yanked at her chains in frustration. "Release me, and while the others are fighting, we can escape."

"I can't," Jiri said. "Ciro will know. He knows everything,

and there is no hiding from those eyes. If I fail, if I run, he won't just make me pay, he'll take out his anger on the souls of my wife and child. I cannot allow that. I failed them before, when I let them die. I can't allow that to happen again."

Jiri was lost in his illusion that his long-dead family would be returned, that they could be threatened by whatever Ciro had become, when in fact the dead were the only ones safe from such a monster.

The sounds from above gradually faded, as the fight waned. Who had won? Did it matter? Even if the invaders defeated Ciro's men, would they be any better? Would their victory mean her rescue, or would she simply exchange one jailer for another?

The door at the top of the stairs opened, and solid footsteps pounded on the stairs. Rayne did not know what fate awaited her, but she was about to find out. Her mouth went dry. Her heart beat in an odd rhythm, as if it might stop functioning at any moment. After all she'd been through, it was unexpected that she could still experience such fear, but there was great fear in the unknown.

A bald and sturdy middle-aged man was the first to set foot in the basement where Rayne was kept prisoner. He held a long-bladed sword stained with blood, and wore loose pants, scuffed boots, and a purple vest which revealed a hairy chest and muscled arms. He'd been cut on one arm but ignored the bloody wound. The man was sweaty and breathing hard as he quickly surveyed the cellar and lifted his sword to challenge Jiri.

"Step aside, you old geezer." His oddly accented voice was rough and too deep. "I don't want to harm you but I will if I must."

"I will protect the prince's beloved with my life," Jiri said, his voice and his sword shaking.

The armed and bloody man sighed. "You can keep the

girl. We have no interest in her. We want the crystal dagger, that is all."

So much for rescue. "Please, sir," Rayne began, wondering if the rough-looking man had a heart beneath that broad, hairy chest.

"Silence, wench," the swordsman said without taking his eyes from Jiri.

"I am not a . . ." Rayne began haughtily, and then they were joined by yet another of the intruders.

This one was not middle-aged or bald. He was, in fact, so handsome he took her breath away. His dark hair was cut very short, and while he had muscles, they were not quite as oddly bulging as those of his companion. He was dressed in a similar fashion, in boots and dark pants and a purple vest over a well-formed but hairless chest. It must be some sort of uniform, but she was not familiar with the markings on his vest. The handsome man with narrowed eyes that seemed to see everything was much younger than the gruff bald fellow, and yet it was immediately evident that this new arrival was the man in charge. "Wench," Rayne finished in a whisper.

The bald man nodded toward Rayne. "I have found Prince Ciro's *beloved*," he said, his tone dry and disrespectful.

"She is promised to the prince; she is his betrothed," Jiri insisted. "Leave her be."

The younger man responded with a slight lifting of his eyebrows, and then he, too, readied his sword.

Jiri realized that he couldn't defeat the two men before him. For a moment, Rayne thought he would surrender, but she'd underestimated his devotion to—or his fear of— Prince Ciro.

"No one else shall have her," Jiri whispered.

The intruders were prepared to fight. They were not prepared for Jiri to turn the sword he wielded on the woman he had sworn to protect. All Rayne saw was the sharp blade of Jiri's sword moving closer to her throat so quickly she couldn't even find the time to scream.

LYR HAD LONG AGO SWORN NOT TO USE HIS GIFT IN BATtle unless there was no other choice. After all, it was an unfair advantage, and there was greater nobility in victory won on an even battlefield.

But when a woman's life was in danger, what choice did he have? He drew his power into a ball in his gut, and waved his sword in a sweeping arc. Time stopped. Time did not stop for him, but all else froze. Only he and those things he touched remained mobile. Above, all was silent, as footsteps and distant banter ceased. The birds which had been flying beyond the small cellar window stilled in midair, their wings and their song immobile.

Segyn had prepared to rush forward, but he would not have been fast enough. The old man's blade had swung too quickly, and the tip of that blade came within a hair's breadth of touching the girl's pale, slender throat.

Lyr stepped toward the girl. He'd been riding for weeks, and with his mission dominant in his mind, he had not so much as thought of a woman until this moment. She was fine, this one was. Very fine. Ciro's wench was petite and dark-haired and fair of skin, with rosy lips and nicely swelled breasts. There was an air of innocence about her, though he doubted very much that air held any truth. She was Ciro's woman, after all, and likely as much a beast as her betrothed, appearances aside.

With an easy hand, he moved the tip of the threatening blade away from the girl's throat and shifted the old man's body slightly. He tipped Segyn's blade aside as well. After all, it was possible the old man might know something about the dagger they had come here to collect, so it was best that he not die immediately.

Before swinging his blade again and setting the others into motion, Lyr took a moment, only a moment, to study the girl. Was she one of Ciro's Own, the soulless creatures Keelia had warned him about? If that was the case, why was she chained to the wall? She was a captive, and this dank cellar was her prison. And yet she was also apparently Ciro's beloved, his betrothed, his future bride.

She had parted her lips to scream, but the old man's sword would've cut that scream short. Now it would not. Lyr studied her fine lips, parted and soft and full and tempting, and though he had promised his mother he would use his extraordinary gift only in cases of dire emergency, he took a little extra time to trace the girl's lips with his fingertip.

"So very pretty," he whispered. "So tempting. Too bad you've aligned yourself with a soulless fiend." Chains or no chains, she was Ciro's and therefore the enemy in this important war.

Lyr stepped back, swinging his sword as he did so and allowing time to move forward once again. The old man stumbled forward and his steel blade met the stone wall. Segyn lurched and tripped, then circled about with an expression of disgust on his face. The girl screamed, but then she stopped suddenly, surprised into silence to find herself still among the living. Beyond the small window, a bird cawed. A step from above which had been stopped in midstride sounded. Lyr easily knocked the old man's once-threatening sword aside, then placed his own blade so that the geezer could not move without bringing about his own death. If the old man moved forward, Lyr's sharp blade would slice easily through his throat.

"I hate it when you do that," Segyn muttered as he righted himself and squared his shoulders.

"I will ask once more," Lyr said. "Where is the crystal dagger?"

"I know nothing of any dagger," the old man responded hoarsely. "You have made a mistake in looking for it here. Now go, and leave the girl and me alone."

Confused still, the girl remained silent. She didn't understand what had happened, and if all went well, she never would. People tended to treat him differently once they knew what he could do. He found it easiest to trust the knowledge of his abilities to a few. The girl before him was attempting to make sense of what had happened; he could see that in her eyes. She'd eventually assume that the old man's aim had been off and she'd only imagined that she'd been about to die.

"I am not leaving without the dagger," Lyr said. Keelia swore the weapon necessary to defeat Ciro was located here in this house. Somewhere. "You can tell me where it is and I will leave you to your business, or I can tear the house apart, stone by stone, until I find it."

The pretty girl squared her shoulders. "You will never find the dagger."

Lyr turned his eyes to her. "Have I been bargaining with the wrong person?"

The prisoner managed to look dignified, even though she was chained to the wall and dirty from a long period of neglect. "Yes, you have. I am Rayne, daughter of the wizard Fynnian and mistress of this house."

"She don't look like any mistress I ever saw," Segyn muttered.

The girl gave Segyn a withering look. "I have been held prisoner against my will for many months. Release me, take me to a place of safety, and I will see that you have the dagger you seek."

"Where is it?" Lyr asked.

"Not until I have your word," she said. "Promise me that you will take me away, that you will not leave me until I am safe, and I will deliver to you the crystal dagger."

Rayne, daughter of Fynnian, was Ciro's woman, but perhaps that was not of her choice. Lyr looked into her dark eyes, trying to find the truth there. Yes, she appeared innocent, but that wasn't what convinced him that she might be telling the truth. The girl was terrified, not of him and not of her jailer's blade, but of being left here to wait for Ciro's return.

"Your father is a wizard, you say. Do you have magic?" It would be good to know what he was taking on, if he chose to rescue her.

"None, much to my father's regret," she said.

Why had he bothered to ask? There was no guarantee that she was telling him the truth. For a long moment Lyr studied the girl. He had been taught not to offer his trust easily, and pretty women were not exempt from his caution. "Segyn, have Til and Swaine search for the dagger. I will wait here."

"Only two of your men to search?" Rayne said, seemingly unworried that they might find what they'd come here for without her assistance. "It won't be easy. You might as well command them all to tear the house apart."

"Two *is* all," Lyr said.

"Did Ciro's soldiers kill the rest?" she asked.

"Ciro's soldiers killed none."

That news did elicit a reaction, from the girl and from her guardian—the old man who remained against the wall with his throat at the tip of Lyr's sword. Rayne's surprise was evident, in her expression and in her words. "Four of you defeated all the men above? It has always sounded to me as if there were . . . many."

"There were eleven," Lyr said. "Twelve if you count this old man."

"Eleven of them and four of you, and yet you defeated them in short order."

"The Circle of Bacwyr does not know defeat, and such odds are not beyond our capabilities."

He could almost see the girl's mind working, and he was so focused on her face that he did not realize what the old man was about to do until it was too late.

Rayne's guardian thrust his head forward so that Lyr's motionless sword sliced through the artery there. The girl yanked against her chains, moving as far away from the grisly scene as possibly. She turned her head and screamed in horror, and when the scream ended, trailing away to nothing, she began to shake.

Lyr drew his sword away, as the old man quickly passed into the Land of the Dead—or wherever his tainted soul might be called—and watched the tears flow down Rayne's face. Were the tears real? His mother and sisters were not prone to shedding tears, but then again, they were unlike other women in his experience.

"Why do you cry for a man who kept you prisoner against your will?" he asked. "Is that the case, or did you choose your current position?"

Rayne, daughter of the wizard Fynnian and the monster Ciro's betrothed, glanced at him with an anger that hinted at strength beneath the petite exterior and feeble tears. "Before Ciro ruined Jiri with false promises and hideous threats, he was a good man. I do not cry for my jailer but for the man I once knew, a man Prince Ciro destroyed months ago."

Perhaps that was the truth, perhaps not. Lyr was oddly undecided about Rayne's character. Why had Keelia not spoken of her when she'd sent him so specifically to this house to fetch the crystal dagger? Why had she not told him what awaited him here? Keelia was a most powerful psychic, and a bit more information would've been helpful.

Ah, if only it could be that simple. If only Keelia and others like her could see which steps should be taken to bring victory, and which should be avoided. Instead they all were meant to stumble along and confront whatever surprises were met along the way. It was the way of life, or so he had been told.

Segyn carried Jiri's body up the stairs. Once there, he would order Til and Swaine to search for the dagger, and he would assist them.

Lyr pulled a chair—Jiri's chair, he assumed by its position—to the center of the room, where he could sit and study the girl who was chained to the wall. While he should join the others in the search, he wasn't certain it was safe to leave this one alone. She said she possessed no magic, but could he believe her? For all he knew, she was a pretty trap, chained to the wall moments before or immediately after he and his men arrived.

There was a brilliantly colored flower which grew near his home, the Ksana. This flower was more beautiful than all the others, and drew the eye with its color and the nose with its sweet scent. But the Ksana was poisonous. A momentary touch, and the skin would turn red and blistered, and if one were so foolish as to lay a petal against the tongue, illness, and possibly death, would soon follow.

As far as he knew, Rayne was like the Ksana flower. Beautiful, sweetly scented, and deadly.

If his men found the crystal dagger, he would not be obligated to accept her proposition and take her into his protection. If they did not . . . well, he would address that when and if the time came.

Rayne yanked against one chain. "Jiri kept the key to my shackles with his belongings." She pointed, and her chains rattled. "Over there."

Lyr nodded his head but did not rise from his chair.

"Aren't you going to release me?" the girl asked, indignation in her sweet voice.

"Not as of yet," Lyr responded calmly. "I haven't decided what to do with you, Rayne daughter of Fynnian."

Anger flashed in her dark eyes. "I thought you were an honorable man."

"I am honorable." He smiled. "But I am not gullible."

Again, tears slipped down her cheeks. Lyr studied the tears, unaffected by the display.

"If you would leave me here, then you are no better than Prince Ciro," Rayne spat in anger.

Lyr's smile died quickly. From all he had learned of Ciro and his plans, she had just uttered the greatest of insults.

2

THE JOURNEY TO ARTHES HAD TAKEN LONGER THAN HE'D imagined it would, thanks to his maddening traveling companion. Diella was insatiable in every way. She needed comfort, food, sex, and the drug Panwyr, and worse, she talked almost constantly.

Ciro would've strangled her with his bare hands if the Isen Demon had not forbidden it.

Diella was as yet unaware that she carried a special child within her. The child was the product of the former empress as well as the body she'd taken. It was the babe of the man Ciro had once been and at the same time it was the creation of the Isen Demon, which now ruled Ciro's body and mind. The child within Diella would not be as powerful or special as the son Ciro and Rayne would make when the time came, but it had a part to play—or so the demon claimed.

"Finally." Diella's single word spoke of disgust and impatience as they topped a small hill on the horses which

had carried them so far. Ciro knew she would not be satisfied with a *single word*, not in this or any other situation.
"At last the palace is before us. I will have a proper bath
straightaway, and new gowns will be made, and I will demand a soft bed with an energetic sentinel and a proper and
thorough fucking."

The body of the young girl Lilia, which had been taken
by Diella's soul months ago, had once been vital and beautiful. The scar Ciro had left on Lilia's cheek did not fade,
but grew deeper and redder with time, as if it had become
infected deep below the flesh. There was still some beauty
left on that young face, in spite of the scar, but the vitality
was being sapped day by day, sapped by Panwyr and hard
living and constant travel.

And by the babe, the Isen Demon whispered. *The babe
takes much.*

Their horses at a standstill, Ciro studied the palace
which rose in the distance. That imperial palace had been
his home, his only home, for twenty-two years, before the
demon had taken him. If there had been much of the man
he'd once been left in his body, he might have felt some
warmth or comfort at the sight, but he felt no warmth these
days, not for anything or anyone. Within the stone walls of
that tall, austere palace there waited his father the emperor,
who would soon be dead. There awaited the throne from
which he would begin his rule.

Suddenly a darkness crept into one corner of Ciro's
mind. He was able to see through the eyes of his Own
when he so chose, and though he could not immediately
tell where or how, some of his soldiers had very recently
been killed. They no longer saw anything. He tried to place
the darkness. His army had suffered some losses in weeks
past as they fought against his father's sentinels, but the
loss he sensed had not come from that quarter.

No, the loss came from much farther away; it came from the mountain home where his beloved Rayne waited for him.

He could not see through her eyes. She was pure; she was not one of his Own. Not yet. Did she live? Or had she died with those whose command had been to protect her at all costs?

Ciro turned his horse about. He was so close to the palace, and Rayne—if she lived—was so far away. But without her, there would be no special son. She was to be his empress; she had been promised to him from the beginning.

She lives, the demon whispered in his mind.

"How can you be sure? If I can't see—"

Do you think you are my only instrument, Emperor Ciro? You might be the strongest, the most promising. You might be my most powerful general in this war, but you are not my only vessel. Others watch. Others will see that your bride comes to you.

The startlingly clear vision in Ciro's mind was one of dark tendrils rising out of the ground all across the country, and beyond. Those tendrils claimed and took charge of willing—and sometimes unwilling—bodies. All across the land, by the sea and in the mountains and in the swamplands, those vessels waited to be called.

Take the throne, and Rayne will be delivered to you in good time.

It was Diella's grating voice which interrupted the demon's promises.

"Stop dithering about. Let's go claim what is rightfully ours."

Ciro would only stand so much, even from this woman. "I will claim what is rightfully mine, and you will take what I see fit to give you."

"Yes, yes," she said dismissively, waving her hand in his

general direction. "Let us go and claim what is rightfully yours, my lord emperor." Her smile was brilliant, only slightly crooked thanks to the scar.

RAYNE WAITED PATIENTLY, QUITE SURE THAT NONE OF Lyr's men would find the crystal dagger.

Her heart beat too fast and hard. It had been a long time since she'd thought about the dagger her mother had made so many years earlier. It had been a long time since Rayne had seen the weapon, and yet the details of the workings remained clear to her. Not only was the hilt made of a murky crystal, but so was the blade itself. The entire weapon had been carved from a crystal which was abundant on this very mountain. Rayne hadn't known it was possible to fashion such a dagger, but her mother, who never seemed to care much for weapons at all, had spent more than a year crafting the dagger this man sought.

She'd also kept her workings a secret, from her husband and the servants of this household. Even after death, Rayne had continued to keep that secret. Until now.

From above, the invaders made horrible, destructive noises. By sound alone she could tell that they tore apart furnishings and broke down walls. She should have been outraged, but was not. This house had ceased to be home long ago, and when she left here, she could not look back with any fondness. Would the soldiers find the dagger on their own? Possible, but unlikely. Her father was quite proud of his ingenious and secret hiding places, and Rayne had one of her own. So had her mother.

Rayne knew that her father likely had many secret hiding places she had never known of. For the most part, she did not wish to know what her father hid from her and others. While he had never confessed that his magic was of the dark sort, she knew Fynnian was not a good man. She knew that her father studied and practiced the darkest of enchantments.

But not her mother. Her mother had been light and good, and since she had crafted the crystal dagger with her own hands, then it, too, must be meant for goodness.

The swordsman who might be the answer to all her prayers seemed quite content to sit comfortably and wait for his men to complete their task. He did not seem the dark sort, but if he would ride away and leave her here, chained to the wall, alone and helpless . . . if he did that, then he was most definitely not an honorable man.

But if he agreed to see her to a safe place in exchange for the dagger, then she'd be in good hands. His four had beaten Ciro's eleven, and when Jiri had turned his sword on her, Lyr had responded very quickly. She'd been so sure she was about to die, and then . . .

"Prince of Swords," Rayne said, making conversation while his men searched above. "What sort of position is that?"

"In Tryfyn, Prince of Swords is the leader of the Circle of Bacwyr and war advisor to the King."

"What is the Circle of Bacwyr?" she asked.

"A brotherhood," he answered simply.

"A brotherhood of warriors?"

"Warriors, wizards, and a few witches."

"And you lead them all?"

He sighed gently, as if he were already tired of her questioning. "I lead the warriors, as did my father before me."

"You inherited the position when he died?"

"My father is very much alive. He stepped down from the position and now serves as an advisor."

"Tryfyn," she said, her tone conversational, as if she were not in chains and he did not hold her very life in his hands. "That accounts for the accent, I suppose."

"I have no accent," he replied. "Yours is quite lovely, by the way."

She did not argue with him that he was the one who spoke oddly, not her. Now was not the time. "You have mighty responsibilities for one so young."

"I was born to those responsibilities," he said, only slightly defensive. "And I suspect that I am older than you."

"Not by much, I'd wager." Since it was clear that he was a bit touchy about his young age, she let the matter die. Since he led men much older than himself, she could see why he might be sensitive about the subject.

Even though he was young, he did not appear to be foolish or capricious. His eyes were quite steady; they were narrowed and piercing and seemed to see all. They did not flicker with uncertainty or flit about. No, they were unwavering, ancient eyes set in a face which had not seen its first wrinkle. He moved as if he were in tune with his body, as if he would never make a misstep or stumble, as if he never wasted a motion or a word. If an artist were to draw the perfect male form, it would likely be just like his, strong and yet somehow beautiful—except for the hard eyes, which were much too piercing to be beautiful.

And yet those eyes were alive and real and she could almost see the soul resting there. In that way, he was very much unlike the man who claimed her as his own, and unlike her own father. She could entrust him with the dagger her mother had fashioned . . . couldn't she?

Certain that the men above wouldn't find the dagger, Rayne attempted to relax. Silent once again, she studied Lyr, Prince of Swords, from his short dark hair down to the tips of his dusty and very large boots. She had been sequestered in this house all her life, and had not known any men of this particular type. Her father's infrequent guests were usually older and more scholarly. In her latter days of freedom she had seen more armed men about the place, but they still had not been quite like this. Ciro had arrived young and handsome and fit, but he had never struck Rayne as being reliable and steady. Instead he was like the plants which grew wild and choked out the flowers, like a vine which sucked the very life from the tree it wrapped itself about. She shuddered at the picture of the face that came to her mind. No, young as he was, Ciro was not of this sort, not at all.

Lyr was a soldier through and through, a fighter, a champion. *Her* champion, perhaps? Was he truly a good man? Was he capable of protecting her from whatever Ciro had become?

What had Ciro become? He was no longer of the natural world, of that she was certain. His promises to eat Jiri's soul and drink his blood remained with her, as if he had just uttered the words in her ears. And Jiri's insistence that she must remain pure so Ciro could give her a special child on their wedding night was just as chilling. Most women might be pleased to know that a handsome prince wished to wed and impregnate them, but they had not looked into Ciro's eyes and seen the darkness there.

If she were not so pure, would Ciro still want her? Could she somehow make herself unattractive to him, and in doing so save herself from his intentions? Surely there were other women in Columbyana and beyond who possessed the pure soul Ciro seemed to need, women who would welcome his attentions.

No. Rayne shuddered. No decent woman would welcome those attentions, not from one such as Ciro had become.

She did wish to marry and have children someday, but she did not wish for them to be Ciro's children. She certainly did not wish to share a bed with him.

Though she was a quiet and well-behaved woman,

Rayne had always kept her eyes and ears open. In the past there had been many female servants living in this house. Her father had even kept a mistress here for a short while, but that odd woman had left in the middle of the night and never returned. In listening to the other women in the house as they spoke of personal matters, Rayne had discerned that lovemaking could be nice enough if the man was gentle and thoughtful.

Ciro would be neither, she suspected.

The man she studied now, the man who held her life in his hands . . . she wasn't yet certain about him, but she did not believe him to be evil, as Ciro was.

Hours passed, and Lyr Hern did not move from his chair, did not seem anxious about whether or not his men would find what they sought above stairs. The light outside Rayne's tiny window died as night fell. Gradually, the sounds from above lessened, as the men from Tryfyn ran out of places to destroy and search.

Segyn, the stocky bald man, finally came downstairs. The failure was easy to read on his face. "Nothing, my lord." His eyes flickered to her. "Should I pry the truth from her?"

It was a fear Rayne had not yet thought to suffer, that they might try to force the information from her through torture or intimidation. Fortunately she did not suffer that fear for very long, as Lyr shook his head at that proposition.

"No. In the morning, Rayne will lead us to the dagger and we will escort her to a place of safety, as she requests." With that, he turned to head for the stairs. "Don't leave her alone. Set up a watch so that she is under constant guard."

"You plan to wait until *morning*?" Rayne snapped, yanking once against her chains. "You're going to leave me here all night?"

At the foot of the stairs, Lyr stopped and turned to face her. "You claim to have been here for many months."

"Yes."

"Then one more night should be of no consequence. Your chains allow you to reach a comfortable-looking bed, and I spot a chamber pot beneath that bed. In a short while I will send down food for you and your guard. Everything you need is here, and knowing you are where you should be will allow me to get a good night's sleep."

Rayne pursed her lips. "You can trust me. You can—"

"Can I?" he interrupted. "No, I don't believe I can trust you, Rayne daughter of Fynnian, betrothed of Ciro."

She could argue that she had chosen to be neither, but Lyr appeared to be a man who did not change his mind often. "I will see you in the morning, then," she said calmly, moving toward her bed. She could endure one more night in this basement. She could wait a few hours before making her escape.

All that was left was to find a way to hide from Prince Ciro. Forever.

ONCE MORNING ARRIVED AND RAYNE WAS FREE OF HER chains, she became more obstinate, insisting that things be done her way. Lyr could've insisted with the tip of his sword that she immediately uncover the crystal dagger, but he did not. He studied her, trying to discern the true aspects of her personality. After all, he would be traveling with her for some time, in order to deliver her to a safe place. And where would that place be? He was not very familiar with Columbyana, aside from the few places he had been to visit family. Perhaps he could take her to the Southern Province and Aunt Sophie's family, but that was very much out of his way if he was to rejoin General Merin and the emperor's sentinels in the fight against Ciro.

Til stood guard at Rayne's door as she bathed and changed her clothes. His men had searched the house well, and there were broken pieces of furniture and holes in the walls to mark their passage. It was a shame, since this had obviously once been a very nice house. In the current situation, that could not be considered of any importance. Ciro had to be stopped, and the weapon which was hidden in this house was necessary.

Lyr paced in the hallway, patient at first, then less and less so as time passed. They needed to retrieve the dagger and begin their travels. Taking the woman would slow them down, and they did not have a moment to waste. He was to collect the dagger, rejoin Merin, and then march on Ciro.

According to the Prophesy of the Firstborn, it would be Lyr who took the demon's life with the crystal dagger. It was his destiny to destroy Rayne's betrothed. Perhaps it would be best that she not realize his purpose in seeking out the dagger.

Finally, she emerged from her room looking fresher and somehow daintier than she had when she'd entered. The dark blue gown she wore was, thank goodness, well suited to travel. The skirt was full to accommodate sitting a saddle and it was not too long; he could see her ankles above low-cut and apparently sturdy boots. Her hair had been pulled back and up in a simple style which would not require constant care. Perhaps Rayne was not entirely senseless, her association with Ciro aside.

Even though she had dressed sensibly, Rayne didn't look at all sturdy. She would not be able to travel at the pace to which he and his men were accustomed, and they could not afford to be slowed in their travels. The sooner he found a place to deposit her, the better.

"The dagger?" he said simply.

She looked him in the eye. "Give me your word that you will escort me to a place of safety."

"Again?"

"Yes, again. You have made it clear that you don't trust me. Why should I trust you so easily?"

"I give you my word, again, and I'm of the opinion that you have little choice but to take me at that word."

Rayne's chin lifted, and she appeared slightly defiant and very annoyed. "Follow me."

She led the way down the hallway, taking her sweet time, walking regally and with a gentle sway of her hips. She walked past disassembled tables and broken vases as if all was as it had been and should be. No, he did not trust her, but she was quite a woman in her own unique way. Why had Keelia not warned him of her? Why had she not told him that he would meet a woman who was trustworthy? Or not. If the danger was great, surely his cousin would've seen some warning. No, Rayne was nothing more than an annoyance, and he did not need the guidance of a seer to know how to handle that annoyance. He would keep his word, but he would also locate the place of safety she sought as soon as possible.

Rayne led him and the others into a large bedroom which was in shambles. She sighed as she surveyed the room, but did not stop to study what had once been a fine bedchamber. Part of the sad state was due to his men and their search, but there was long neglect at work here also. The men who had been living here for a long period of time, Ciro's Own, he assumed, had not been concerned with cleaning during their time in this house.

Rayne pushed aside a broken chair and gently kicked away a table leg. The tapestry which had once hung on the stone wall before her already lay on the floor, dusty and torn. "This was my mother's room," she explained as her pale fingers traced the grout between large gray stones. "After she died, my father refused to allow anyone to change things. He was not a loving man, but I do believe he cared for her in his own way. Otherwise, he would've turned the room into a study or a library, he would've married again and put another woman here, don't you think?" She glanced over her shoulder.

Lyr had walked with her into the room, but his men remained in the hall and at the doorway. "I have no idea what your father was like, nor do I care. He aligned himself with Ciro, that is all I need to know of him."

Again, Rayne sighed. "Are all men so dreadfully single-minded?"

Lyr did not bother to answer as Rayne's hand stilled on the wall.

"It's been a long time since I opened this secret hiding place. There are many like it throughout the house, but this one was my mother's. My father was a bit distrustful, and he kept many secrets."

"Even from you?" Lyr asked.

"Always from me," Rayne said so softly Lyr was certain that only he heard her response. "My mother kept her own secrets, but she shared them with me. I haven't been in this room for many years, but I remember well the last time we were here together." Her fingers pressed and then slapped again seemingly ordinary stone. She worked at the stone above and below the one she had chosen, with no results. "I know it's right here," she said, frustration creeping into her voice.

Lyr began to suspect that he'd been tricked. There was no secret hiding place, and this woman had no idea where the crystal dagger was hidden. Perhaps she thought he would take her with him in any case. Perhaps she thought him incapable of returning her to her basement prison. If that was her way of thinking, she did not know him at all. He would send someone back to release her when he was a few hours away, but if she did not produce the dagger, he would not take her with him.

Not that he could afford to leave this house without the crystal dagger.

"Rubbish," Rayne snapped, slapping her hand against the stone wall.

If all else had not been silent, Lyr would not have heard the gentle clicking noise or Rayne's sharp intake of breath. She worked at the stone again, and this time it swung open. The stone—which was not a proper stone at all—was hollow, and inside there rested a large blue gem on the end of a gold chain. He saw no weapon of any kind.

Rayne reached into the hollow rock. She took the necklace in her hand, and studied the gem as she removed it. "This was my mother's," she said softly. "She always said it would be mine one day. I had almost forgotten it." She dropped the jewel into a deep pocket of her gown, and then she reached again into the hollow in the wall, her hand delving into the shadows.

With reverence, she removed a weighty object wrapped in purple velvet. She held it with both hands, though it was not very large and did not appear to be horribly heavy. Rayne turned, and offered the object to him on outstretched hands. "If my memory has served me well, this is what you seek."

Lyr stepped forward and took the purple-wrapped object from Rayne's hand. She seemed oddly glad to be rid of it. With his back to his men, Lyr peeled away the fine fabric. Sunlight streaming through an uncovered window hit the crystal and blinded him for a moment. He closed his eyes and turned about so his body would block the sunlight, and with dots dancing before his eyes, he looked down at the weapon in his hand.

He had never seen anything like it, and for a moment he was awestruck. The hilt and the blade were carved from one piece of crystal. In some places the crystal was murky gray and pink, in others it was completely clear. The blade seemed to be very sharp, and he wondered how such a weapon had been crafted without destroying the stone from which it was made. It appeared to be fragile and mighty at the same time.

And then the colors inside the crystal began to move, drifting like clouds across the sky. A moment later, the weapon spoke to him in a voice only he could hear. In his mind it whispered, *I have been waiting for you, Prince of Swords.*

Lyr quickly rewrapped the weapon, and once it had been covered, the voice—and the certainty that the weapon was alive—was stilled.

"My mother made that dagger," Rayne said in a lowered voice.

"How?"

"I remember watching her work," Rayne said. "She began with a large crystal and gently worked away those pieces which were not necessary to the finished weapon, or so she said. Late at night in my room, by early morning's light in the garden . . . she worked."

"For what purpose?" Lyr asked.

For a moment, he thought Rayne would not answer, and then she said, "My mother was very much opposed to violence of any kind, but she said one day this weapon would be needed." Rayne shrugged her shoulders. "I was young. That is all I remember." She looked him in the eye. "I have never trusted another with this secret, but I trust you, Lyr Hern. Do not disappoint me."

Lyr did not want to be made to feel as if he owed this woman anything. "You mentioned that there are other such hiding places in this house," he said sharply, ignoring her offer of trust.

"A few, if they have not been found and ravaged in my father's absence."

"Show Segyn where they are." He turned to his first in command. "Use your discretion in choosing what to take and what to leave behind."

"Yes, my lord," Segyn responded. "M'lady, after you." He gave Rayne a sweeping bow and stepped aside so she could move into the hallway.

When he was alone, Lyr studied the silent object in his hand. He considered unwrapping the weapon to see if it would speak again when revealed, but in the end he decided not to.

He had always known that the crystal dagger he was meant to collect would possess some magic, but he had never expected that it had a life of its own.

Keelia was anxious to leave the palace in Arthes, but she had vowed to remain with her cousin Ariana as long as she was needed, and she was still very much needed.

When they'd arrived at the palace weeks earlier, Ariana's first responsibility had been to dispatch her younger sister Sibyl and their brother Bronsyn. Their brother Duran, who had returned to Ariana's army in the company of Lyr and a handful of Circle warriors, was to escort his younger siblings to safety before returning to the fight. Duran, a fine sentinel, was still irked that Ariana had sent him away before marching off to fight Ciro, but that didn't stop him from doing as he had been told. Keelia suspected that he'd expressed his anger to Ariana privately, but would not allow others to witness his demonstration of emotion.

Sibyl had served her purpose, keeping the emperor alive even though her talents as a healer were not enhanced as Ariana's were. The younger sister did have healing gifts, and she'd used them well.

Emperor Arik was now remarkably restored. It had taken more than one healing session with Ariana, and the sessions always left her horribly drained. But they had worked well, and Arik was fit once again.

And still, Keelia saw death around him. No matter what she or Ariana did, he would not live to see the first snow of winter.

Keelia stood at the window of her fine suite and looked to the east. "He watches," she said softly. "He watches and waits."

Joryn came up behind her and wrapped his arms about her waist. "Do we stay here and fight him?"

"No." Some things were meant to be and there was nothing to be done to change them. Some decisions made for the right reasons would lead to disaster. "Ariana is most desperately needed with the sentinels. Much as she would like to stay here and keep watch over her emperor, it is not meant to be." She glanced over her shoulder, glad for the strength Joryn gave her. "She cannot save him from what is meant to be, and neither can we."

All they could do was warn Arik that Ciro was no longer his son, that the thing inhabiting his child's body was a demon bent on destruction. The emperor's guards could be warned, the emperor himself could be warned, but in the end it likely wouldn't matter.

Ciro was coming, and he would take the palace.

3

SINCE LYR AND HIS MEN NEVER BOTHERED TO ASK IF ONE of those oddly disguised hiding places had been located in her bedchamber, Rayne didn't feel as if she were lying when she neglected to guide them to it. It wasn't as if what she'd retrieved from that particular space was of any consequence to them. They were personal items, keepsakes which had belonged to her mother. A few pieces of jewelry. A journal her mother had kept when she'd first married—a journal Rayne had read again and again, each time becoming entranced by the words which were filled with light, filled with the woman she remembered.

Words which abruptly stopped, midway through the journal. Rayne had often wondered why, but in her heart she knew. At this point, her mother realized what kind of man she'd taken as her husband, and she no longer wished to preserve her dreams and thoughts. The journal of those happier days was a wonderful remembrance of her mother.

The jewelry she might need to sell in order to survive, at least for a while.

Since Rayne had never been beyond the walls of her father's house, she wasn't sure how she would live after Lyr and his men left her in a safe but strange place. Perhaps someone would take her on as a housemaid, or she could find work on a farm of some sort. She'd always loved working outdoors, tending her garden and watching things grow, and she really wasn't afraid of hard work. Yes, that seemed almost an ideal solution. A farm. A simpler life.

First, she had to make her way down the mountain, and that was not as easy as she had thought it would be. While she had ridden on occasion, her outings had been limited to a small enclosed field beyond her garden. She was not an accomplished or adventurous horsewoman, and the trail which led from the house where she'd lived her entire life to the valley below was steep and treacherous. She held on to the saddlehorn tightly, waiting for the moment when she'd be thrown from the gentle mare.

Neither Lyr nor any of his men seemed to have trouble keeping their balance. They did not slip and slide, they did not even wobble. Annoying as he was, she could not help but think that she'd chosen wisely in picking her rescuer. Lyr Hern was more than capable. The dagger her mother had fashioned was in good hands.

Her entire life was about to change. Rayne was certain, deep in her heart, that she would never make the journey back up this mountain to the only home she had ever known. Her father had left here with Ciro, and she had no doubt that the man who claimed her as his beloved was not only dark, but *evil*. Wrong to the pit of his soul. Even if her father managed to come to his senses and extricate himself from the prince, a return to their previous lifestyle would not be possible. Unless Lyr and those he fought alongside defeated Ciro completely, she would never be entirely safe.

Jiri had been insistent that Ciro planned not only to wed her, but to give her some sort of special child. Rayne shuddered and almost slipped off the saddle. She could only imagine what sort of child a monster like Ciro would consider "special."

Lyr remained as silent as she, but his men spoke often. Riding all around her, one directly ahead and one behind, with Segyn and Lyr leading the way, they bantered. They laughed. They spoke nonchalantly of battles to come and relived old ones. Even though she was located in the midst of them, they ignored her completely. Lyr was well ahead at the front of the party, so that all she could study of him was the back of his head and his squared shoulders. Since his hair was cut so short, she could see the strength in his neck and the muscled curves of his shoulders. Studying him, she was certain she had never before known a real soldier. Not Ciro, not any of her father's men. None were like this one.

Perhaps she thought so highly of him because he was her only chance at survival, and believing him to be extraordinary offered her momentary relief.

As they reached the end of a particularly difficult stretch of the trail, and the path leveled for a distance, Lyr turned to look at her. His stony expression was difficult to read, but she suspected that if she had fallen from the mountain and perished, he would not have shed a single tear for her.

A soldier such as this one, a fighter through and through, would likely not shed a tear for anyone.

THEY MADE CAMP MILES EARLIER THAN WOULD'VE BEEN necessary if they didn't have a woman in their party. Lyr pushed the annoyance aside. Bringing Rayne along was unavoidable. Without her he would not have the crystal dagger in his possession, and the weapon would be necessary when he faced Ciro.

He should not ponder what might take place when that meeting occurred, but he couldn't help it. Though he had trained all his life in order to reach this position and this level of skill, he was not a battle-hardened warrior like Segyn, who was older and had fought among the clans before peace had been forged. Even if he had been more experienced in true battle, he had certainly never faced anyone—anything—like Prince Ciro. Keelia said the prince was possessed by a demon who collected souls from his victims, who drank blood, who would turn the world to darkness, given the chance.

Segyn was currently on watch, while Swaine and Til slept. They had spent many nights on the ground, and had no difficulty making themselves comfortable for the few hours of sleep they would be allowed. Even Rayne had settled down very quickly, though he suspected she was not accustomed to such conditions. At least it was not too cold nor too hot. The weather, in fact, was quite nice tonight.

Rayne seemed harmless enough, but he still did not trust her. Ciro claimed her as his betrothed. Why would he claim Rayne as his own if she was not as dark as he? Why would he so fiercely protect her, sparing a dozen men he could've used in battle to watch over her? It did appear that she'd been imprisoned, held against her will, but Lyr had been taught not to rely on what things *seemed* to be.

All he could see of his charge at the moment was her back and a long expanse of silky dark hair. When loose, it would fall past her waist, but she usually had it tied up this way or that. Had Ciro chosen his intended bride simply for her beauty? There were many beautiful women in the world, so that seemed unlikely. Had he chosen Rayne for some magic she'd hidden thus far? That seemed most likely. Ciro probably wanted to merge his own dark power with whatever gifts the wizard's daughter possessed.

As he watched, Rayne rolled over. By the light of the low fire he could see that her eyes were wide open. She was not having such an easy time sleeping, after all. For a long moment she watched him. He did not look away; he did not pretend that he hadn't been watching her. After a short while she sat up slowly and studied the rest of the camp. She looked at the two sleeping soldiers and watched Segyn pace near the most vulnerable section of the perimeter.

Instead of assuring herself that all was well and lying down once again, Rayne left her makeshift bed and walked toward Lyr.

He stiffened his spine and steeled his resolve. No matter what she said, he would take her no farther than the closest safe farmhouse or village—whichever came first. He would not, could not, personally deliver her to Prince Ciro. The sooner she was out of his care, the better.

She sat on the ground near him, but not too near. "I cannot sleep," she confessed, keeping her voice low so as not to disturb the others.

"We will ride again as soon as there's light in the sky, whether you sleep well or not."

She sighed. "I was not asking for special treatment, just . . . just . . ."

"Just what?" he snapped.

Her eyes caught and held his. "I need someone to talk to, and you claim to be an honorable man. My mind is spinning with questions and possibilities, and that is why I can't sleep. You're not sleeping either, and I thought that perhaps if we talked for a while, my mind would settle."

"Fine," Lyr said. "Talk."

He did not expect her to smile so widely, not after all that had happened. And yet she did smile. "You are not much of one for conversation, are you?"

"No."

"Why not? There's much to be learned in vibrant conversation with another person."

"I have two younger sisters, and they talk enough for all of us."

"Sisters," she said warmly, the word rolling off her tongue with what seemed to be joy. "Tell me about them."

He did not trust her enough to share family secrets, and he wasn't certain it was safe for her to possess too much information about him or his family. "I'd rather not. Instead, why don't you tell me what thoughts are keeping you from sleep?"

She seemed disappointed, but not horribly so. "Before you showed yourself to me, while you battled Ciro's soldiers above my head, Jiri revealed some information that raises more questions for me than it answers."

"Such as?"

Her brow wrinkled a little. "What does it mean for one's soul to be pure?"

He was surprised by the nature of the question. "I suppose that depends on your religious beliefs." There were many different religions practiced in Columbyana and Tryfyn, some worshipping The One God, others worshipping many gods. All of them believed in the existence and the importance of the soul and the afterlife, but the Prince of Swords had not undertaken a study of theology in his years of training. "They all strive for purity of the soul, I suspect, unless the religion is of a dark sort. I have heard of such dark religions."

She looked into the shadows beyond their camp and nodded, but she did not seem satisfied with his answer. "If one wanted to tarnish a pure soul, how would they go about it?"

"Perhaps you should ask your sweetheart," Lyr said darkly. "I believe the tarnishing of souls is one of his attributes."

Again, Rayne looked at him boldly. "I know you don't trust or believe me, but I will tell you again that Prince Ciro is not my *sweetheart*." She pursed her lips tightly. "Jiri said . . ." She stopped speaking and again pursed her lips. "Never mind. I'm wasting my time speaking to you. You're not going to believe anything I say, no matter how hard I try to convince you that I did not choose to be affiliated with Prince Ciro."

"In a few days we will find a safe place for you, and I'm certain you will find many fine conversationalists there."

She looked disappointed, though there was no reason for her to be disappointed in him. His obligation was to escort her, not to charm her with insightful conversation and ease her bedtime fears. Asking how one might go about tarnishing a pure soul did nothing to convince him that she was not willingly aligned with the enemy.

"You know much of Prince Ciro, it seems," she said, and her eyes widened a little. "What can you tell me of my father?"

He could easily lie to her and tell her he knew nothing of the wizard. Until now it had been easy enough to avoid the subject, simply not telling her all that he knew. But Lyr did not tell falsehoods, not even to make his own life easier. If she had not asked, then he could not consider his silence a lie. But once the subject was broached, he had no choice.

"I was told by a powerful seer that the house where I was to collect the crystal dagger was once the home of a wizard who is now deceased. I'm sorry."

Tears filled her eyes, but did not fall. "Do you know who killed him?"

"No."

"It wasn't . . . you, was it?"

"No. From what Keelia said, I believe your father was killed before I even knew of this battle."

Rayne's head dropped. "I'm not surprised to hear that he's dead," she whispered. "My father was doomed from the moment he involved himself with Prince Ciro."

"Are you similarly doomed?" Lyr asked without kindness.

This time when Rayne looked into his eyes, tears ran down her cheeks. "Yes, I believe I am. If Ciro is as power-ful as Jiri claimed him to be, then there's nowhere I can hide that he won't find me. If he wants me badly enough, then there is no safe place."

So, that was her game. She wouldn't be satisfied to be deposited at a farmhouse or a small village. She was going to claim that there was no safe place for her, and therefore in order to fulfill his part of the bargain, he would have to keep her with him.

Pretty as she was, vulnerable as she seemed to be at the moment, that was impossible. The sooner he was rid of her, the better. "Then you'd best hope that this dagger does what it's supposed to do. If that is the case, you won't have to worry about the prince's intentions much longer."

By the light of the fire, her eyes became livelier. "The crystal dagger is to take Ciro's life?"

"Yes." He watched her for some reaction, and saw only apparent relief.

"I should not wish anyone dead, but when we're speak-ing of Prince Ciro, when it means an end . . ."

"Try again to sleep," Lyr said when Rayne faltered. "I need a couple of hours myself. Morning will soon be here."

"Yes. Yes of course." She rose silently and returned to

her bedroll, again settling down with her back to him. While she had boldly looked him in the eye more than once on this night, she did not do so again.

SHE WAS ALONE. ENTIRELY, COMPLETELY ALONE. NOT THAT she'd expected her father would be of any help where Ciro was concerned, but still . . . he was her father. He *had been* her father, if Lyr was correct about the house belonging to a dead wizard.

Whether or not Ciro had been the one to kill her father, he was certainly responsible. Rayne believed that to the pit of her soul. Her supposedly pure soul.

Soul, heart, and body, Jiri had said.

Was wishing Ciro dead enough to tarnish her soul or her heart so he no longer found her desirable? Surely wishing another person dead was a sin of some kind. What kind of trade would she be making if she ruined her soul simply to make herself unattractive to the monster? She'd be trading one damnation for another.

But at least it would be a damnation of her own choosing.

The path they traveled was not as arduous as it had been in the past two days, and Rayne no longer felt as if she were in danger of plummeting to her death. And yet today she trembled. She'd never been truly alone in her life. Her childhood had been a good one, with a loving mother and a protective—if often absent—father, and many attentive servants. After her mother's mysterious illness and resulting death, her father had not become more loving, but he had remained protective, as a father should be. As she'd grown older and taken over the duties as woman of the house, she'd had not only her father but the companionship of servants who were more than servants to her. They were her family as much—perhaps more so—than her father.

And now they were all gone, all gone thanks to Ciro and his soldiers, and she was entirely alone in the world. She had nowhere to go, no one to turn to. She couldn't even engage her reluctant rescuer in a decent dialogue to pass the hours of an unbearably long night.

Last night, the second night since their departure, she hadn't even attempted such foolishness but had pretended to go directly to sleep. If anyone had heard the tears she tried to hide, they hadn't let on.

As sunset colored the sky before them pink, she thought of ways in which she might tarnish her soul or her heart enough to make herself unsuitable for Ciro's intentions. Were the vengeful thoughts enough? Or did she need to take her plans further? What sins would tarnish one's soul?

Blasphemy, murder, theft, coveting, an abundance of arrogance, wanton destruction of beauty . . . lust.

She blushed simply thinking about such things, but also realized that now was not the time for timidity. If she did not want to end up married to a monster, trapped in his life and his bed and bearing his children, then she had to do something.

Not murder. She set that possibility aside quickly. The very idea of taking another's life was repugnant. Lyr and his men had killed in battle, but their cause was good. She didn't think that sort of killing counted as a sin, but even so . . . she didn't think she could lift a hand in that situation.

Blasphemy might be easy enough, but would that alone be enough?

Jiri had also insisted that she be pure in body, and she knew very well what it would take to undo that particular purity. Still, perhaps that could be called upon as a last resort. Surely a lesser sin would do the trick.

Rayne turned her head and looked at the soldier who rode closest to her. Til was nice enough, though he was also tough and she did not fool herself into thinking he considered her anything other than cargo to be transported from one place to another. He would be handsome enough for a man of his age if not for the scars on his arms and chest and the crookedness of his oft-broken nose. He wore his long brown hair in a sloppy braid.

She lifted her chin. "When are we going to damn eat?"

His reaction was subtle, but there *was* a reaction. Deepset eyes sparkled. "I beg your pardon, m'lady?"

"When are we going to damn eat?" she asked again. The heat of a blush rose to her cheeks.

"We'll have a quick bite in a couple of hours," he said. "Pardon me for saying so, m'lady, but if you wish to pepper your language with curses, it is best to do so with vigor and without the blushing."

"I did not know there were rules."

"Not rules so much as commonly accepted procedures," he said seriously. "For instance, if you wanted to make a point at this time, you should say, 'Damn it all, you cursed ass-kissing scalawag, when are we going to fuckin' eat?'"

She felt herself blush again, and she knew the reaction showed when Til grinned widely. "I'm not sure I can say that," she confessed.

"If you wish to take up cursing, you should attempt to do it well," Til said, a touch of censure in his voice. "Cursing is like swordplay or a woman's sewing or any other skill. One must throw oneself into the activity with enthusiasm, or else why bother to curse at all?"

"You do have a point. Perhaps, as this part of the journey is less arduous and demanding, you might give me . . . lessons."

"Lessons on cursing, m'lady?"

"Yes, please. If you wouldn't mind."

"Fuck no, I don't mind."

Rayne wrinkled her nose. "I do hate to be finicky, but can you teach me to curse without using *that* word?" She had heard the cook rail against a stableboy once for using that word, and had come away certain it was not a word fit for a lady's ears. It wasn't as if she hadn't heard enough cursing from the servants when they thought she wasn't listening. It was one of the advantages to being quiet and unobtrusive. "A few damns and sh . . . shits should be sufficient." She hoped that was the case.

Til sighed. "It won't be the same, m'lady, but I can give it a try."

"Thank you," she said, certain that she had found her first true friend among the Circle of Bacwyr warriors. "You may begin."

ARIK WAS NOT SURPRISED WHEN THE HIDDEN DOOR which opened from a secret stairway into his bedchamber opened and Ciro emerged. His son knew all the hidden passageways and secrets of this palace which had always been his home. Before she'd left the palace, Ariana had warned him many times that though Ciro might appear to be his son, that was no longer true. She said that Ciro's body was now home to the Isen Demon, and would show him no mercy.

But as Arik looked into Ciro's eyes, by the light of the candles which kept his room from darkness, he saw only his son. Twenty-two—no, now twenty-three—years old, a young man still, in spite of his responsibilities as prince and his position as next in line for the throne. Handsome, with much of his mother in his features. He certainly had her hair, straight and fair and spun like gold, and he had her pale blue eyes. He'd grown in his time away from the palace, grown taller and broader, as young men sometimes did.

Ciro smiled at him, and all Arik saw was his son. Not a demon, not an ambitious prince. He saw the child who had sat on his knee, who made friends among the servants and sentinels' children. He saw the baby he'd held in his arms at birth, and the young man who had studied so ardently to become a worthy ruler. He saw it all as if it had happened yesterday, not years past. Had he spoiled his son? Yes, he had, but that did not mean what stood before him was a monster.

One shout, and a dozen sentinels would rush into the room and place themselves between Ciro and Arik. The emperor considered raising his voice, but then Ciro stepped toward him gently, smiling the entire time.

"Father, I've missed you."

Arik sat up and swung his legs over the side of the bed. "I've missed you, son. I swear, I believe you've grown quite a bit since last I saw you." Ciro had always been thin, but he was not too old to have a growth spurt, and apparently that had occurred.

He stood, glad that Ariana's healing work had made him stronger so that he could stand on his own and face his child. "We have fallen upon difficult times. I beg you, tell me that what I hear is not true."

Ciro hung his head. "I swear that what you hear is not true, Father. A demon did try to take me, but I fought it off. I gathered all the strength you gave me to my heart and I drove the demon away. I have come home to ask your forgiveness for the injustices I have committed."

Arik sighed in relief. Ariana had been wrong, they had all been wrong. Yes, Ciro had fought a difficult battle, but he'd won. He'd bested the demon and returned home, and soon all would be as it should. He would sit on the throne for a few more years with his son at his side, training for the day when Ciro would take that duty. That right.

A young woman stepped through the doorway and surveyed the room with critical eyes. She was pretty enough, but there was a nasty scar on her face and she was much too thin. Her clothes were ragged and dirty, but then she had been traveling. He supposed that explained away her state.

"Who is your friend, Ciro?"

"This is Diella."

An unfortunate name. "My brother was once married to a woman by that name, when he was emperor. If what I hear is correct, she seduced a sentinel and tried to have my brother killed."

The young woman grinned, crookedly thanks to the scar on her cheek. "Actually I seduced many sentinels, and once I tried to kill that bastard Sebestyen myself."

For a moment, Arik did not understand. His mind didn't know how to accept her words. By the time he began to make sense of her claims, Ciro was upon him. The child, the man, moved quickly.

Ciro—whatever Ciro had become—was very strong. He clamped a powerful mouth down on Arik's throat, he broke the skin and slurped hungrily at the blood that poured from that wound. Arik tried to shout, and could not. His voice was frozen, as was his body. He was able to shift his eyes to the side and see that Diella watched with an evil smile on her face.

Darkness crept upon Arik quickly as his blood was drained. He should've remembered all of Ariana's warnings. He should've been stronger of spirit when he'd looked into his son's face. Perhaps he had been fated to this moment. What man can look into a face of a child he loves and see the demon?

Was anything of Ciro left in the body that restrained and attacked him? His son would never do something like this, not to him, not to anyone. Ciro was a good man, a good, noble prince.

Arik forced a word past his numb lips. "Son."

Ciro yanked his head away from Arik's throat. Blood stained his lips, and darkness filled his eyes. Black had taken the place of his mother's pale blue. "Father," he responded without emotion, and then bloody lips curved into a smile.

"Finish it," Diella ordered sharply. "The sooner it's done, the sooner you'll be emperor. Taking the palace is a major victory."

"Maybe I should keep him alive for a while," Ciro said thoughtfully. "Maybe I should allow the emperor to survive long enough to see all that his son has become."

Diella scoffed. "Don't be ridiculous. Finish him off so we can get started." She surveyed the room. "Is this the nicest room, do you think? I don't care for the colors. I do prefer blue."

Suddenly Arik wished for a quick death. He did not want to see all that his son had become. He did not wish to watch as evil took this palace where he had worked so hard to bring goodness.

"I haven't taken his soul yet," Ciro said casually. "I think I'll let him live awhile longer."

Diella spat on the floor. "You're only saying that because I told you to finish him off. Well, fine. Play with him all you'd like, but I am taking control, and I will have the proper bath I've been denied for so many weeks."

Ciro seemed to have forgotten Arik, yet still the emperor could not move. "That body you've taken has likely never had a proper bath, and I will be as happy as you are to see that task accomplished."

Diella ignored the insult. "So we leave the emperor alive for now. What is our next step?"

Ciro sat on the side of the bed, dropping Arik's limp body beside him. He closed his eyes and lifted his chin. "Now I call my legion to my side. Ciro's Own will soon rule the palace. They will soon rule all of Arthes. Many of them are already here, waiting. Waiting for this moment." He grinned, and his body twitched, and Arik finally accepted that if there was anything left of his son, it was buried so deeply in this damned body it would never again see the light of day or goodness.

Ciro looked down at Arik, and the emperor could feel his son—whatever his son had become—pushing into his very mind. He fought, but it was difficult and painful. Was that why he had ignored all of the warnings? Was it the demon who had pushed memories of the past into Arik's mind?

"Do you know where Ariana has gone?" Ciro asked. "That bitch has been snatching away souls I once called my own. She's making it very difficult for me to attain the strength I should now possess. What of the army? Do you know of their plans?"

No matter what happened, he would not tell. To foolishly sacrifice his own life was bad enough, but he would not aid the demon in defeating the others. Arik attempted to shake his head, and managed little more than a tremble.

Ciro did not seem concerned. "I can get the information from you, Father, one way or another." The eyes which were sometimes that lovely pale blue went black once more.

Again Arik wished for a quick death, but death was not coming for him. Not yet. This thing had other plans for him.

Arik had been fighting death for months, and now . . . now he prayed for it to come. Death would be easier than watching a thing which had once been his child destroy everything he had worked for. Death would be easier than looking into those black eyes.

4

LYR NARROWED HIS EYES AND STUDIED HIS CAMP. ALL was not as it should be on this cool autumn night. There had been no sign of trouble from Ciro's followers thus far, and thankfully Rayne had not attempted again to draw him into friendly conversation.

But she had been speaking regularly to Til and Swaine, who now smiled at her on occasion and asked too often about her comfort and her disposition.

If they began to care about her, would they protest if she balked at being left behind?

It didn't matter. They were his soldiers, and no woman would come between Circle Warriors. Would innocent-looking Rayne be foolish enough to try to seduce one or both of the soldiers to her side? If so, she wouldn't be the first woman to use her body to bind a man to her, to make him her slave.

Circle Warriors were not easily swayed, but neither were they made of stone.

Segyn had walked the horses to a nearby stream. He could've ordered one of the other men to take care of that chore, but Lyr's first in command had always been fond of animals and had been caught speaking to them on more than one occasion. He took some comfort in the chore, so Lyr allowed him to do as he wished. Swaine and Til prepared supper for all, such as it was. The meal consisted of dried meat and hard biscuits, and until they came across a village where they might purchase fresh food, it would serve them well enough. Til gave Rayne a plate and nodded toward Lyr. Lyr was not blind to the fact that both of his men were suppressing smiles, and not doing a very good job of it. Had Rayne's seduction already begun? Were they so totally entranced by her? She was the kind of woman who could entrance a man if she wished.

Rayne walked toward him with the tin plate held steady in both hands, as if she were serving a fine meal instead of dried food that wouldn't be at all damaged if she tossed it to him from the opposite side of the camp.

When she was close, Rayne spoke. "Here's your damned supper, m'lord. I hear it tastes like shit, you cranky old bastard." Her face turned bright pink, and her nose twitched a little.

Lyr lifted his eyebrows. "I beg your pardon?"

"I said, here's your damned—"

Lyr took the plate from her. "I don't need you to say it again."

"Then why did you ask?"

Guffaws burst from Til and Swaine as they released their contained laughter. Til snorted, and Swaine slapped his knees in childish delight.

Rayne turned to her new friends. "How did I do?" she asked primly.

"Well," Til said between snorts, "it was a fine start,

though I think your voice could use a bit of a Tryfyn accent when you say 'old bastard.' It should sound more like *ol' bastid*," he said, exaggerating the inflections.

"Ol' bastid," she repeated as she returned to her compatriots. She lifted her skirts in a ladylike manner as she stepped over a fallen tree limb dainty as you please. No matter how she tried, the vile words she spoke still sounded prim and proper.

Lyr set his plate aside and stood, and in a few long strides he had joined his men and the maddening woman they escorted. "Explain," he said simply.

" 'M'lady wishes to know how to curse properly," Swaine explained. "We've been giving her lessons."

"Lessons on cursing," Lyr repeated. "May I ask why?"

"No you may not," Rayne said with her nose in the air. "My reasons are none of your concern."

Til shook his head. "You missed a perfect opportunity for a natural 'damned' in that sentence, and if you'd thrown in a—"

Lyr lifted his hand, and his man instantly went silent. All was silent, heavily so. The faces of his warriors went still as they realized the depth of his anger. Why was he angry? Passing the time teaching curse words to a lady who apparently wanted such instruction was hardly an offense. What was her reasoning? What did she have planned? He was quite certain she had some nefarious plan at play.

The first sound to break the silence was Rayne's heavy sigh. "Well, damn," she said, and the curse sounded almost natural flowing from her tongue. "I'll be happy to tell you why I asked for such instruction. It was entirely my proposal. It certainly wasn't Swaine or Tiller's idea."

"Tiller?"

"It's the name me mother gave me, m'lord," Til said,

"silly as it is. M'lady asked for my true name, and I saw no reason not to tell . . ."

Lyr took Rayne's arm and led her to the place where he'd left his supper sitting on the ground. "You two go help Segyn with the horses. You can eat when that's done."

"Yes, m'lord," they both said, happy to be released.

Lyr sat on a nearby fallen log and gestured for Rayne to join him. She did so, moving primly and with a propriety he had seen only in the King's court. He'd never cared for his regularly scheduled and necessary visits to the court. Advising the King in military matters was part of his duty, but as Tryfyn was at a time of peace, he had not been required in the palace often for matters of business. No, his visits there had been of the social sort, and that had left him with a distaste for those who appeared proper to one's face while plotting behind one's back. There were many women of that sort, a fact which he had already discovered.

"Why would a lady need lessons on cursing?" he asked, maintaining what he thought was a magnanimous calm.

"I told you, I need to know how to tarnish a soul. You were very uninterested and unhelpful, I might add, when I shared that concern with you days ago."

He was confused. "You're going to tarnish someone's soul by cursing at them?"

Again there was that disgusted sigh. "I would never try to taint someone else's soul. That would be horribly wrong."

At last, he understood. At least, he thought he did, odd as it seemed. "You're trying to tarnish your own soul."

"Yes."

"May I ask why?"

For a moment her lips were pursed and unfriendly, and then her mouth softened. "I suppose it won't hurt to tell you. Maybe you'll have some ideas. I find cursing horribly uncomfortable. There must be a better way."

She looked him in the eye. "Before Jiri died, he told me that Prince Ciro wants me for my pure soul. Then he said I must be pure in heart, soul, and . . . and body." She blushed, more than a little. "I don't understand why exactly, but it seemed very important. He said that's why none of the others were allowed in the basement in the months I was imprisoned there. Once the servants were . . . gone"—she dropped her eyes in sadness or respect—"I saw only Jiri."

"I'm not even sure that Ciro has a soul," Lyr confessed. "Why would he wish yours to be pure?"

Rayne lifted her chin, trying for an appearance of dignity and strength. It hurt her efforts that her chin trembled. "Ciro plans to marry me, as you know. Jiri also mentioned something about . . . about a child. A special baby." Again, she blushed. "I don't want to be Ciro's bride, and I certainly don't want his child." She shuddered. "Maybe if I'm tarnished, maybe if I don't possess the pure soul and heart he seems to be infatuated with, he'll leave me alone. I'm sure there are other women who will suit his purposes if he isn't quickly defeated."

She did not mention tarnishing her body, which would be easy enough to accomplish, so he suspected that it was the soul Ciro concerned himself with most. That made sense, as the demon was an eater of souls.

A decided chill walked down Lyr's spine. If Rayne was telling the truth, and he suspected she was, there was more at work here than Ciro's lust or obsession with a pretty woman. Keelia had told a tale of a Caradon wizard in the Mountains of the North, a wizard who'd had dark plans to give *her* a special child. The child of man and demon, a baby who would be more powerful than anyone could imagine. More powerful and more evil, a child who would rule the dark world Ciro and the Isen Demon wished to create.

Rayne was meant to be the mother of just such a child.

If he were to do his right and proper duty, he'd kill her now. He could hold her and slit her throat, and she'd die before she knew what had happened. That would be best, for her, for the war, for the fate of the world.

And yet he couldn't do it. For the first time, he considered that Rayne might truly be an innocent in all this. Perhaps it was his task to protect her, just as it was his task to wield the crystal dagger. If that was the case, he couldn't leave her with just anyone.

Lyr also knew he couldn't take Rayne directly to Ciro—and he knew he had no choice but to face the prince.

The crystal dagger, which he'd strapped close to his thigh, hummed. He heard and felt it, but Rayne didn't seem to hear anything at all. She didn't look around for the source of the noise. Instead, she looked deeply into his eyes as if judging his reaction to her claims.

"I would not lie to you," she said softly. "You saved me from imprisonment, and have kept your word to me. You could've taken the crystal dagger and left me in that house alone, and then what would I have done? I can't fight you, I can't force you to do anything against your will. I can only trust you, Lyr Hern."

Lyr wished for Keelia's guidance, but Keelia was not near. He briefly placed his hand against the humming dagger, wondering if it would speak to him as it had in the past. If it spoke to him with words he did not wish to hear, would he listen? Should he attempt to ask for guidance? No, he was not a man to be incessantly guided by others. This decision was his to make, it was his alone. The solution to his dilemma was simple, and would not require him to go much out of his way. Having Rayne along would slow the journey, but if she was meant to give birth to Ciro's child, then he had two choices. He could kill her, or he could take her to Ariana and Keelia and entrust her to their hands.

And if he did not succeed in his mission to defeat Ciro, then one of them would have to kill Rayne. She and Ciro could not be allowed to come together and make that special child.

HE WOULD HAVE TO MOVE VERY CAREFULLY WHEN THE time came. Phelan knew what the Prince of Swords could do. He'd seen the displays of magic and swordplay.

Before the Isen Demon had called, Phelan had more than once seen time stop at the hands of the young man who led this party. He never felt as if time had been lost, but one moment the young man was in one position, and a moment later he was not. In the blink of an eye, the Prince of Swords might be at your very back, and you would not know he was there until it was too late.

A useful gift, one he wished he himself possessed.

He'd had no doubts about killing those of Ciro's Own who'd guarded the woman. What choice had he had? None at all. That had not been the time to reveal himself, to rise up to fight alongside those the Circle called enemy. If he'd given himself away too soon, he, too, would be dead, and then who would be left to deliver the woman to Emperor Ciro?

Yes, emperor. Another step had been taken. Another victory had been won.

Though Phelan had hidden himself for years among noble warriors, he'd always been rather fond of the killing that came with battle. There was no need to admit such to others, of course, but when in battle, he felt a rush like no other. On some occasions he had not stopped when the battle had ended, but had continued on late at night, in dark alleyways and the homes of welcoming strangers. When there was no enemy to be killed, he imagined his own enemies in the bodies of drunken bums who would not be missed, or in loose women who plied their trade in dim alleyways.

He'd often silently bemoaned the fact that there was not enough battle in Tryfyn to suit him, and yet he'd somehow known that a proper battle was coming.

When the demon had come for him, it had been no surprise at all. Phelan had welcomed the joining with the demon, and he'd gladly taken on this assignment to watch and listen and even guide. He'd been concerned when they'd confronted the Queen of the Anwyn, that powerful seer, but the demon had promised to protect him from her sight, and it had. It had protected him very well.

The demon had considerable powers, and was able to protect some of its secrets with a dark magic the Queen and those like her would never understand. In Phelan's mind he likened this secrecy to a thick black smoke which concealed many of those secrets the demon did not wish to be known.

For now, all was favorable. The party traveled in the right direction, and while they remained on constant guard, there had been no skirmishes along the way. Ciro's Own was keeping their distance until called.

Ciro's Own. One day Phelan would have his own army, and they would answer only to him. That would be his reward for delivering the woman, pure and untouched, to the emperor of Columbyana. Phelan's Own, Phelan's Legion, Phelan's Army. There was time still to decide what they might be called.

No one among them knew him as Phelan. He'd hidden his true name, as well as his true nature, for many years. Soon he would reveal himself and take his reward.

Ciro's bride was a fool if she thought a few clumsily uttered curse words would touch the brightness of her soul.

WHEN SHE SAW THE FARMHOUSE IN THE DISTANCE, Rayne's heart dropped. It had been several days since they'd headed down the mountain, and she'd known this time would come, but still . . . she wasn't ready. Her mouth went dry and her heart began to pound. Thinking of taking on a job for strangers where she might work for her keep had seemed like a fine idea from a distance, but looking at the small dirty farmhouse a touch of reality intruded. It would be hard work, and even if the people there appeared to be kind on meeting the travelers, who knew what they would be like after Lyr and his men rode away?

She thought of her mother's jewels, keepsakes which would do her no good in a place like this. She needed to be deposited in a town, preferably a large town where she could sell her valuables and rent or buy a small house or a decent room and think about how she might hide until the fight with Ciro was over.

Lyr saw the farmhouse and stopped on the narrow roadway to study it more intently. He finally turned to Swaine. "See if they are willing to sell us food. I'm mightily tired of dried meat."

Swaine nodded and headed in that direction. At Lyr's order, Tiller followed.

Segyn sidled up beside his commander. "M'lord, will we be leaving the girl here?"

Rayne held her breath, but not for very long, thanks to Lyr's curt and immediate response. "No. I don't like the look of this place. It's too remote. Why would decent folks settle here? We'll find a more proper situation further down the road."

Segyn nodded, seemingly agreeing with Lyr, and Rayne's heart soon resumed a normal rhythm.

While waiting for the others to return, Lyr dismounted. He walked directly to her and offered his arms. "You might want to stretch your legs while we wait for the others to return."

"Thank you." She accepted his help, and was glad to feel her boots hit the hard ground. Too many long days of riding were not agreeing with her, but she didn't dare to complain. She lowered her voice. "I thank you also for not leaving me here."

Lyr didn't look directly at her, which was odd since he usually had no qualms about staring her down. "I can't be certain it's a safe place. I did give you my word."

"Yes, you did."

"We should probably move more toward civilization before settling you with a proper keeper. Don't you agree?"

"Yes. Yes, I do."

While she knew Lyr Hern to be a capable fighter, she hadn't always felt that he had her best interests at heart. Not at all. For the first time since she'd met him, she sensed a real change in his attitude. He did care for her well-being. He would not abandon her.

The man who had rescued her truly was a champion.

Rayne pushed down the little rush of . . . something . . . that made her feel almost giddy. It would be foolish to become attached to a man whose only wish was to deposit her in a place where she'd be out of danger. It was noble of him, but he would likely have the same care for any other man or woman in his charge.

Even though she'd been shielded from much of life's

harsh realities during her lifetime, she was no fool. She knew why Ciro had looked at her the way he sometimes did, and why he grabbed her with clumsy hands that attempted to touch her where no man should. A pawing of her breasts, a hand thrust among her skirts and between her thighs. She always moved quickly when serving his tea, so those unpleasant touches did not last too long. Over the years other of her father's visitors had often looked at her with leering glances that turned her stomach, most particular since she'd turned fifteen. At first she'd merely thought them odd men, but after speaking with a few of the maids and catching the cook and the gardener in the pantry . . . she knew exactly what was on their minds.

She'd complained to her father once when an elder visitor had attempted to grab her, but her father had told her that she should be flattered, that their guest showed her attentions only because she was beautiful. How could a man be so protective in some ways, and so uncaring in others? How could he suggest that she be *flattered*?

During that particular man's visit, Rayne had not passed a single night in her own bed. She'd hidden each night in infrequently used guest rooms or with the servants, and she'd known, by the way the man glared at her over breakfast, that he had discovered she'd not been in her own bed.

Lyr Hern did not leer, nor did he grab. She almost wished that he would, but then of course, he would not be the man she was coming to admire.

He was very handsome, not many years older than she, and . . . oh, he was striking. Not only handsome, but well built and graceful and strong. He was not at all like those men who had stared at her as if they were starving and she was a meat pie, and if he ever thought to grab at her in an inappropriate way, he wouldn't paw roughly, she imagined, but would be possessed of gentleness and kindness. His touch would be skilled and caring. If Lyr were a gardener and she were a cook . . .

Rayne closed her eyes tightly, but that did nothing to chase away the image in her mind or the odd clenching in her lower belly.

"Are you all right?" Lyr asked, sounding concerned.

"Yes," she said primly. "I'm fine."

"Why are your eyes closed?"

"I'm . . . tired." It was a silly explanation. She was standing on the road, rigid as a board.

"You need to get to sleep sooner after we stop at night," he said, sounding relieved that exhaustion was her only complaint.

"I will try," she promised.

Lyr moved away. A moment later she heard him speak to Segyn, and she opened her eyes slowly. She'd been trying so hard to tarnish her soul with cursing when she wasn't at all good at it, and suddenly lust touched her, unbidden. Was it lust that she felt? Or was it simply gratitude?

It didn't really matter. The only man she'd ever been attracted to in that special way had absolutely no interest in her as a woman. To Lyr Hern, she was an obligation, a package to be delivered and deposited and forgotten. A man like him, with his fine looks and his important position, probably had many women at home, women who would know what they were doing if he did grab or leer. No, he had no use for a woman like her.

Well, damn.

THEY WERE DAYS AWAY FROM THE PALACE, AND DAYS more still from Merin and his army, when Keelia suffered a startling vision of Ciro in the palace their party had left behind. She was overwhelmed with sadness, and filled with horror. She had not met Prince Ciro before the demon had taken him, so she didn't know if he had always been bad or if he was as much a victim in this war as any other soldier who fell. It didn't matter. Whatever the prince had been before, he was now an enemy like no other, and only his destruction could bring peace.

Joryn and Sian were busy setting up camp, while Ariana tended horses and Keelia got ready to prepare their simple supper. The meat was freshly caught, the vegetables purchased in a small town they'd passed through that afternoon, the fire had been built by Joryn with a flick of his fingers. As Queen, she had not been called upon to cook, but of late she'd been forced to develop many new skills.

She didn't want to tell Ariana what she knew, not yet. Her cousin was emotionally attached to the emperor; she had gone to great lengths to save the older man from the sickness the Isen Demon had given him. Even though Keelia had warned Ariana that nothing she did could save Arik in the end, she would be distraught. There would be enough pain in the days to come. This pain could wait.

A moment later, Keelia glanced up to see her cousin standing over her, a frown on Ariana's pretty face. "What's wrong?"

Keelia sighed. "I forget sometimes that your empathic abilities were heightened along with your gift for healing." She forced a smile. "A forgetful seer. How very unfortunate."

"Don't try to make light or change the subject. Queen or not, you can't lie to me."

"I don't lie."

"No, but you do conceal on occasion."

Keelia set the makings for their supper aside and faced her cousin. Yes, she was Queen. Queen of the Anwyn, a psychic like no other, a shape-shifter not yet accomplished in her new skills, and a soldier in this blasted war just as

Ariana was a soldier. "Fine. If you will not allow me to spare you, then I will tell you all the truth you seek." She reached out and touched her cousin's arm, her caress kinder than the tone of her words. "Prince Ciro is in the palace. Arik did not take your warning to heart and . . ."

Ariana's face fell. "He's dead, isn't he?"

"Not yet." And that was a pity for the emperor, who would be better off if he had died quickly.

Ariana turned about sharply. "We're going back," she said. "If Emperor Arik is still alive, we can save him. We can . . ."

Keelia caught her cousin from behind and turned her about. "We cannot save him. No one can. If we turn back, your efforts will be wasted. We must move forward."

Ariana did not cry. She had seen too much horror, too much sadness, to sob for one more death. But tears glistened in her eyes. "He was always kind to me."

"Emperor Arik was a good man."

"I can't bear the thought of Ciro in his place."

"That was meant to be. How long he remains there is not yet known. That's why we must move forward."

Ariana's fears as a soldier were replaced by her fears as a wife, and Keelia saw those fears long before Ariana spoke of them. "Before we left, Arik signed the papers naming Sian as his illegitimate son and his chosen successor. By rights, when Arik dies, Sian will be emperor."

"I know." She and Joryn had been two of a few trusted witnesses to that document.

"If Ciro finds those papers—"

"When," Keelia interrupted in a sharp voice. "*When* he finds the papers."

Ariana's face went deathly pale. "He will send his cursed soulless soldiers after Sian, won't he?"

"Yes," Keelia whispered.

"When?"

Some information came to Keelia with such ease, she did not even need to reach for it. She simply knew, as surely as she knew the sky was blue and Joryn's eyes were green.

But other knowledge did not come to her so easily. It came like a puzzle, incomplete and difficult to piece together.

She closed her eyes and thought of Ciro, Emperor Arik, and that paper naming Sian Sayre Chamblyn as his son and successor. She saw, in her mind, the way Arik's hand had shaken as he'd signed that paper. She saw where he'd hidden it, after all the witnesses had departed.

"Three days," she whispered.

"Three days!" Ariana snapped. "That's not—"

"Three days after Arik dies, Emperor Ciro will find the hidden document that threatens his right to sit on the throne." Keelia opened her eyes and looked squarely at her cousin, so Ariana would have no doubts as to the seriousness of what she saw. "And when that happens, he will send everything he has after your husband."

5

Since they'd ridden away from the farmhouse, Rayne had been looking at him oddly. No, not oddly, exactly. He knew that moony expression; it was simply unexpected from her.

It wasn't as though Lyr didn't enjoy the company of beautiful women, as any other man would, but he divided the segments of his lives very neatly and he did not allow them to mingle in a way which would make his life messy and complicated. As Prince of Swords, he had access to women whose duty and skill was to give and take pleasure. There was a time and place for those women. It had been mentioned more than once that when the time came for him to marry, he might wed one of the King's five daughters. The princesses were fine women, but they were not of the same type as the women with whom Lyr sometimes passed a night—or a day or two.

When he was in the midst of a mission, he did not think of either type of woman, neither concubines nor princesses, and he had never been entrusted with a mission of such importance. There was no pleasure in war, no pleasurable moments of respite—not when his mind and heart must be focused only on victory. To allow his mind or any other part of his body to wander might mean defeat, and they could not afford to lose this war.

And yet the glances Rayne had begun to cast his way reminded him of the princesses *and* of the concubines. It was impossible that she might be like both, and yet he could not help but wonder . . .

No, he could not wonder. She was likely trying to seduce him with those looks, as she had seduced Til and Swaine with her silly lessons in cursing. Lessons she had apparently given up. Both of the soldiers had finally told her that she did not curse well and should probably abandon the attempt.

Maybe she was suffering from an abundance of gratitude, and had twisted that gratitude into something it was not. He had never been so desperate as to take advantage of a woman who did not completely understand what she was getting into, and gratitude? It was a poor reason for that inviting glance she was casting his way.

It did not matter where her thoughts had taken her, he could not allow himself to become entangled with Rayne, daughter of a dead magician, beloved to a monster, future mother to a dark fiend if he was not able to protect her from her fate. Since he might be called upon to take her life, it would be best to ignore those meaningful glances she had begun casting his way.

The journey had been uneventful thus far, and Lyr was getting restless. The back of his neck itched, as did his spine, and he felt tension all through his body, from the short hair on the top of his head to the tips of his toes. Had there been time, he would've stopped and expended energy in sparring with the men, but they moved endlessly forward without time for any of life's pleasures, large or small.

Rayne was becoming more accustomed to sleeping on the ground apparently, since for the past two nights she'd nodded off quickly and remained asleep until one of the men awakened her to resume the journey. She wasn't getting enough rest—none of them were—but she never complained. Not to him, at least. He was not a part of the conversations she had with his men. Cursing lessons aside, Til and Swaine remained smitten with her.

If her death became necessary, would they protect her? Would they choose to fight against him if he had no other choice but to kill?

At the moment Til and Swaine were sleeping. Segyn patrolled the perimeter of camp regularly, and so did Lyr. In an hour or so they would be relieved by the others. Even though all had been peaceful thus far, they could not let their guard down.

Certain that the perimeter was secure, Segyn joined Lyr at a distance from those who slept. The older man, the scarred warrior, had been at Lyr's side for so many years he wasn't sure he could remember when Segyn hadn't been around. As a teacher, a warrior, and in recent years a friend, Segyn had always been a part of Lyr's life.

His voice lowered, Segyn said, "She is not for you, boy."

No one but Segyn would dare to address the Prince of Swords as *boy*, but Segyn often did—when no one else was around to hear. Lyr did not take offense. "I don't know what you're talking about."

Segyn snorted. "I am not blind nor an idiot, and no one knows you the way I do, except maybe your family, and even then—"

"Yes, yes, you know things even they do not," Lyr responded impatiently. Segyn had accompanied him when he'd first drunk too much whiskey, and he'd stood in the hallway when Lyr had lain with his first woman. Though his father was often open in discussing such matters, it was Segyn who was willing to discuss specifics, who was willing to answer the questions Lyr didn't dare ask a parent.

"The world is full of pretty girls," Segyn whispered. "This one would be more trouble than most."

"I understand that well, and I have no intention of serving as anything other than an escort."

Again, Segyn snorted. "She keeps making eyes at you and you have begun to look like you're about to explode."

"I'm perfectly in control," Lyr insisted. The older man's response was not unexpected, and Lyr added, "And if you snort at me again, I'll drop you in rank and put Swaine in your place for the remainder of the journey."

"You will not," Segyn said with confidence, but he did not snort again.

The night was very quiet. Til snored a bit, and on occasion a small critter scurried in the forest beyond their camp, but for the moment the silence was heavy.

"I mean no disrespect, m'lord," Segyn said seriously, "but you don't know what kind of trouble a woman like that one can bring you."

"I have no intention—"

"Let me finish, just in case your mind wanders in an unfortunate direction in days to come."

Lyr nodded crisply, giving his permission.

"You are a fine leader. You're a gifted swordsman and I've never known one more dedicated to his people and his destiny, but as a man . . . as a man you're not quite done."

Lyr studied Segyn's rough profile by the light of a low-burning fire. "I am not a loaf of bread."

"Are you not? Are we all not such? The dough is your

basic composition, the gifts from your parents, whether those gifts be magical or as simple as the color of your eyes and the size of your feet. As years go by, your mind and body are molded. Kneaded. Shaped. You rise, perhaps, and then you bake for a long while until you're done."

"Is this some sort of kitchen philosophy?"

"I had an affair with a cook once. A kitchen helper, more rightly. It lasted several years. I was not much older than you when it began." He cut his eyes to Lyr with censure. "While the love lasted, it was wonderful, but in the end it was quite ugly. You could say I was burned. You, m'lord, have never been burned. You haven't even been toasted, if truth be told. Women adore you, no man can best you sword to sword, your family loves you, and you have many physical gifts—strength, beauty, a steady hand. You have never known the heartache of betrayal, the agony of loss, the sting of rejection. Perhaps you never will. Perhaps your life has been blessed and you will never know any of those pains, but if you never know loss, then you will never be *done*."

"What is the purpose of this conversation?" Lyr asked impatiently.

Segyn was silent for a long moment. "I do not wish to see you burned at this time, boy." Again, his tone was that of friend and mentor, not subservient. He nodded toward a sleeping Rayne. "That woman could singe the hair off your very head. I am glad to hear that you are not so foolish as to think that the two of you might—"

"No, I am not so foolish."

"If you think of changing your mind in that area, speak to me and I will tell you all the ugly details of what happened with me and my kitchen maid when I was not much older than you."

"Did she singe the very hair off your head?" Lyr asked,

and he smiled when Segyn responded by rubbing a hand on his bald scalp.

"That she did, boy. That she did."

THE TERRAIN WAS SO DIFFERENT FROM HER MOUNTAIN home that Rayne was fascinated. To the north were distant mountains, while grassy plains spread far and wide. To the south the landscape was entirely flat, and in the distance she saw what appeared to be low-lying water and stark, tall trees.

Swampland. She had read about it but had never thought to see the swamp firsthand. As far as she was concerned, the narrow, infrequently traveled road brought her close enough to the swamp for study. In the books she'd read, there had been much about snakes and large ratlike creatures and a reptile called croc which was capable of snapping off a man's head with its sharp teeth. The drawing in the book had shown a large mouth opened wide, and there were rows upon rows of teeth.

She did not wish to see a croc. That one drawing would suffice.

Tiller rode close by, taking an interest in her even though she had given up on her cursing lessons. If it was necessary that she tarnish her soul, she'd have to find another way. If the curse didn't come from the heart, would it affect her soul at all? She thought not. She thought that perhaps whatever sin was practiced had to be embraced for it to touch the soul. Whether for good or for ill, whether an act of kindness or a transgression, one's actions had to come from the heart.

As they often did, her eyes wandered to the man who led their party. Lyr had barely looked her way in the past two days. Was he angry with her? Bored? Annoyed? At times he seemed to be all three at once.

"He's to marry a princess, you know."

Tiller's words took her by surprise. Rayne's head snapped around to face her escort. "I beg your pardon?"

"The Prince of Swords, Lord Lyr, he is to marry one of the King's daughters. Sylia, most likely, though some say Princess Erinda is the most beautiful and they would make the better match."

Rayne wished she did not blush so easily. A heat rose to her cheeks, but she ignored the telling sign and kept her voice distant, as if she were not at all interested in the subject. "How very nice for him."

"Nice indeed," Tiller said. "To have one's choice of princesses would be an honor for any man."

Rayne's lips pursed. She had never actually given any consideration to a future with Lyr, but she had admired him, and to have any and all possibility of more snatched away was annoying. Even though he was only the object of a fantasy, she did not want a future wife intruding on that fantasy.

"He has a choice, you say. Do the princesses themselves have no say in the matter?"

"Of course not," Tiller said, as if such an idea were unthinkable. "And that is just as well, I suppose."

"Why?" She could not help the word that sprung from her mouth. What woman would not want a man like Lyr Hern as her husband?

Tiller looked away before he turned to her again. "His family is rather . . . odd."

"Many men have odd families, I imagine." None odder than her own, with a wizard father who couldn't decide if he wanted to guard her from all harm or offer her up to his compatriots like a tasty supper, and a mother who was, perhaps, not all that she'd appeared to be.

"He has Anwyn cousins who shift into wolves at the

rise of the full moon. His mother and his sisters are witches, and quite powerful ones at that. I hear one of his aunts is not safe to be around when she is angry—or aroused—as her very state of mind can affect the weather and the crops and the fertility of a woman's womb. His eldest cousin died and returned from the Land of the Dead," he said in a lowered voice, as if he were in awe. "Almost all of his cousins possess some sort of magic. Since the King and his daughters have no magical abilities, marrying into such a family might be a bit daunting, don't you think?"

"I imagine so," she said softly.

"Your father was a wizard," Tiller said. "Are you . . ."

"I am like my mother, without magical abilities. And I like it that way, though I imagine there are times when having unnatural powers would be convenient." In truth, she did not like what magic had done to her father. Would he have been a better man if his desire for power hadn't led him astray? Would he have been a better father? As she turned her attention to the back of Lyr's head, she asked, "What is his ability? I haven't seen him practice any sort of magic, and we've been on the road for many days."

"He does not use his gift often," Tiller said. "But I have seen it once before. Well, as much as any man can *see* what he does. He is a sight to behold when he uses his magic."

"What does he do?" Her father had practiced spells for as long as she could remember, and she had never cared for them. She hadn't cared for their unnatural way or the very stink that had risen in the air as her father worked.

"He stops time," Tiller whispered.

Rayne's head jerked about. "No one can stop time."

"He does. He stops time for all but himself, and he moves among us while we are stuck and he is not. He might be right before you, and then a blink of the eye later

he's gone. He might be to the right or to the left or gone altogether. It's quite alarming."

Rayne recalled the moment in the basement when she'd
been so certain she was about to die. Jiri's sword had been
flying toward her throat . . . and then it had not. Had Lyr
used his magic on her, on all of them? Had he saved her
life with his gift for stopping time?

Knowing what he could do shouldn't make him less attractive, but it did. Heaven above, she was tired of the
machinations that came with power and the actions men
would take to achieve it. She was sick of manipulations
and secrets and enchantment. From here on out, she
wanted to know what was real and what was not. A simple
life, that's what she wanted . . . if she was lucky or smart
enough to escape the plans Ciro had for her. A simple life,
where she would never need to question what was real and
what was not. A simple husband who would like her. Who
would even perhaps one day love her. Simple children who
would not wield magic or be sought and used for their
gifts.

Lyr, with his nicely crafted body and eagle eyes and
ability to halt time, was not at all simple.

SHE WAS TOO OLD FOR CONSTANT TRAVEL, FOR SLEEPING
on the ground, for wearing the same frock day after day,
for eating only what they could carry or catch.

"I have been horribly spoiled in the past few years,"
Isadora said as she knelt beside the stream to catch a handful of water and bring it to her face. The splash was re-
freshing and rejuvenating.

It had been a long time since the Fyne sisters had spent
this much time together, and as the days passed Isadora realized how very much she'd missed Sophie and Juliet.

They were all older, but they had not changed so very much. The youngest sister, Sophie, was still unendingly optimistic and sunny, and Juliet was down to earth and intuitive. Isadora herself was the eldest sister, the caretaker of them all, the practical one. No, they had not changed very much at all.

Sophie laughed as she copied Isadora's actions bringing a handful of water to her face. "I know what you mean. My ass aches from riding in the saddle, and my feet ache from walking. But what choice do we have?"

"None."

Refreshed, the sisters sat by the stream, enjoying the beauty of this secluded place and the rest for their bodies. Isadora looked at Sophie and shook her head. Her sister had aged remarkably well, particularly when one considered that she'd given birth to and raised nine children. Three were a handful for Isadora and she could not imagine managing more, but then she'd never had Sophie's patience.

They were no more than three days from the coastal town where Juliet was quite sure Liane had settled. Their seer sister was also certain that Liane had changed her name and the names of her sons, but those names were not a part of that which she could discern. It was a large port town, so finding Liane could take days, or even weeks, more.

Sophie leaned back on her hands. "I never would've imagined that we'd search out Liane for the purpose of putting one of Sebestyen's sons in the palace. What if they're both like their father? What if they both claim the throne and we exchange one war for another?"

"From what we have heard of Ciro, Sebestyen himself would be a better emperor." She snorted in disgust. Perhaps Sebestyen had tried to redeem himself in the end, but he had been a horrid, horrid man and a terrible ruler. "I think you should all move to Tryfyn," Isadora said. "The

King is a good man, and when Lyr marries one of his daughters, we'll be family and he'll be glad to welcome you all."

"I did not know Lyr was betrothed," Sophie said with excitement. "What is her name? Is she mild tempered or fiery? How old is she? When will the marriage take place?"

Isadora sighed. "He has not chosen which princess he will marry, so I can answer none of those questions."

Sophie was so silent, Isadora was compelled to turn her head to meet her sister's stare. The accusation was evident.

"You are speaking of an arranged marriage," Sophie said in a lowered voice, as if anyone else were close enough to hear.

"Lyr is Prince of Swords," Isadora said calmly. That should be explanation enough.

"So was Lucan when you met him."

"That was different!"

"How so?"

Isadora waved a dismissive hand. "Can't we discuss something more pleasant, like . . . like war or demons or Sebestyen's sons?"

"I knew it!" Sophie grinned widely. "You don't like the idea of an arranged marriage for your children any more than I do." She nodded her head. "It is best to marry for love and love alone. That's what I want for my children, and I'm sure that's what you want for yours. We were lucky enough to marry for love, so we know how important that is."

"He might come to love one of the princesses." Isadora turned her gaze to the rushing water. Yes, of course she wanted her children to marry for love, but there were also obligations to consider. "When did I get so staid and un-bending?"

"You were born staid and unbending," Sophie said with

a sister's love. "It suits you." With that said, she asked brightly, "I wonder which of us will be a grandmother first?"

"Bite your tongue," Isadora said sharply.

Sophie laughed. "I wouldn't mind at all being a grandmother, and when the time comes, I'm sure you'll love it just as you loved being a mother. More so, from all I have heard from women who have grandchildren."

Fortunately Juliet arrived, and Sophie said no more. Grandmother! Isadora wasn't certain she was ready for that. Was she so old? Yes, she had a few strands of gray in her hair and the lines at the corners of her eyes had grown more noticeable of late, but . . . *grandmother*?

Juliet, who was more hot natured than her sisters thanks to her father's Anwyn blood, did not splash water onto her face. She walked into the stream. Since her skirt was much shorter than was fashionable or proper, she didn't have to worry about soaking her clothing. With cool water rushing against her legs to just above her knees, she turned to face her sisters.

"A race, eh? Don't forget about Keelia." Her smile was wide, as if she, like Sophie, thought being old was grand and wonderful.

Isadora sighed. So much for letting go of the subject of her age. "The years go by so fast," she said. "I blink, and my children are grown, or almost grown. And no matter how old they get, I still worry about them." She caught Juliet's eyes. On occasion her sister had assured her that Lyr was alive and well, though his mission was a difficult one and the outcome was still to be decided. "What of my son?" she asked simply.

Juliet closed her eyes and her face became very peaceful. Beyond peaceful. She took a deep breath and lifted her face to catch the rays of the sun. She did not immediately answer, as she usually did. In an instant, Isadora began to worry. Juliet saw something terrible and did not want to tell. Lyr was hurt, or in danger, or . . . dead.

"Tell me now," Isadora insisted.

Juliet's eyes opened, and she frowned. Not an encouraging sign. "I can't decipher what I see when I reach for knowledge of Lyr. All I see is a loaf of bread being thrust into a raging fire. Does that mean anything to you? Do you understand the symbolism?"

"No," Isadora whispered. "But I don't like it. I don't like that image at all."

EVEN THOUGH THEY'D MET NO RESISTANCE SINCE LEAVing the house where he'd retrieved the crystal dagger, Lyr did not allow himself to relax. If anything, he'd been feeling more anxious of late, more on alert. Maybe it was simply the tension of being in the company of a woman for such a long period of time. Though women came and went on a regular basis, only his mother and sisters were constants in his life.

As the moon was bright and almost full, they rode into the night. Their mission was an important one, and every step took them closer to the end—whether that end be for good or for darkness. Lyr could not help but think of what failure would mean. His friends, his family, his men—all could and would fall victim to the darkness. His sisters were young and silly and a continual annoyance, but they were his annoyance and he did not wish to see them live in a world where they weren't safe, or worse, where they might perish at a dark hand.

And Rayne . . . Ciro's plans for Rayne were not of her doing; she had no choice in the matter. If she lived and

Ciro won, then her fate would be worst of all. If he had to take her life, he'd be doing her a favor, he supposed.

Not that she was likely to see things in that way if he was forced to hold a knife to her throat.

It helped him to think of the worst. Imagining failure steeled his resolve, and it took his mind off other things, like the manner in which the woman who rode behind him had worked her way under his skin.

Segyn was right. She could burn him, given half a chance.

Not long after darkness fell, Rayne guided her horse forward, bringing it and herself to Lyr's side. "I have been seeing more homes in the distance, all to the north. Did you come this way on your journey to my home? Is there a large town nearby?"

There was a decent-sized village perhaps a day's ride ahead, and if he had not known too much about Ciro's plans for Rayne, he would have happily left her there. How would he explain to her that he wouldn't be leaving her anywhere? He did not lie, but this was one truth he could not share.

"There is a town ahead, where we can buy supplies and perhaps rest for a short while, but I won't be leaving you there."

"Why not?"

Lyr took a long deep breath and chose his words carefully. "It is not the best place for you. Trust me in this, Rayne. I promised to see you to a safe place. The town ahead is not such a place."

She nodded her head agreeably. "All right. I will trust your judgment in this matter. It's just that I know I'm slowing you and your men down. You must be anxious to join the fight. I know Tiller and Swaine are."

"We will arrive in the place we are supposed to be when the time is right."

"That's very philosophical of you," she said lightly.

"Man can only control so much of his destiny. That is not philosophy; it's fact." Anxious to change the subject, he said, "I notice that you've given up swearing."

"Yes, I have. It was not for me. I will find another way if I must."

If she tarnished her soul so that it was no longer what Ciro needed in order to make that special child, maybe Rayne would be safe. Maybe he would not have to see her in Ciro's grasp or take her life, and she could have what she wanted—a quiet life in a simple place, where the monster who called her "beloved" would never find her.

He did not think it would be easy to tarnish such a soul. Though he did not see the purity of which she spoke, he knew Rayne was a good person through and through. She had a kind heart and an easy way about her, and she would never knowingly harm a living thing. She was good, in a world where true goodness was sadly rare.

"We will think of a way," he said in a lowered voice. He nodded at the blue gem which lay against her chest, catching the moonlight. "I see you have taken to wearing the necklace which was stored with the crystal dagger."

A small hand rose up and touched the stone against the swell of her breast. "Yes. It reminds me of my mother, and I wish to feel closer to her now. I've been thinking about her a lot lately."

"She was . . . not like your father?"

Rayne shook her head. Many strands of fine dark hair had come loose from her once-staid fashion and fell around her face and down her back. She was mussed, she was wrinkled, there was a smudge of dirt on her cheek. And still, she was more regal than any princess.

"She was not at all like my father. If she had been, I do not think the dagger you carry would do you any good at all against one such as Ciro. I think it was her goodness which makes the crystal dagger a weapon for light."

"If that is the case, I owe your mother a great debt."

Rayne's pretty brow furrowed. "I suppose."

He could not stand to see her frown so fiercely. "Why does that supposition make you scowl? Your mother's goodness is a fine thing, is it not?"

Rayne brushed a wayward strand of hair away from her face, as if it had begun to annoy her. "As we ride for hours on end, my mind wanders. It flits from one place to another, and a thousand questions fill my head. The question that has been haunting me all day won't go away. How did my mother know, all those years ago, that the dagger would be needed now, eight years after her death?"

The answer seemed simple enough to Lyr. "Perhaps she possessed a magic she did not share."

"Perhaps," Rayne responded. Her hand gripped the blue stone as they rode forward in the night. "I did think she shared everything with me," she added in a lowered voice.

They rode for a while longer without speaking, and then Rayne spoke once again. "Save me from him, please," she said simply.

"If I can." He would not promise her more than that, because he wasn't certain anything more was possible.

6

IN THE MIDST OF ONE OF HER LONG, FREQUENT BATHS, Diella frowned at her slightly rounded stomach. In the body which had been hers many years ago, a body which was now dust, she had never conceived a child. This body, however, was apparently more fertile and had caught some man's seed. She was not overly concerned, as there were many ways to rid oneself of an unwanted child. Diella gave a passing thought as to whom the child might belong to, and then dismissed the query as unimportant. She would not be saddled with any man's child!

Perhaps the pregnancy was the reason for her recent pallor and weight loss. Some women plumped up immediately when they caught a seed, but not this body. She could see the bones in her wrists and her legs were too thin, and it took more cosmetics every day to make her look beautiful. She would have suspected the truth earlier but she'd continued to bleed, though irregularly and very lightly.

A trip to Level Seven would cure all her ills.

Much had changed in the years that had passed since she'd been empress, but the location of the palace witches had not. The emperor's quarters were no longer at the top of the palace, on Level One, but farther down. The lift which had once carried those of importance up and down was no longer operational, so of course, the emperor had moved his offices and personal quarters. There was no collection of concubines on Level Three, though the baths there were kept open. Some days she made use of those baths, but on other days—like today—she preferred a small tub in the privacy of her room. She was so tired that making the trip to Level Three seemed too much a chore.

That was the child's fault, she decided, and would soon be an unpleasant memory and nothing more.

Diella left the tub and dried herself with a soft towel, noting the changes in her body as she took care of that simple task. She was downright bony, even though she'd been eating very well since Ciro had taken the palace. Her color was not good at all. There was a touch of yellow under the skin, and this young flesh she had stolen was actually beginning to wrinkle. That was entirely unacceptable.

Leaving her hair damp, she donned a crimson robe that fell too loosely on her body and exited her chambers. This was not a task she could trust to anyone else, even though she did not relish the idea of climbing two flights of stairs to reach Level Seven.

Diella did not rush, but walked slowly and deliberately up the stone staircase. She met no one. Since Ciro had taken over the palace, many of the sentinels had either deserted or been executed. Soldiers, Ciro's Own, took their places in short order, but those soulless soldiers had a tendency to remain near to the man they worshipped.

A few sentinels, those who were touched by the demon or simply craved what Ciro promised, had remained. They were her favorites, as they still possessed a bit of themselves and had not given their souls over to the demon. They were healthier, prettier, and they gifted her with more of their attention—which was, after all, what she needed most.

Stop.

Diella was surprised by the voice of the demon, as he rarely spoke to her anymore. She had served her purpose in leading Ariana and her army to Ciro, and a lavish life in the palace was her reward.

"I want no man's child," she said aloud.

You carry no man's child.

Diella stopped climbing and caught her breath. "It isn't possible that the child is yours. You're . . . you're . . ." In another place, unable to touch her, not of this life.

Mine, yours, Ciro's, Lilia's.

Diella sat. Her legs were about to give out on her, in any case. She did not mind at all doing the demon's work in exchange for this new and healthy—well, once healthy—body. But to carry its child? To give birth to a baby who would be both human and demon?

"I don't want it," she whispered.

What you want has never mattered. What you want doesn't matter now. You will carry and birth this child, even if I have to order Ciro to put you in Level Thirteen for the next five months. Is that what you wish for, Diella, do you wish to go home to that dark hole beneath the palace?

She shuddered. Nothing was worse than the emptiness that was Level Thirteen. Nothing.

"I won't raise this child," Diella said as she descended the stairs, Level Seven forgotten. The Isen Demon would never allow her to rid herself of the life inside her. Still, she would not sacrifice her entire new life for a child. "Once it's out of my body, someone else will have to care for it."

That is my plan, Diella. All you are asked to do is nourish and birth my daughter, Ksana.

"Pretty name," Diella said. "Isn't that a flower?"

A poisonous flower, more beautiful than any other and deadly to the touch.

Diella placed a hand over her slightly rounded stomach. If the child was actually poison to the touch, how would she survive the months to come?

I will protect you. All you need do is nourish Ksana and deliver her into this world. When that is done, your obligation to me is also done. Others will be waiting to take her from you, to raise and educate her.

As much as she hated the idea of being pregnant for the next five months, Diella was pleased to know that she'd be released from her allegiance to the Isen Demon. It was a fair enough trade, she supposed.

RAYNE'S EYES WERE WIDE AS THEY RODE INTO THE TOWN. It was her first foray into such civilization. The four men who served as her escort surrounded her, Lyr in front, Segyn behind, Tiller to her right, Swaine to her left. They kept a sharp eye on all those who were in the streets and on the shaded walkways before shops and businesses.

The soldiers who escorted her were an awesome sight, and that was undeniable. What must these four men look like to the farmers and shopkeepers of this village? The men shaved quickly every three or four days, but they were all due for another and looked rather rough at the moment. They were well armed and carried their weapons with the ease of warriors. They were straight of spine and hard of eye, and showed no softness, no kindness, in their exterior presentation.

Perhaps the Circle Warriors were as foreign to the villagers as this village was to Rayne.

The buildings which lined the street were not what she would call attractive, but they were sturdy and well kept. The people were much the same. They looked to be hardworking people, many of them a bit the worse for wear at the end of a long day. She hadn't seen her face in a mirror in a long while. After these days of travel, she imagined that she herself appeared to be a bit worse for wear.

One building was very noisy, and beyond opened doors she saw many men and a few brightly dressed women who seemed to be having quite a lot of fun. They laughed and drank, and there was loud, crude music and boisterous dancing that caused the women's colorful skirts to swirl and flip.

She had never danced. Reading about it was not the same as witnessing the vigorous activity. The dancers, so briefly glimpsed, seemed gloriously happy.

Two brightly dressed women who wore an excess of cosmetics stepped from the building and toward the party which moved slowly down the street. "Would you care for some company, gentlemen?" one of them asked. Then they both smiled widely and the other bright woman said, "We'll be right here all night."

Tiller looked at the ladies and his eyes sparkled. Swaine smiled and blushed. The pale complexion which suited his wiry red hair reddened easily, she had found. Lyr and Segyn ignored the women. Neither of them blushed.

Though she did glance at the women, Rayne made a point not to look too hard. Innocent as she might be, she knew what they were offering. If they weren't moving straight through this village, would any of the men take the bright women up on their offers?

Of course they would.

Lyr had said they'd buy supplies, but Rayne was certain that when that was done, they'd continue on for a while longer. It was not yet dark, even though the sky was gray and night would soon be here. Lately they had been traveling well into the night, and she suspected tonight would be no exception.

But instead of taking them to a shop which would supply what they needed, Lyr led the party to a large building at the end of the street. Three stories high, it was almost as large as the home where Rayne had been born and raised, though it was not nearly as nice. Like the other buildings in town, it was made of wood and was plain in design, though there were pretty curtains in all the windows. Someone had expended some effort to make the place hospitable.

Lyr looked past Rayne to his most senior officer. "Obtain two adjoining rooms. If such rooms are not available, we will continue on."

"We're stopping for the night?" Segyn asked as he dismounted. "We get to sleep in a real bed?"

"Only if they have adjoining rooms," Lyr responded, and then he glanced at Rayne. "It wouldn't be wise to be separated. We'll sleep in shifts and there will be no drinking or whoring."

The two younger men looked disappointed, and Rayne suspected they were not saddened because they could not *drink*.

Segyn returned moments later, nodding his head to let Lyr know that the rooms had been obtained. The men all dismounted, and even though they could not have their fun, they were glad of the chance to sleep indoors on a soft mattress. The food would likely be significantly better than the dried meat and hard biscuits which had become their daily fare.

Lyr assisted Rayne from her saddle and handed the horses over to Swaine for tending. "You go nowhere without an escort," he said in a lowered voice as he led her into the inn. "One of us will keep watch on your door all night, so you need not be afraid."

"I'm not afraid," she said, and it was true. As long as Lyr was with her, she had nothing to fear. Who could get past him? No one. He would not allow anyone to harm her.

He collected keys and directions to the second-story rooms from the innkeeper, a stout older woman who was pleased to have the guests. Perhaps this village was not a popular place for travelers to stop. In any case, she seemed almost giddy as she announced that she'd serve supper in three-quarters of an hour.

Lyr took Rayne's elbow as he guided her up the stairs to the second floor. She enjoyed the possessive sensation of his hand on her arm, the strength that radiated from him to her in a way that was somehow very personal. The touch elicited an unexpected tingle that crept up her arm and warmed her entire body.

They were alone, the innkeeper left behind and the men taking care of other chores, so she felt free to ask him a question which might otherwise be embarrassing.

"Those brightly dressed and painted women we saw on the street, are they available for the purposes of sexual relations?"

Lyr's hand instantly grew hot, and she was certain she felt a twitch. "You need not worry about such women. They will not come here. They will not bother you."

"I'm not bothered by them, just curious."

"Such curiosity is unnecessary."

They reached a door, and Lyr chose the correct key.

Rayne put a hand on his arm to stop him from opening the door. "To give oneself so freely, without love or commitment, do you think it a great sin?"

Lyr's narrowed eyes met hers. She had never felt that gaze so intently. "You're not thinking of joining them in order to tarnish your soul, are you?"

"Of course not," she said primly. "As I said, I'm simply curious."

"Women and curiosity are a dangerous mix," he mumbled, and then he crossed his arms over his chest. "If you must know, such women do not *give* anything. They sell."

"They sell sex?"

"Yes," Lyr said through gritted teeth.

"Why? If they enjoy sex so much, as they certainly seemed to do when they issued their invitation, then why do they not simply get married?"

She could see the coiled tension in Lyr's neck and shoulders, in the cut of his fine jaw and the flaring of his nose. "When we reach our destination, you can ask one of my cousins. This sort of questioning is best asked of a woman."

"But I wish to ask *you*."

"What have I done to invite this regrettable circumstance?"

Life was short, achingly so. She did not know what tomorrow would bring, so why was it necessary to live by strict rules which might not serve her at all well? "It occurs to me that if I am not a virgin, Ciro might not want me. Perhaps that is part of the . . ." She stopped, as Lyr's face was turning an odd shade of purple. "Are you all right?"

"Not at all."

"Are you sick?"

"No." The shade of purple seemed to lessen slightly.

"Good. Jiri mentioned that Ciro wished me to be pure in

all ways. Soul, heart, and body. In any case, it has occurred to me that I can't be considered entirely pure if I've had sex with another man. I don't know with any certainty, but Jiri was quite adamant about keeping the other soldiers away from me. I know I take the risk of finding myself with a child and no husband, but wouldn't that be better than the alternative? In fact, that might be best. If I'm carrying another man's child, I can't carry Ciro's. Demon or no, I can only carry one child at a time."

"You've given this some thought," Lyr said in a lowered voice.

"Yes. There isn't much to do as we travel but think." She did her best to keep her voice detached and cool. "Since you saved me, perhaps you wouldn't mind having sex with me so as to make me unacceptable as Ciro's bride."

"No," he whispered.

Rayne wrinkled her nose. She had not expected him to refuse. "I can pay you," she said with a touch of excitement. After all, he had said those bright women received money for their sexual companionship. Perhaps Lyr expected the same.

"No!" he said again, more adamantly than before.

She looked away from him and to the lamps that burned down the long hallway, trying her best to hide her disappointment. "Then perhaps you would be so kind as to order one of your men to do the deed. I will close my eyes, and I promise not to peek. We can do what needs to be done in the dark. I don't even have to know which man you send if he doesn't speak, so there will be no awkwardness in the days ahead."

"Do you really believe that losing your virginity will save you from Ciro's intentions?"

"Maybe. Maybe not. I don't know what else to try at

this point. Will you help me? Will you send one of your men to me?"

She was disappointed that Lyr had refused the chore himself, but she wouldn't let that disenchantment show. She had begun to consider the others friends, and surely it was better to lie with a friend than to blindly choose a man at her final destination, wherever that might be. Once she was no longer fit to be the mother of Ciro's child, maybe she would be safe. When that was done, she could begin her simple life. Did it really matter which man did the deed? Surely not.

Lyr opened the door to her room and ushered her inside. He examined the room thoroughly, which took mere moments as it was small and had only one tiny window which overlooked an alleyway. She had begun to think he wouldn't even answer her question, but as he was exiting the room, he stopped in the doorway and looked directly at her. A muscle in his jaw twitched.

"After supper, I will send someone to you, if that is what you wish."

She could not speak, so she nodded once.

"Be certain, as there will be no turning back once this is done."

Again, she nodded. "Who will you send? I . . . perhaps it's silly of me, but I've changed my mind. I would like to know."

"I haven't decided." Lyr slammed the door behind him so hard Rayne felt the walls around her shake.

HE COULD AND SHOULD SEND ONE OF THE MEN TO Rayne's room. It wasn't as though Til or Swaine would refuse such an order. They were already smitten, and what man would refuse a beautiful woman when she made such a request? Maybe she was right, and losing the purity of her untouched body would be enough to save her from Ciro. Even the possibility was enough to give it a try. It wasn't as if she had decided to soil her soul with murder or hate.

No, she wished to taint herself with physical love. Perhaps it would be enough that she was no longer a virgin, but he doubted her soul would suffer. Everything she undertook was open and honest, and there was no darkness in that. Would it be enough to take a lover? Would knowing another man had touched her make her unattractive to Prince Ciro?

It was Lyr's watch, and he paced the hallway making almost no noise. The others slept, crowded together in one bed and happy for the comfort of a mattress, even if it was just for one night, even if that bed was shared. Rayne slept alone . . . or was she waiting for the man he had promised to send to her? Was she awake behind that door, perhaps naked, perhaps anxious, perhaps scared?

Perhaps she had changed her mind.

He unlocked and opened her door, slipping silently into the darkness. There was no light. The lone window at the back of her room was covered by a thick and dark shade that kept out the little bit of moonlight that otherwise might've seeped into the room. Lyr waited for a moment until his eyes adjusted to the darkness, and then he moved toward the bed in the center of the small room. He could see little in this darkness, where no moonlight lit his way. Lamplight from the hallway through a crack in the door, and a small amount of moonlight through a slit in the shade, were all that lit the room.

Rayne's breathing was even, and he suspected she'd fallen asleep. After all, it had been a while since she'd eaten a good meal and rested upon a mattress. He could walk away and she would never know he'd come . . . but he didn't walk away.

Lyr sat on the edge of the bed, and Rayne's breathing changed. She sat up quickly. "I dozed off. I thought no one would come."

"Have you changed your mind?" he asked softly.

She gasped, and then breathed deeply. "It's you."

It would be best if she did not know he couldn't bear to send anyone else to this place. He couldn't explain that oddity, but it was undeniable. If he could've come to this bed and made love to her without ever revealing his identity, that would suit him just fine, but that didn't seem practical—or even possible. "Yes."

Rayne drew her covers down. "I came to bed without clothes," she said, obviously nervous. "I thought it would be best. Easiest, I suppose, is the right word. It might be difficult to wrestle with clothing in the dark, but I suppose we will have to deal with yours. Some of them anyway." Her voice was soft, quick, and high. "You'll have to tell me what to do, or show me. Guide me, use your hands or . . . whatever . . ."

His *whatever* was hard, and he could think of nothing but sliding inside her soft heat.

Lyr leaned forward and silenced Rayne with a kiss, taking her mouth with his and swallowing her surprised gasp. Yes, she gasped, and twitched, and moaned. She moaned like a woman pleasantly surprised by the sensations of a kiss. She was naked beneath him, and while he could not see her as he'd like, he could feel her very well. One hand rose up and settled on his arm, warm and soft, with a woman's gentleness. In no time at all her mouth began to move against his. She needed no instruction when it came to kissing.

Segyn was right about this one; she could burn him well.

* * *

THE KISS WAS MORE PLEASURABLE THAN RAYNE HAD EX-
pected it would be and she threw herself into it heartily.
Lyr kissed her with skill and gentleness, but also with a
passion she'd not expected. This was a chore which could
be quickly done without any kissing. At the moment it did
not feel like a chore, not at all.

Lyr had apparently shaved since leaving the supper
table. His face was smooth. She touched his face and his
jaw as they kissed, allowing her fingers to trace the sharp
ridge of his jawline and the unexpected softness of his
cheek. He was wonderfully warm, and she even liked the
simple sound of his breathing so close.

She was no longer alone. For the moment she was a part
of something larger and better, as if nothing mattered but
this bed and this man who had come to it. Lyr placed a
hand on her breast and caressed, and she was taken aback
by the sensations that danced through her entire body. He
brushed a thumb over the nipple and her response was so
intense it surprised her.

In the midst of the pleasure, Rayne suffered a moment
of doubt. Even though he touched her with such tenderness
and skill, Lyr did not care for her. This was a task to be
done, a necessary action which might save her from Ciro.
It didn't feel like a necessary action and nothing more.
She'd been grabbed in the past by men who cared nothing
for her, and this was different. She and Lyr shared a bond.
Man to woman, in the dark, there was something beyond
what she knew to be real. Flesh to flesh, his hand on her
body and their mouths linked, they shared something powerful. She felt it, but did he? Was she anything more to him
than one of the bright women who offered themselves to
any man who passed by?

Her doubts did not last. Lyr was kind and thoughtful, and at the moment that was enough. It had to be enough.

He laid her back on the bed and continued to kiss her, while his hands explored. She'd not expected this much attention. She knew the basic hows and wheres of sex, thanks to overheard conversations among the female servants, but no one had ever talked of what happened beforehand. Her body felt very warm and heavy, her heart beat steadily but too fast. And inside . . . inside she trembled and ached.

A man you barely know is about to be inside you.

The thought crossed her mind but was easily dismissed. She knew Lyr as well as she knew any man. He was noble and strong, he was serious and dedicated. His eyes were unflinching and as sharp as those of a hawk, and his touch revealed a kindness he did not express in any other way. Yes, he would one day marry a princess, but he was not married *now*. *Now* he was hers.

Lyr removed himself from her and very quickly undressed. She had wondered if he would simply open his trousers to take her virginity, but apparently he did not believe in half-measures in any area of his life. He had devoted himself entirely to this necessary deed, and she could only admire him for that. She could only be glad that he was the one.

She could confess to herself, though not to him, that she'd caught herself fantasizing about Lyr on occasion. Not about this, which was a new experience for her, but about small things like seeing him smile at her, or having him take her hand as she stepped across a rugged patch of land . . . or of being held by him. She had fantasized more than once that he might wrap his arms around her and hold her close, offering a much-needed comfort.

Lyr not only undressed, but set aside his weapons—

including the crystal dagger, which was always on his person. When he was naked and the implements of death had been put aside, he joined her on the bed. He pressed his naked body to hers and kissed her again, only this time his mouth was on her throat, and then on her tender breasts. Rayne forgot everything else and allowed herself simply to feel. She felt as if she were falling, falling quickly toward something she could not wait for. Her body rocked toward his, her hands settled on strong shoulders and gripped the flesh which was like and yet so unlike hers.

He was determined to leave no part of her body untouched, unkissed. He had fine, full lips, and he knew how to use them very well. Those lips trailed across her chest and her belly, on her throat and the side of her neck. Soon she could not see or think, she could only feel, and what she felt was beyond her imagining.

Lyr spread her legs and touched her where she was wet for him, where her body pulsed and ached and screamed. A finger slipped inside her and she caught her breath as her back came up off the mattress and her hips jerked. A deep tremble grew and fluttered. Lyr did more than ensure that her body was ready for his, he aroused her. He teased her entrance until she shook to her bones and could not take a proper breath.

And then he was there, above her, pushing himself inside her, filling the aching emptiness slowly. His size was unexpected, but she did not hesitate to accept him and, indeed, to demand all he had to give.

He didn't move quickly, as he could've, but gave her body time to adapt before pushing deeper and breaking through her maidenhead.

Nothing mattered beyond this room, beyond this bed, beyond these two joined bodies. He stroked her slowly, moving in and out, almost leaving her and then plunging deep. The tremors she experienced grew sharper and quicker, and she found that her hips naturally moved in a rhythm that met his thrusts and urged him deeper and faster.

And then it happened. A powerful release fluttered, not only there where Lyr touched her but everywhere. She gasped and then lost her breath. Her body lurched and quivered, and she found herself holding her lover tightly as the pleasure she had not expected wiped away every other thought.

He drove deep again and then went still, quivering and filling her with the seed that might save her from the fate Ciro had planned for her, finding his own release and pleasure. As he gave her that gift, her hand settled possessively on the back of his head, and her fingers touched short strands of thick hair.

His head settled beside hers, and in a gruff whisper he asked, "Did I hurt you?"

"No," she answered breathlessly. "You did not hurt me. In fact, I was pleasantly surprised. Sex is quite fun, isn't it? I didn't ask you here for purposes of fun but out of necessity, but since you're here and we do seem to get along so well . . ." She wrapped an arm possessively around Lyr to touch his finely sculpted back and raked her foot along his leg. "Stay with me for a while?"

7

LYR THANKED THE STARS THAT IT WAS HIS CUSTOM TO ride at the front of their party. He didn't think he could look at Rayne and not somehow reveal that he'd been affected more than he should've been by their encounter last night. He'd gone to her bed intending to do what had to be done and nothing more, but when he'd found her waiting, naked . . . soft . . . *his* . . . everything had changed.

Maybe it would make a difference to Ciro's plans that she was no longer a virgin. She was so trusting, even in bed, even when she moaned his name and lifted her hips to his, that he was almost certain there was nothing she could do which would tarnish her heart or her soul. Lyr didn't know what criteria a demon would use when choosing a wife, but if bedding Rayne last night meant he wouldn't have to kill her, then he could not be sorry. As if bedding her had been a chore . . .

He'd do the same again, given the same circumstances. There was no way he could send one of these men to her bed, not when he had begun to feel so blasted proprietary about her. The unexpected sensation was a temporary inconvenience and would not last. He'd saved her, she'd helped him find the dagger, he'd given her his word that he would see her to safety. What honorable man wouldn't feel a bit proprietary?

A bit. Ha.

Segyn left his post at the end of the party and joined Lyr. "Something's wrong with m'lady," he whispered, so none of those behind them would hear.

"What's the problem?"

"I don't rightly know, but she's been acting strangely all day."

"Strangely in what way?"

"Look at her."

Lyr hesitated, then turned his head about in a casual manner. Rayne looked fine to his eyes. A bit tired thanks to a lack of sleep, a little wistful, maybe a touch too happy with an added bit of color to her cheeks . . . "She looks fine to me."

"She has not engaged Swaine or Til in conversation all morning, and you know how she likes to chatter nonsense. She thinks it makes the time go by faster." The older man rolled his eyes, expressing his opinion of that idea.

"Maybe she's run out of things to say," Lyr offered logically.

"Unlikely, m'lord. There have been many times when she's been content to chatter and say nothing at all. I suspect she might be up to something, and so her mind has wandered elsewhere."

"What might she be planning?"

"Escape, perhaps. You didn't see fit to leave her in the village. Perhaps she'd just as soon settle there as continue on with us. We've been traveling at a steady pace for more than a week now, and she is unaccustomed to such travel."

"She did not wish to stay behind," Lyr said confidently.

"How do you know?"

"We discussed the matter."

Segyn gave one of his snorts. "And of course she wouldn't *lie* to you and agree to whatever you might say and then turn around and do something else entirely."

Lyr studied Segyn's rough profile. "You do not think highly of women, as a whole."

"Not particularly."

"Well, you can take my word as truth in this matter. Rayne did not wish to remain in that village. She is not plotting escape."

A moment later Segyn said, "Women and war do not mix well."

Lyr could not argue with that statement. "Is that what happened to your kitchen maid? War came between you?"

"That is a tale for another time, boy." With that, Segyn turned his horse about and returned to his post at the end of the line.

IT WAS ALL RAYNE COULD DO TO KEEP HERSELF FROM humming as she rode along. She did smile on occasion, for no reason at all, and she found herself staring more often than usual at the back of Lyr's head. More than once she willed him to look back at her, to smile—as she had fantasized that he could—to give her a nod that no one else would understand.

But the only time he looked at her was at the urging of Segyn, for some reason. And even then, there was no expression of softness on his face, no acknowledgment of what they had shared last night—and this morning.

Perhaps the events of the past few months had changed her outlook on the world, but it seemed a waste not to embrace such wonders as the pleasure of physical love. Lyr had warned her sternly that no one else was to know of their liaison, and he had assured her it would not happen again. At the time she had nodded agreeably, but in truth she did not understand why. He was not promised, not as of yet. She was betrothed to a monster, but that was not of her choosing so she should not be bound by that promise. They were free for now, and they were wonderfully compatible. So why did he insist that there could be no more?

It was very wanton of her to wish for more, but she could not deny that she did. Perhaps those wishes alone would tarnish her heart, but she didn't think so. How could something so beautiful be a sin? How could the joining of two people, two souls, be anything less than pure?

Lyr didn't love her, and she could not say that she loved him either, but that didn't mean there wasn't some enhanced level of caring in what they'd shared.

And would share again, if she had her way. She'd lived a meek life, and look where it had gotten her! It was time to take the chances she had never before taken, to demand that which she knew to be right.

When they stopped to allow the horses to rest, she casually made her way to the edge of the road, where Lyr stood alone. "It's a lovely day for traveling," she said, her voice loud enough for the others to hear if they wished to listen.

"Yes, it is." He turned and looked at her, and if she wasn't mistaken, there was a touch of pain in his piercing eyes, eyes which were more narrowed than usual, as if he were looking into the sun.

"I'm much the better for my night in a proper bed." Her smile was innocent as she rocked up onto her toes and back down again.

The pain in Lyr's eyes increased, and she could not help but notice that the deep blue of his eyes was the color she had always imagined the sea to be, though all she had was a hand-colored picture on which to base that assumption. Would she ever see the ocean? Would she ever dance? Would she live to love and bear children and laugh without fear?

Rayne took a step closer and lowered her voice. "Do you know what I have learned from my time as Ciro's prisoner, from my days when I thought I was doomed?"

"I have no idea, but I imagine you're going to tell me whether I want to hear or not."

She didn't allow his dour mood to dampen her enthusiasm. "Every day is a gift. *Every day*, Lyr. We cannot live our lives based on what we plan for tomorrow or next week or next year, because those days might never arrive. Life is meant to be lived to the fullest, to be grabbed with joy and wonder and . . . and embraced."

"When did you come to this enlightenment?" he asked dourly.

"Very early this morning," she confessed, "as you were kissing the back of my knee and trailing your fingers—"

"Enough." He lifted a hand to emphasize the single word. "We did what had to be done and that is all."

"We did much more than was necessary, Lyr Hern, and you know it. Do I frighten you in some way?"

"Of course not."

"Were you . . . displeased?" She knew he had not been, but wanted to hear him say so himself.

"No, but—"

"You are so dedicated to your duties as Prince of Swords, I imagine you often neglect Lyr Hern the man."

"They are one and the same," he said.

"Are they?" she asked. "Truly?"

She would've asked more questions, but Swaine joined

them to inquire about the route they'd take that afternoon and into the next morning. Apparently there was an alternate route to the one they'd traveled on their way to her home, one which might be a day or two quicker. Rayne knew that revealing the nature of her relationship with Lyr to his men would without question end all possibilities of more, so she allowed the subject to drop *almost* entirely.

"Every day," she said simply, and then she walked away.

Behind her she heard Swaine ask, "Every day what?"

"I have no idea," Lyr responded convincingly enough. "You know how the woman rambles."

Rayne could not help but wonder if their new route would take them into more villages, where there would be more inns and more beds—and privacy. As long as his men were watching, Lyr would reveal nothing of his feelings for her or for anyone—or anything—else.

TO THOSE WHO DID NOT KNOW OR ACCEPT THE NATURE of the war at hand, it appeared that Prince Ciro had returned home to comfort his ailing father. Arik, drained of much blood but still possessed of his soul, hung to life by a thread—but he did as Ciro instructed when his recently returned son pushed into his weakened mind.

Arik told the priests that his illness necessitated a passing of the throne to his son, and they agreed. Father and son made a few public appearances from the balcony outside the emperor's chamber, where Arik passed a scepter with trembling hands, and a priest placed a crown on Ciro's head.

It felt good.

When Ciro had come to Arthes, he'd expected to find more resistance among the people there, but he quickly discovered that there were many who chose to turn a blind eye to the truth. They did not believe what they'd been told. They did not believe that a demon could possess their prince. They wished only to live their simple lives undisturbed by politics, and he allowed that foolish wish to continue. For now. After he won, after all the armies that opposed him were defeated, they would discover the truth for themselves. By that time, it would be much too late for resistance.

Ciro continued to study the priests at his leisure, in no hurry to oust them all from the palace. There were only a few pure souls among them, and many of the souls he glimpsed were almost as dark as his own. Those were the ones he would call to his side as his power grew.

Emperor Ciro walked past those of his Own who guarded his father's newly appointed chambers. They bowed, as was right and proper, as he walked through the door to the small, plain room which was intended for a minor servant.

His father sat in a small hard chair, bound tightly even though any movement was increasingly difficult for the rapidly aging man. It was important that the former emperor not forget who was in power here, that he not begin to think that he might have a chance at escape.

If the former emperor were able to speak freely, those Columbyanans who were so anxious to dismiss the idea of evil in the palace would believe. That could not happen.

Alone with his father, Ciro pulled up a chair and unbound one feeble hand. "How are you feeling today, Father? Poorly, I see by your color and the fading light in your eyes." Ciro pulled his father's thin wrist to his mouth and nipped the vein there, licking at the blood which seeped out too slowly. The old man didn't have much to give.

Except the soul, which Ciro was saving for later . . . but

not much later. As soon as he had what he wanted, the old man's soul would be his.

The former emperor sobbed as Ciro tasted, a shadow of the man he had once been, the shell of a rebel who'd taken the throne from his legitimate half-brother.

Ciro didn't take too much blood, as he was not yet ready to remove his father from this world. There was still much to be learned from the old man, who had thus far been able to hide any knowledge he possessed. There was strength in the old man still, but it wouldn't last.

Arik would die broken, with *nothing* left of the man he had once been.

"I can take your soul at any time," Ciro said as he laid his father's limp hand on his lap. "It is gray, tarnished by the lives you have taken and the lies you have told, darkened by your thirst for power and your willingness to start a war to get what you wanted."

"I did what was best for Columbyana," Arik whispered, as a whisper was all he had the strength for.

"You did what was best for Arik, you selfish bastard." Ciro smiled. "Now, let's move on to the current war, shall we? Where is your army, Father? I imagine they'll be here soon enough, but it would be nice to know when they might arrive so I and my men can be prepared. None can challenge me for the right to the throne as you challenged your brother, but I imagine there are those who will fight me in any case." If he knew precisely where the army was located, he could place his Own between them and Arthes. With luck, they'd never reach the palace.

He expected some kind of protest from his father, but the old man remained still. In fact, there was an unexpected jolt of life in the shriveled body.

"What are you thinking, old man? What has you believing there is even a shred of hope that I won't win this war?"

Was it his imagination, or did his father attempt to *smile*?

Ciro grasped his father's chin and yanked the old man's head up so their eyes met. He felt the demon rise up, and knew his own eyes turned black as night. "Tell me."

He pushed into the old man's brain. Feeble as he was, Arik fought hard to hide his thoughts. The former emperor began to ponder on days past to conceal anything of importance. He thought of Ciro's mother, and another woman Ciro did not know. He thought of Ciro as a baby, as a child, as a young man untouched by demons. He thought of redberry pie, and jokes told to him by a minister of finance with whom he had been friends.

Ciro pushed harder, trying to make his way past the memories to see the present, to see what made the dying man smile.

He grasped his father's throat tight. "Tell me what I need to know. Show me what makes you smile when the loss of your very soul is at hand."

A few words trickled through, as Arik began to tire. *Brother.* His own brother, Sebestyen, who'd been dead all these years? No, Ciro's brother . . . a half-brother he had never known existed.

Babies. Whose babies? Whose? *Sebestyen's sons.*

"There were no babies. Sebestyen's whore and his get are dead and have been for a very long time," Ciro whispered as his grip tightened.

Arik closed his eyes. A peacefulness settled over him quickly. He spat out one, slightly garbled message. "You are not emperor. You are not my son."

And then he was gone. His soul, his life, his memories, and his knowledge. Gone.

In anger, Ciro picked up his father's body, chair and all, and tossed it across the room. Arik felt nothing. Arik was gone sooner than Ciro had intended, leaving annoying and unanswered questions in the wake of his departure.

Brother.

Babies.

FROM A DISTANCE, THE VILLAGE LOOKED NOT SO DIFFERent from any other. It was only as they drew close that Lyr sensed a wrongness. All was silent. Too silent. As they rode closer, he saw that many of the buildings in the village had been burned, and no attempt had been made at repairs.

As they rode down the main street, he realized why. There was no one left to make those repairs. If anyone had lived through whatever fight had taken place here, they'd departed long ago.

Months ago. Remains had turned to bones. Weeds grew among the ruins. Lyr possessed no psychic powers, but he could feel to the pit of his soul that in this place a terrible thing had happened, and this plot of land would never be right again. No one would build where this village had once stood. No one would so much as try to make use of the wood that remained of the few buildings that had not burned.

It was a ghost town, and they'd best ride straight through.

It was Swaine who asked, "M'lord, should we search for usable supplies?"

"No," Lyr said crisply. "We want nothing that comes from this place. Keep riding."

He wanted to look back to see how Rayne was reacting to the scene, to the charred remains and the bones, to the heavy air of wrongness, but he didn't. He didn't dare let on to her or anyone else that he was concerned about how she might feel at this moment, or any other.

His plan was to ride straight through without stopping, to emerge on the other side and leave the damned village behind. He would not so much as glance back.

Rayne had other plans.

First he heard her gasp, and then he heard the collective protest of his men. All of them shouted. *No. Don't. It isn't safe.* Lyr turned about to see that Rayne had already slipped from her saddle and was running toward a corpse that lay half in and half out of the doorway to what might've once been a public house. A skeletal arm was outstretched. Fire had burned away clothing and flesh, but the afternoon sunlight slanted down at just the right angle to sparkle on a wide gold bracelet and a golden ring which dangled on bone.

Whoever had done this—Ciro and his Own were the likeliest culprits—had not been concerned with taking valuables. The bracelet and ring would be worth a small fortune to a farmer or a shopkeeper, but they had been left on the victim as if unimportant. If anyone had stumbled across this scene in months past, they'd run from it without looting the bodies. Anyone who passed by here would sense the same wrongness which had been so apparent to Lyr.

When Rayne dropped down in front of the corpse and sobbed, Lyr knew what they had found. Her father. He dismounted and walked toward her, touched by the sobs but unable to show it, wishing desperately that they had taken a different route. She already knew that her father was dead. There was no reason for her to see what had become of him.

"Get back on your horse and forget what you've seen here," he said, his voice low and steady.

He was prepared for Rayne to argue with him, but he was not prepared for her to jump up and hurl her body at his, holding on to him and sobbing even harder, clutching at him as if she'd fall to the ground if he pushed her away. For a moment he didn't know what to do. This was highly improper, and his men were watching.

There was nothing he could do but put steadying arms around her and offer comfort. Offering comfort was not his strong suit, but he did the best he could. He patted her back, then ran a hand up and down. He murmured a senseless "It's all right," when nothing in this world was all right at this time and they both knew it.

"You told me he was dead," Rayne said, her voice broken and sad, "but to know that he died like this, to be burned and left behind without a proper burial, to lie in the open this way and . . . and . . ."

"Forget what you've seen." Comforting finished, Lyr tried to remove Rayne from him and turn her toward her mare. "What remains of your father is not your father, do you understand that?"

Rayne refused to release him, and he could not bring himself to forcibly push her away. "He was not a good man." Her sobs lessened in intensity. "But there were times when he was a decent father. I think he loved me." She sounded less than certain.

"I'm sure he did," Lyr said, though he could not at all be sure that a man who would leave his daughter chained in the cellar and promised to a demon had any love in his heart.

Her grip lessened, and Lyr felt a rush of relief. She was going to release him. She had come to her senses and would back away.

"We will bury him, won't we?" Her head, which had been pressed against his chest, tipped back so she could look him in the eye. "I can't leave my father this way."

"We don't have time . . ."

She moved well away from him, finally. "You go on,

then," she said, anger taking the place of her sorrow. "I'll bury him myself."

"You know very well I can't leave you here," he said in a lowered voice.

"Then help me bury my father." Her eyes, still wet with tears, pleaded with him. They were the sort of eyes that might break a man's heart if he allowed.

Lyr looked up and down the street. Fynnian's body was not the only one that had been left to rot. Would burying the victims of the slaughter make it a better place? Would anything or anyone heal if they made that effort?

He finally set Rayne aside as he turned to the men, who watched too closely. They had never seen the Prince of Swords offer solace to anyone, and he could not help but notice the curiosity in their eyes. He ignored those glances. "Find some proper tools. Shovels, picks, anything that will move dirt. We'll dig one grave."

Segyn's mouth was set in a grimace that spoke of disapproval as he repeated Lyr's original protest. "M'lord, we haven't the time for—"

"We'll make the time, and we'll all do our part. Cover your hands and faces as you work. These bodies have been here a long while and those which were not burned might be diseased."

"I'll dig," Rayne said, most of the teary sadness gone from her voice. "I know I can't do as much as the four of you, but—"

"You will not dig." As the men moved away to find the tools they'd need, Lyr turned to face Rayne. "You may say words over the grave if you'd like, but you'll have to make them quick."

"I don't mind helping," she said. "In fact, I insist. I'm the one who made the request, so I'll—"

Lyr was unaccustomed to having his commands questioned, and Rayne questioned him constantly. He was mightily tired of it. "You will not dig your father's grave. Mention it again and we'll leave him where he lays."

Rayne pursed her lips to keep from saying more and then dropped her head as if to stare at her feet.

"Help me lead the horses to the other end of town," Lyr said in a kinder voice. He tried to imagine finding his own father in such a state and could not. No matter what sort of man he'd been, Fynnian had been dear to his daughter. "We will dig the grave there, away from the scene of their deaths. You have spoken often of your garden. Perhaps you would like to gather a few plants with which to mark the grave."

Her head popped up quickly, and he saw the light of pleasure in her eyes. That light should not bring him even a tidbit of joy, but it did.

"Yes," she said. "I would like that very much."

They gathered the horses, and as they walked the animals down the street of the dead village, Lyr felt compelled to add, "Don't move too far away from us as you work. What happened here took place long ago, but I don't like the feel of this village." He did not add that he didn't want her out of his sight.

Rayne nodded and then she said in a lowered voice, "You're a good man, Lyr Hern."

"No, you are a good daughter. I would not stop to take on this chore if you had not insisted."

She didn't look at him as she answered, "A good daughter would've stood up to her father when she realized he had chosen the wrong path. A truly good daughter would have tried to save her father before a day like this one arrived. I was too meek, too . . . too afraid to do what I knew to be right. I won't be afraid again." A touch of steel entered her soft voice.

Lyr didn't tell her that every warrior knew fear. The trick was in not allowing that fear to rule all else.

At the moment his own fear was a new one. He didn't know that he could save Rayne from Ciro. He didn't know if he would be called upon to take the life of this woman who had the power to make him do things he knew he should not do.

His fear for her was much greater than any he had ever known for himself.

8

LYR AND HIS MEN WORKED HARD, AND THEY FINISHED their unpleasant chore much sooner than Rayne had expected they would. She took Lyr's advice to heart and remained nearby as she did her own digging. Even if he hadn't told her to stay close, she would've done so. She felt safer in their presence . . . in Lyr's presence, more rightly.

She chose two small bushes she knew would flower in the spring, and also unearthed two evergreen plants. It was possible that no one else would ever know these bushes marked such horror, but she would know. Maybe her father would know, if his spirit survived and watched over her.

Somehow she thought his spirit would have better things to do. Though she tried to convince herself that he'd loved her, in truth she had never been very high on his list of priorities. In death would he be sorry for the choices he had made in life?

When the remains had been covered and nothing more than a mound of recently turned dirt marked the spot,

Rayne set the chosen plants on the sites where she wished them to be. One each of the evergreens at the foot and the head of the grave, the two plants which would flower in the center. Each of the men made a move to assist her, but she shooed them away. They had done their part and needed to rest. This was her contribution to the chore, and she wanted to accomplish it alone.

As she dug holes for the plants with the simple tools Swaine had given her, she hummed a spiritual tune her mother had taught her years ago. Odd, but she'd forgotten the song until now, though her mother had sung it often. It seemed fitting, as if the serene words might lift away some of the pain of this place. She dug, and hummed, and when the song was done, she spoke to the plants. They were living things, after all, different in many ways from animals and humans but still very much alive. Her escorts, all four of them, sat, rested, and watched. They did not speak. Perhaps they were too drained from their unpleasant chore.

At the center of the large grave she dug a suitable hole and placed the roots of the first of the flowering plants there. She used her hands to cover the roots, and then she moved a short distance away to do the same for the other plant. She could not tell if the blooms on this wild flowering plant would be white or lavender, but she hoped for the latter. This dull place needed some color, even if it lasted only for a week or so once a year.

It would be best if someone were here to water the transplants and tend to them until they were well situated in their new sites, but that was not possible. She would have to trust that rain would fall and the roots would remain healthy and reach deeper into the earth.

"Grow for me," she whispered. "Take root, be strong. Flower." She dug her hands into the dirt, wishing she could share her will for life, that she could send that will into the soil itself. She wished that she could somehow assure, even though she would never pass this way again, that the plants which marked this grave would thrive.

Just a few inches from her nose a leaf twitched. The wind, she thought immediately before several more leaves began to twist and dance. She felt no wind in her hair or on her face, though she would have welcomed a breeze since her physical efforts had caused her to perspire.

She did not remove her hands from the dirt, but remained very still as the plant began to grow before her eyes. It was as if a season passed in the blinking of an eye. The thin limbs grew longer, and buds appeared, growing as she took one long, deep breath.

The buds opened, revealing large, healthy lavender blooms. It was as if time rushed forward.

Time. Was this Lyr's doing somehow? Her head snapped up and she found that all four men had risen and moved closer to her, and they stared at the plants, which were growing at a rapid rate. Judging by the expression on Lyr's face, this was not his doing. He was stunned.

Somehow she had done this herself.

Rayne removed her hands from the dirt, and the growth stopped. The blooms looked healthy, and they were decidedly fragrant. She stood and brushed the loose dirt from her hands, and absently brushed away some of the soil that had stuck to her skirt. There was no quick fix for the dirt which was lodged beneath her fingernails.

It was Segyn who spoke first. "I did not know you possessed such magic," he said, his tone reverent.

"Neither did I," she said.

Her gaze was drawn to Lyr, who stared at her with those narrowed eyes which always seemed so calculating. She knew him well enough to realize that he did not entirely believe her.

* * *

PHELAN WASN'T SURE HOW TO PROCEED. SOMETHING HAD happened between Rayne and Lyr, or else it was about to happen. He was not blind to the silent exchanges where eyes met eyes, and who wouldn't question the way the slut had so easily thrown herself into m'lord's arms when she'd found her father's body?

The Isen Demon wished the woman to be pure in all ways, but was it already too late for that?

No, the demon whispered. *Emperor Ciro is concerned with purity of the body. I care most ardently for the brightness of her soul. That is what matters to the babe she will carry.*

Phelan cared nothing for Ciro and what he wanted, but he did want to please the Isen Demon. How else could he get all that he wanted when the world turned to darkness?

"Now?" Phelan whispered. "Do I take her now?"

Soon. When the opportunity arises, take it. Kill the warriors, take the woman, bury the crystal dagger deep.

Soon. Phelan was anxious to make his move, but considering what Lyr was capable of meant he had to plan carefully. While the other slept, perhaps. Then again, if he could catch the Prince of Swords unaware, that would do just as well. His limbs tingled with excitement as they rode away from the mass grave where the woman had demonstrated her magical ability, an ability she claimed she'd known nothing about until this very day.

He was not concerned by the demonstration of magic. Forcing a plant to bloom out of season couldn't exactly be used as a weapon, not against him and certainly not against the Isen Demon.

Soon.

He could hardly wait, and in truth—why should he? The

sooner he had the others out of the way and Rayne in his grasp, the sooner his charade could end. Yes, it was time.

IT HAD BEEN DIFFICULT FOR LYR TO KEEP HIS QUESTIONS to himself as they traveled well past dark. It would not do for his men to realize how curious he was about Rayne's supposedly newly discovered powers. How could she have possessed such a gift and not known about it until now? She'd mentioned often that she kept a garden. Did she not find it unusual that she could ask her plants to grow and they obeyed?

He needed to know the details of her gift. Was she a fertility witch like Aunt Sophie? Would she get pregnant if he sneezed in her direction, or were her gifts exclusively directed to plant life? He had given little thought to babies when he'd lain with her. It wasn't as if women regularly found themselves with child after one night. Yes, that was possible, but he considered it unlikely.

Unless she was like Aunt Sophie.

Segyn and Swaine slept, and Til kept watch. Even though their journey had been uneventful, they were all unsettled by the day's findings. The destroyed village, the sense of dread that still lived there, they reminded them all of what they were fighting against, and how difficult that fight would be.

Rayne tried to go to sleep, but it was obvious by the way she tossed and turned on the ground that she was not sleeping—and sleep was not coming anytime soon. The discovery of her father's body and the revelation—or unintentional display—of her magical talents left her unsettled.

Lyr was a bit unsettled himself, truth be told.

He made his way to her by moonlight alone. His night vision was quite sharp, and on a night like this one there was no need for a fire. So far their journey had been blessed with good weather and a lack of obstacles, but he didn't think that was likely to last.

Lyr leaned down, knowing Rayne was awake. "I would have a word with you," he whispered.

She rolled over to look up and directly at him. Yes, she looked innocent enough. "A word?"

"A word." He offered his hand to assist her, and she took it. That simple touch, her hand in his, was like taking lightning into his palm. On his palm and in his blood and into every nerve of his body. He tried very hard not to let his reaction show. His response was entirely physical in any case, and in the end unimportant.

He drew Rayne to her feet and led her away from the camp. They would not go far, but he didn't wish to wake those who slept. Til watched as Lyr and Rayne walked away from the small camp. He nodded in acknowledgment, and then glanced at the sleeping soldiers. Tonight his job was an easy one, and he was likely grateful for it after a day which had not been at all easy.

Lyr and Rayne walked into the deeper shadows of a forest, where the leaves were turning red and gold and blue. Soon those leaves would fall and cover the ground and the trees would be bare, but on this night the trees were lushly alive.

"You said you had no magic," Lyr said, his voice soft and accusing.

"I didn't. At least, not that I knew of."

"You made those plants grow and bloom. Is that not magic?"

"Of course it is, but it's not something I've ever been able to do in the past." She bit her lower lip. "Not that I was aware of, in any case. Maybe it's my father's bracelet or his ring."

"You have them on you?"

"Yes. Tiller said it was all right. He helped me—"

"I told you to take nothing," Lyr interrupted. He'd told Til, too. Everything about that ruined village reeked of darkness, and it should've all been buried with the remains.

"I have nothing of my father but for those two things," Rayne argued. "Surely it can't matter—"

"They come from a dark place, Rayne. Surely you realize that as well as I do."

She dropped her head. "The truth is I might need them to live on, once you leave me elsewhere. I have some of my mother's jewels, but I don't know how long the proceeds from their sale might last."

Lyr took her chin in his hand and forced her to look him in the eye. "I will not let you starve or live beneath yourself," he promised. "I will not simply drop you in a strange place and leave you to your own devices."

"I thought that was the plan," she said. "How else am I to hide myself?"

"I don't have all the answers," Lyr said, "but I do know that I won't leave you." He felt his brow knit. "Was that the reason you asked me to have sex with you? Did you know that once that was done, I would feel responsible for you to the pit of my soul?"

"No," she whispered. She lifted her skirt. Even in the dark, Lyr could see the fabric bag that was strapped to her thigh. She carried her valuables much as he carried the crystal dagger, close against the skin.

She opened the bag and drew out the two gold pieces. "Do you really think there's darkness in these?"

"Yes, I do. I learned at an early age that good and evil both remain in the things they touch."

Rayne did not ask again. She drew back her hand and threw the jewelry she'd taken from her father deep into the forest. The gold pieces made soft sounds as they broke through limbs and leaves and finally landed on the ground a good distance away.

"If they are the reason for my ability, then it is now done," she said without regret.

"And if they're not?"

Rayne placed one hand on Lyr's chest. "Maybe it was you. Us, more rightly. I swear, I did feel as if I reached another place in my very soul when I . . . well . . . when we . . ."

"After what we shared, I would say there is no need for shyness."

"I suppose there's not." She took a deep breath. "The pleasure I experienced in your arms was not only of the body, it touched my soul. I felt it there, I'm sure of it. Perhaps my gift was resting there until you roused it."

"That is unlikely."

"Is it? Is that theory any more unlikely than a magic that might've been trapped in two pieces of gold?" Her hand settled boldly on his penis, and he grew quickly. "I believe there is more magic in what we shared than in any wizard's words or talismans. I believe the magic of the universe might awaken at the soft sound of two bodies coming together."

"It was only—" Lyr began.

"It wasn't *only* anything," she said breathlessly. "Tell me you don't want me again. Tell me you have not thought endlessly of being inside me again."

It had not been Lyr's intention, when he'd led Rayne into the darkness, to do anything but talk. But the way she touched him, the way she spoke so seductively and innocently, changed his intentions.

"Do you want me now?" he whispered, leaning down to kiss the side of her neck.

"I do, more than ever. More than I thought was possible."

There was no soft bed, no undressing or arousing or games. He was hard, she was wet, and it seemed they tumbled together without thought or design. She freed him, he lifted her skirt, and moments later he took her with rough tree bark at her back and her thighs wrapped about his hips.

Last night her room had been dark. Tonight the moonlight illuminated her, and her worse-for-wear traveling dress covered the skin he longed to see. He had touched her delicate flesh, he had reveled in it, but he wished to *see*. He wished to see the swell of her breasts as well as touch it. He wished to study the dip of her waist and the curve of her hip. Even now he could be still and remove her gown, showing patience and restraint and care, but he did not.

Lost in her tight warmth, he forgot all else. There was no gentle instruction of a virgin, not tonight. It was as if they'd become animals, as if they'd lost control and obeyed the commands of their bodies without the interference of their minds. Lyr never lost control. Never.

If losing control meant this kind of intense pleasure, he should allow himself the satisfaction more often.

Rayne moved against him, she moaned as she ground her hips against his and very quickly found release. She gasped and clutched at his hair. Her thighs tightened around him and he felt her tremble in every bone of her fine body. Her inner muscles spasmed around him and he climaxed in response.

To the soul, she'd said, and at the moment he could not argue with her. This was certainly unlike any controlled, well-planned liaison he'd shared with any woman in the past.

As Lyr returned to the world, he noticed that leaves fell all around their joined bodies. Red leaves, plump and colorful, dropped en masse, though the color was not easy to see at night. Rayne lifted her face and smiled as the leaves rained down.

She took his face in her hands and kissed him. The kiss was deep and enthusiastic and filled with emotion. Her lips danced over his, her tongue fluttered and explored. The rustle of falling leaves surrounded them, and Lyr felt them pile up at his feet. He heard a sharp cracking sound, a crackling of the bark as the tree grew more quickly than was natural. The rustling sound was like the wind, or the rush of a brook, but there was no wind, no rushing water. There was only Rayne, daughter of the dead wizard Fynnian, betrothed to Ciro, lover to Prince of Swords.

"I do not think it was my father's gold that awakened my magic," Rayne whispered as the leaves fell. After a hard day where there had been no joy, Lyr heard joy in her voice.

RAYNE WAS GLAD TO PUT MILES BETWEEN HER AND THE village where her father had died. As she rode along, she wondered if Lyr had any idea that he had helped her so much when he'd led her into the forest last night. Not just for sexual pleasure, not that she was complaining, but for the simple and wondrous act of being with a friend.

Lyr was her friend, wasn't he? Perhaps the only true friend she'd ever had.

Tiller sometimes looked at her and almost smirked, as if he knew what had happened last night. He'd been too far away to do more than suspect, and in truth she didn't care. Lyr did care, however. He'd made it clear his men were not to know the true nature of their relationship.

Friendship.

Scx.

Love?

Maybe.

When they stopped for an afternoon break, Segyn left

the care of the horses to Til and Swaine and swaggered to her with a smile on his face. "Do you think you could make any bush grow the way you made the flowers grow?"

"I don't know," she said honestly. "The ability is . . . new. Untested. I honestly don't know what I can do."

"I ask because I spotted a yettle bush right over there." He pointed to the south. "Have you ever had a yettle berry?"

"I've never even heard of them," she confessed. "Are they tasty?"

Segyn rolled his eyes. "Tasty indeed. Sweet as pie with just a touch of tartness to tease the tongue. They're very rare. I had wondered if there were any yettle berry bushes left in the world, that is how rare they are. They sprout early in the summer, but it occurred to me that if you can make flowers when there should be none, perhaps you could make berries as well. I suspect Lyr would enjoy a bite of something sweet on a warm afternoon."

The very thought made Rayne smile. Lyr didn't take time for many pleasures; she had learned that about him. If she could feed him a few sweet berries when there should be none, what a gift that would be.

Segyn led her to the bush, and Rayne knelt down before it. Lyr was not about, so if she was successful, the berries would be a surprise. Lyr had gone to the stream where Til and Swaine had taken the horses, and there he would likely shave quickly with a small, sharp knife. Last night his beard had been quite rough, so it was time. He would return with smooth cheeks, and she would feed him sweet berries—if she could make her magic work again.

She pressed her hands into the dirt at the base of the bush. She could almost feel a part of herself seeping into the soil, feeding the plant with a magical energy. "Can you give us lovely berries, even though the time has not come?" She began to sing, as she had yesterday, and in moments the growth began. The leaves quivered, and soon small blooms opened. The blooms dropped, and berries appeared. At first they were red, and then they turned a dark purple.

And then the growth stopped.

Rayne began to pick while Segyn looked on. "There are so many! Everyone will be able to have a few, and if they'll keep well enough, perhaps we can pack what's left for later today and tomorrow." She looked over her shoulder to a smiling Segyn. "Would you like to help me pick?"

"After you take some to m'lord, I will pick some for myself."

Rayne had so many berries she ended up carrying them in the folds of her skirt. Til and Swaine should have some fruit, too. After all they had done for her, she was glad to be able to give them something, even if it was just a handful of berries.

There was a rough path of sorts that led to the stream. She arrived just as Lyr was washing off his freshly shaved face, and with a smile she presented the berries, which rested on her skirt, to him. "Yettle berries," she said. "Segyn says they're very sweet and tasty."

Lyr studied the fruit. "I have never had these berries."

"Neither have I, but Segyn says they're sweet as pie and that's good enough for me."

Lyr took a handful of berries and popped one into his mouth. Another followed, and then he smiled. Lyr did not smile often, she knew that, so this smile was particularly gratifying. While he ate, she offered Til and Swaine some of what she'd gathered, and they both took greedy handfuls.

They had both taken big bites, tossing several berries at a time into their mouths, when Lyr fell.

Rayne turned, not sure what to think of what she'd just seen. Lyr *fell*, landing on his face. He was so graceful, she had never seen him so much as stumble. The breath he took—face in the dirt—was a labored one, and a moment later his hand opened to spill berries across the ground.

"Are you choking?" Rayne dropped to her knees. The berries she'd caught in her skirt scattered, rolling away from her as she turned Lyr onto his back. His face was taut and slightly contorted, and his hands were clenched. His throat worked oddly, and for a moment she believed that he was truly choking.

And then Tiller fell, followed by Swaine.

Rayne looked at the berries she'd dropped. They were poisoned! How could Segyn have made such a mistake? She screamed for Lyr's next in command and in very short order he was there, as if he had been waiting for her call.

"I think this is the wrong sort of berry," she said frantically. "They all ate a few and then they fell, and . . . I think they're dying."

"You didn't eat any?" Segyn asked.

"No, I was—"

"A lady always serves others first."

How could he be so calm? "Do something!" she commanded. "They're dying!"

"They're not dying," Segyn said in an even voice as he stepped past her and drew his sword. "Not yet."

9

LYR COULDN'T MOVE. HE COULD BARELY BREATHE. HIS arms and legs felt heavy, as if they were not his own.

She'd poisoned him. Just as he'd feared, Rayne had never been who she'd appeared to be. She'd seduced him, made him care about her, and now she was going to kill him for her true lover—her beloved Ciro.

Segyn stepped into the clearing. He obviously hadn't eaten any of the poison berries. Rayne spoke to him, but Lyr could barely hear her treacherous words. His blood was rushing so fast he couldn't understand what she was trying to say. Making excuses, no doubt. Trying to explain away why three men lay helpless while she looked on.

Segyn saw through her. The Circle Warrior drew his sword. Lyr tried to shout *no*, but he wasn't sure why. Rayne had poisoned him and his men, so it was right that Segyn kill her. And still, he wanted to scream *no*.

Segyn walked past Rayne to the bank where Til and Swaine lay, no doubt as helpless as Lyr. He couldn't see them, not in this position, and he couldn't turn his head for a better view. Segyn was likely checking to see that they still breathed, that they could be saved. Could they? Could any of them be saved?

With effort, Lyr shifted his eyes just enough to see Segyn raise his sword and bring it down again, not once but twice.

Rayne screamed. Lyr heard that well even through the rushing of blood in his ears.

And then Segyn moved to Lyr. He stood above, his sword grasped easily in one hand. For a moment the Circle Warrior studied Lyr from that position so far above, and then he smiled widely and something in Lyr's heart died. Segyn was his friend, a man he trusted above all others, and somehow he had done this terrible thing. Not Rayne, but Segyn. Or were they working together? Had Rayne seduced Segyn as well? Had she been playing a deadly game from the moment they'd found her bound and supposedly helpless? It didn't matter how this had come to be. Segyn's participation was a betrayal of the worst sort, a betrayal that cut to the core.

Rayne threw herself at Segyn in an apparent rage, but the large man pushed her aside with little expended effort. Rayne landed on her backside in the dirt, and Segyn spun about to point the tip of his sword at her chest. Lyr could not yet hear, but he managed to read Segyn's lips.

Move and I'll gut you.

So, they weren't working together after all. It was just Segyn, only Segyn, and somehow that was worse.

When Rayne was still and properly warned, Segyn turned his attention to Lyr again. He leaned down, bringing his face closer to Lyr's, and shouted to be heard. "Where is the crystal dagger?"

Lyr would've shaken his head, but still could not move.

"Of course, you can't tell me just yet." Segyn dropped to his haunches, casual and easy as if he had not just murdered two comrades and now threatened a friend. "I could search for it, but in a little bit you will be able to speak again. Before you can move, you'll regain your hearing and your speech." Again, there was that smile which was not Segyn's and yet . . . was. "I had planned to wait awhile longer before making my move, but when I saw the yettle berry bush so near to the place we stopped, I decided it was meant to be. That isn't a plant you see every day, after all, so it seemed quite fortuitous. I've worried quite a bit about how I might kill you without taking the chance that you'd stop time for me in the midst of an attack. You're such a light sleeper, especially when we're traveling."

Apparently Rayne moved, because Segyn's head snapped around. This time, Lyr could hear his words. "You likely know I won't gut you, not before Emperor Ciro gets his hands on you. I will, however, make you *very* uncomfortable, and I will gut your lover slowly while you watch, rather than offering him a quick death. So sit yourself down and don't move until I tell you to move! Don't look at me that way as if you think you can fight me. What are you going to do, pelt me with berries and flowers?" Segyn laughed harshly at that concept.

Lyr wished he could see Rayne, but he could not. At the moment he could see nothing but blue skies above and the face of a traitorous friend.

Segyn returned his attention to Lyr. "We have a little time, and I did promise to tell you about my kitchen maid, didn't I? It's a tale I've often longed to share, but could not. Not until now." He leaned slightly closer, as if to make sure no detail was missed. "I made use of her, the same way you have taken to making use of Emperor Ciro's bride, and she loved me. She loved me even more than you love me. You do love me, don't you, m'lord? Not the way she did, of course, but as a young man loves a father or an older brother. You trusted your life to me, more than once."

Yes. Lyr still could not speak, but the word echoed in his brain.

"She saw in me the man I wanted her to see, just as you did. I showed her only the face I wished the world to know. I was a lover, a friend, a trusted companion, and she never saw beyond what I wished her to see. It's been difficult, as you can imagine, hiding my true self in the midst of wizards and seers, with witches all around. I had to become someone else for a while, and let my true self sleep." He smiled a chilling smile. "I killed her. She was my first. Like you, she didn't see it coming. Even when I wrapped my hands around her throat and squeezed, she thought it was a joke. Up until the moment she died, my little kitchen lover did not think me capable of taking her life. She was wrong."

Segyn slapped Lyr's cheek soundly, but Lyr felt nothing. "Can you speak yet? I need that dagger so I can dispose of it properly." He opened Lyr's vest and patted down the sides of his pants. His hands skimmed right over the dagger, and yet he seemed not to feel it. Segyn's speed and clumsiness or magic? Lyr had never known Segyn to be clumsy.

"We can't have just anyone stumbling across that special weapon," Segyn said. "It's on you somewhere, I suppose. In your boot? A hidden sheath? Maybe in your saddle bag, but I doubt it. You wouldn't want to walk away from such a treasure, not even for a moment. Besides, I've already searched your saddlebags, while the berries I pointed out to Ciro's bride filled your stomach and did their work. You can tell me where the dagger is and we'll make this quick, or I can tear you apart until I find it."

Again, Segyn's head snapped around to look at Rayne. "What do you think you're—"

It happened so quickly, Segyn was cut off in midsentence. A thick length of vine twined around the arm which held his sword. The massive, muscled arm was yanked up and the weapon was tossed aside. Other vines, also thick and moving quickly and unnaturally, wrapped snakelike around Segyn's legs and his other arm, yanking the traitor away from Lyr, throwing him down to the ground with force, and then pinning him there. Leaves twitched as if alive, dancing around the stem, which pulsed gently.

When Segyn was restrained, Rayne rushed forward and leaned over Lyr. "We have to get out of here. Can you move yet? Can you speak?"

No.

"I don't know how long the vine will hold him."

Segyn shouted. He screamed and howled like a trapped animal. "There is nowhere you can go that you'll be safe, boy. If you escape me now, an army will come after you. They'll be ready for you and your tricks, and they'll find a way to stop you just as I did. You'll sleep, or you'll let your guard down, and they'll be there. When that happens, the demon's soldiers will take her from you and they'll leave you in pieces on the road. They're coming for you. They're coming soon and you won't know they're before you until it's too late! Can you hear their hoofbeats on the road?"

Lyr began to feel a tingling on his face as Rayne tried to help him into a sitting position. He was too heavy for her, and he ended up lying on his side. He almost wished she had left him where he lay flat on his back, for now he had a gruesome view. Til and Swaine had been ruthlessly murdered while helpless, killed by a man they had trusted just as Lyr had.

"Shut up!" Rayne screamed as she scurried about gathering berries dusted with dirt. She'd dropped them on the ground, but now she gathered a handful and rushed toward Segyn.

When she got close, she stopped, afraid to move any closer. Like him, like Swaine and Til, she'd trusted Segyn, but that trust had died a quick and certain death. She dropped down and thrust her fingers into the dirt, and segments of the vine which imprisoned Segyn crept toward her. Moving like a snake, the vine crept closer. Though it was unnatural and, to Lyr's mind, inexplicable, she was not afraid. A sturdy leaf growing from the stem plucked a berry from Rayne's hand. One and then another, the leaves plucked until her hand was empty, and then the vine moved toward Segyn.

Knowing what she intended, what the unnatural plant itself intended, Segyn tried to clamp his mouth shut. He was no match for the vine which moved at Rayne's command, a creeping and oddly strong plant which pried his lying lips apart and force-fed him the paralyzing berries. Purple juice spewed from his mouth and down his chin, but some of the berries made their way past stubborn lips and clenched teeth.

In moments Segyn dropped to the ground, not dead but helpless and no longer fighting against the plant which restrained him. The berries had paralyzed him and the vine continued to bind him.

Again, Rayne attempted to help Lyr up. He was beginning to feel again. A tingling sensation rippled in his arms and legs, and breathing was easier. The paralysis caused by the berries was temporary, which meant Segyn would be mobile again very soon.

"We must hurry," Rayne said as she tugged at his hand. "Please tell me you can move, please tell me we won't be sitting here when Ciro's soldiers arrive."

Lyr wasn't sure that part of Segyn's speech had held any truth. He'd confessed that he'd chosen this moment to reveal his true nature because they stumbled across the berries. That was happenstance, so it couldn't be possible that a planned attack was about to take place.

Still, Lyr didn't know what to believe at this moment. He'd trusted Segyn without question, and that trust had been horribly misplaced. The older man was right. Lyr had loved him, like a brother or a second father, like a friend who would never do what he had done.

With great effort and Rayne's help, Lyr rose to his feet. He moved slowly and clumsily, as if there were rocks and grit among his bones.

"Hurry." Rayne tugged on his arm. "We must leave before Ciro's soldiers arrive. You are in no shape to fight an entire army."

He was well trained, and he had an extraordinary gift, but Lyr had never attempted to fight an army on his own. He'd never even imagined he might be called upon to face such a task. In the weeks to come, he would need to rest, even if just for short periods of time. If the opposing army—or a single soldier—came while he slept, he might be killed before he had a chance to stop time. There was no one to watch his back, not anymore. There was no one but Rayne.

Rayne's grip steadied him as he drew his sword and stepped toward Segyn.

"What are you doing?" she asked.

"I'm going to kill him."

Her grip tightened. "You can't kill him. He's helpless, and . . . and no matter what he's done, he's your friend."

Lyr turned his head to look down at Rayne. Her cheeks were damp with tears, and she was very pale. She wanted to escape this situation, to ride away quickly and forget all that she had seen here.

He did not have the luxury of taking escape.

"If we leave him alive, he will come after us. He will tell Ciro's men of your talents, and they will be on guard. He will tell Ciro that you are no longer the pure maid he chose as his betrothed."

If Lyr thought he could ride away from the bound man and never face the consequences of that weakness, he would gladly do so. He did not wish to take the life of a man who could not defend himself, but when he looked at what remained of Til and Swaine, when he looked at Rayne and wondered what Ciro's soldiers would do to her if they got the chance, he knew he had no choice.

His sword was heavy, much heavier than usual thanks to the weakness in his limbs, but he was able to lift it enough to point the tip at Segyn's heart. Segyn could not speak, could not move, but his eyes spoke of fear. Even a fiend could fear for his own life apparently.

Lyr trembled, a combination of a lingering weakness from the poison berries he'd eaten and the realization of what he was about to do. This was Segyn . . . and yet it was not.

He pushed the blade forward cleanly, into Segyn's chest, into the black heart which was capable of unspeakable treachery. He did not immediately turn to face Rayne, the woman who continued to hold on to him. Lyr could hear Rayne's tears; he did not wish for her to see his.

SINCE THERE WAS A SMALL CHANCE THAT SEGYN HAD been right in telling them that Ciro's army was close, Lyr changed his course of travel. Instead of taking infrequently traveled roads, he turned into the forest itself. He explained to Rayne that he'd studied the maps of Columbyana carefully before starting his journey to retrieve the dagger he now possessed, and while the roads they'd been upon for many days were the easiest route to the site where Ariana's army should be at this time, the swamp which lay beyond the forest was a more direct route. If they didn't run into trouble along the way, they'd reach Ariana and General Merin more quickly, and he now felt an urgency to do just that.

Rayne was not at all anxious to discover what awaited in the swamp.

Lyr hadn't said a word since they'd left the others behind, all dead, and Rayne had remained silent as well. She didn't know what to say to take away his obvious pain. Maybe some things could not be helped with words of comfort. Maybe some pain went too deep.

Instead of the regulated column of five, they were now two. Lyr had freed the other horses, mounts which were no longer necessary as the men they had carried for such a long time were dead.

It was difficult to travel in the forest after darkness fell, so they had no choice but to stop. Here the moonlight did not light their way. Instead it was caught in the leaves overhead, and as the pathway they made was not free of obstacles, they were forced to rest, no matter how much they wanted to move onward and away from the scene of betrayal and death.

Lyr saw to the horses first, then he built a small fire in the clearing where they would make camp until morning. Still, he did not speak. He unpacked food and handed Rayne some, but did not eat himself. After inadvertently feeding Lyr poisoned berries, she found she could not urge him to eat. Tomorrow, perhaps, if he did not display a return of appetite of his own accord, she would find a way to suggest that he take some nourishment.

It was bold of her, perhaps, to seek him out, but Lyr was her lover, and they were now alone in this endeavor. What sense did it make to settle on the ground far apart, alone and cold and shaken to the core? Rayne sat next to Lyr, who was near the fire staring at the flames, and without hesitation she placed her head in his lap. She wasn't sure how he would react, since he was obviously shaken, but he didn't order or push her away. Instead he settled one hand in her hair and seemed grateful for the touch, however innocent.

After a while, he finally spoke. "Segyn said I would be burned one day," Lyr said softly. "I thought he was speaking of you, or perhaps of women in general, but in the end he was the one who did the deed himself. I wonder if he would think me done now."

"Done?"

"Finished. Burned. Done."

She didn't exactly understand, but in a way she understood enough. Until now, Lyr had never been hurt. Not like this.

A moment later, the first raindrop fell. Lyr made a snorting sound of disgust. "Not a drop of rain since we left your house, and now, on this of all days, it begins."

They were almost sheltered by the trees above, but there were gaps where raindrops could fall through, and when water gathered on the leaves, it would drop upon them in streams. Rayne worked her fingers in the dirt. Directing the growth of the berries this afternoon had been relatively easy, but calling on the vines to entrap Segyn had drained her. She didn't know if she had any magic left, but she tried. She whispered to the dirt and the trees and the bushes, she asked them to provide for her shelter. In a matter of moments they closed in around her and Lyr. The overlapping leaves formed a shield which protected them from most of the rain.

"Your gift is much more useful than mine," Lyr said. "At least, it has seemed so since revealing itself."

"You saved my life with your gift," she said.

"And you saved mine with yours."

They lay down on the ground together, the leaves forming a sort of tent around them, and Lyr wrapped his arms about her. Again he was silent, and she hated the deep quiet when she knew neither of them were near sleep.

"I once thought all magic was bad," she said. "Of course, I only had my father as an example, and magic twisted him horribly. The more power he possessed, the more he wanted. He was a wizard by birth and in that he had no choice, but he did have a choice in how he used what he'd been given. I thought all magic corrupted those it touched, but you don't seem to be damaged by your gifts. I don't want to be corrupted by mine," she added softly. "I don't want my soul to be tainted by a greedy darkness."

"I thought tainting your soul was what you wanted."

"No," she whispered. "For a short while I thought that was the way, but the spirit, the soul, is too important to treat in such a manner. I think I knew that all along, but my fear of Ciro made me desperate." She stroked her hand against his back. "I don't feel desperate anymore, Lyr. I don't know if I will be forced to hide or to fight, but I won't give him my soul in any way."

"I think that's wise."

Now was likely not the time to tell Lyr that she would gladly give *him* her soul. As she finally drifted toward what she suspected would be an uneasy sleep, it occurred to her that perhaps she already had.

After a long bout of silence, Lyr whispered, "I'm sorry."

"Sorry for what?" Rain pattered on a roof of entwined

leaves, lulling her, pulling her toward dreams. She would sleep tonight, after all, and she would likely have horrible nightmares.

"For a moment this afternoon I suspected you. I thought you were the traitor. I thought you had killed me with those poison berries."

Her heart became heavy, even though she understood why Lyr had believed her to be guilty. She had been the one to give him the berries, after all. "I will never hurt you," she whispered.

"I know that now, I truly do."

Rayne buried her face against Lyr's chest and held on tight. She listened to the patter of rain above their heads, and sleep came.

CIRO HAD DISCOVERED THAT HE DIDN'T NEED MUCH sleep since the demon had taken him. When he did sleep, he had vivid dreams that he knew were not exactly dreams. They were uncontrolled glimpses through the eyes of others who were connected to the demon, and so to him.

What he saw on this night terrified him. Rayne was not where she should be. She was in the care of another, in the embrace of a warrior who thought he could protect her.

A warrior who had already taken that which should've been Ciro's to take.

He came awake instantly and in a rage. Rayne would still wed him, she would give birth to their son as he and the Isen Demon had planned, but in many ways she had been ruined by the man who now protected her. Her time as his wife would not be as pleasant as it might've been if she'd waited for him. She would pay for her sin a thousand times.

She thought to soil her soul but she only made it brighter.

"How?"

The demon did not answer, but Ciro knew. Love. Rayne thought herself in love with the man who'd taken that which was rightfully his.

His empress had been fouled by another man.

She is still capable of carrying our child. She is the one.

Ciro knew that to be true, but anger filled him. First his father dies with his soul intact, and now this. His power grew every day, he had never imagined that he might possess such power, and still all did not go as he planned. If Ariana had not taken back so many souls, would he be strong enough to end them all? Would the demon have reached his full power if not for the witch's interference?

All is not lost.

"Show me something which proves that to be true."

The room, Ciro's fine bedchamber, melted away and he found himself standing by a stream. The image looked almost real, though on occasion the view shimmered as if to remind Ciro that he was not actually in this place. In the moonlight, three dead bodies were illuminated. Two lay by the stream, while another was caught in tangled vines that wrapped around his body and held him as steadfast as any chain.

"Where is the hope in this?" Death was everywhere, and more was coming. Ciro was certainly not appalled by the death of his enemies, but he did not see the hope in three dead soldiers, either.

The body which was caught in snarled vines twitched, and one of the men Ciro had thought dead sat up and took a deep breath. The bald man placed a hand on his chest, where blood had dried on his skin and his vest, and then he laughed. He laughed loud and long as he ripped the vines away. When one hand was free, he drew a knife and began to cut at the plants.

"Why should this insignificant man's survival take away my pain?" Ciro asked.

The bald man did not hear or see him, Ciro knew that. The bald man did not know that he could be seen, either.

Phelan will take your bride from the man who dared to join with her when she is rightfully yours. Phelan will capture the warrior who thinks he can kill you and take your place in Rayne's bed. Phelan is one of us, and we are harder to kill than most yet know.

That was true enough. Ciro had received more than one wound that would've been the death of him if not for the demon's strength and magic.

"I want the warrior to suffer."

He has, and he will.

"I want to kill him myself, and I will take his soul."

If you are strong enough when you meet him, you will take it.

Apparently the warrior had a white soul, and no matter how strong Ciro grew, the white eluded him.

With a suddenness that startled him, Ciro found himself back in his chamber, with a few pots of oil burning to create light in the darkness of night. Knowing that the man who had violated his virgin bride would die did ease the sting, but the dissatisfaction of having his plans spoiled was not so easy to dismiss. He dressed quickly and left his bedchamber, hoping to find some solace in the offices of the emperor, where he now held court, issued commands, and took blood and souls from those who dared to speak against him.

Yes, all in all, being emperor was pleasant enough.

In the dead of night, Ciro found little comfort in this official room. It was cold and without blood, and his anger at knowing another man had touched Rayne did not entirely abate—justice promised or not.

Only one thing would ease him, for a while. The drug Panwyr.

Ciro opened the top drawer of his desk, where he kept a healthy supply of the drug both he and Diella needed. In a drug-induced state he would envision fucking Rayne and then killing her. He would envision tearing her lover into small pieces, and it would seem almost real. It would seem real enough until the two came to him and his plans for them became true.

In his anger Ciro pulled too hard and the drawer flew out too far and too fast. The drawer came out of the desk entirely, swung to the side, left Ciro's grip, and landed on the floor with a sharp crack.

Ciro snatched the drawer from the floor, his eyes on the undamaged Panwyr, but his attention was averted when his fingers brushed against a thick sheaf of paper which was attached to the bottom of the drawer.

Curious, he snatched the folded papers from the drawer's underside. For a moment, at least, the Panwyr was forgotten. He unfolded the papers to reveal his father's handwriting.

I, Emperor Arik, name my illegitimate son Sian Sayre Chamblyn as my successor . . .

There was more, but Ciro read that first line many times before he allowed his eyes to move down the page. Not only had his father named this bastard as emperor, he'd coldly dismissed his own son, his own Prince Ciro, as a monster.

The papers could and would be destroyed, but first Ciro made note of the signatures at the bottom of the document. Chamblyn himself. The witch Ariana, who had also taken the name Chamblyn. There were other names . . . names he did not recognize. Names which did not matter.

Ciro built a fire in the stone fireplace, and as soon as it

was blazing, he dropped the document on the flames. He watched it burn, pushing away the too-human sensation of the pain of betrayal. This was the brother his father had sought to shield by hiding his thoughts. A brother who might attempt to claim what Ciro had taken.

Chamblyn would take *nothing*. Very soon, Ciro would have his bastard half brother brought to him. In pieces, if necessary.

10

THE SWAMP WAS AN ODDLY NOISY PLACE, CONSIDERING no humans but the two of them dared to travel through it. Birds chirped and animals hidden from their sight screeched and growled. Fish splashed. On the far, marshy bank, a large reptilian creature left the water to catch the sun and watch the travelers. All the creatures kept their distance from the intruders and their horses. Lyr imagined it was possible no other human had ever passed this way. Their path took them across an unfriendly landscape, with stark trees more dead than alive rising from the stagnant water.

The horses plodded through that shallow water on occasion, and when it was possible, they walked along a bank which was often too soft and slippery for the horses to safely tread upon. It was a treacherous path for any traveler, that was certain.

Ciro's men would not find them here, and if they did, Lyr would know long before the enemy soldiers were in sight. Sounds traveled a long way in this flat, echoing swamp, and his ears were alert. He would not sleep, and this path would take them to Ariana's army quickly. Lyr dismissed the horrors of past days and looked ahead. All that mattered was getting Rayne to safety and killing Ciro and the demon who lived within him. There had been a time when killing the enemy would've been first on his list of priorities, but no more. Until Rayne was safe, he could not face Ciro.

Rayne would not be truly safe until Ciro was dead.

"You haven't spoken in two days," Rayne said, her own voice not much more than a whisper.

"We must be quiet so I can listen for what might lie ahead."

"Nothing lies ahead in this place," she argued, and he could hear the shudder in her voice.

"I have heard that there are those who live in the swamps of the Southern Province," Lyr said, though it was not those few residents who caused him to be on alert.

"Why would anyone live here when they could live elsewhere?" Rayne asked. "Why would they live in this swamp where creatures slither in the muddy water and the smell of decay is always present?"

Lyr's eyes cut to the left, and he allowed himself to see beyond the obvious for a moment, to see beyond his initial impressions of desolation. "You are the one who is connected to the earth, so you should see what I see. You should see more."

"I'm too frightened to see anything beyond what's beneath my feet and on the opposite bank," she said, and about that time another of the reptiles slipped into the water. "What do you see that makes this place worth inhabiting?"

Glad to turn his thoughts to simpler matters, Lyr lifted

one hand and pointed into a thick stand of trees. "There. Do you see the growth amidst those trees?"

Rayne turned her head and silently studied the area for a moment. "Those are unusual flowers, and very beautiful. I did not say there was no beauty here, but it is overwhelmed by . . . by . . ."

"See that tall plant with the thick stem?" Again, Lyr pointed. "It looks very much like a cor shoot, and is most likely edible. The water is filled with fish, and I have spotted other edible plants along the bank as we've traveled. One who lived here would never have to toil at a farm, or worry about hunger, no matter what the season. The silence might be comforting, I suppose, to those who have become accustomed to it, and there is beauty in this place if you can see past the danger."

The stark trees, the still water, the long-legged birds, red and white, even the reptiles . . . they were picturesque in a new way. Maybe he saw some beauty here because the landscape was so different from what he had known. Then again, perhaps the starkness of the place spoke to him at this moment when he felt desolate through and through, as if every bit of life had been sucked from his soul.

Segyn had betrayed him, and in answer Lyr had driven a blade through the helpless man's heart. There was no honor in that, but neither would it have been wise to allow Segyn to live and come after Rayne again. The man he'd called friend for as long as he could remember had ruthlessly murdered two fellow Circle Warriors and attempted to kill Lyr as well.

Lyr had great responsibilities thrust upon him. He had been born to great responsibilities, but none as important as the one he now embraced. Rayne, Ciro, the crystal dagger, those were all in his hands, but when he allowed his mind to go back to that afternoon by the stream, they all faded into nothingness and he felt only pain.

Burned.

"I'll admit, you're right that there is some beauty here," Rayne finally said, her voice remaining soft as if to raise it in this desolate place would bring Ciro and his army down upon them. "But it is also frightening, especially those reptiles. They have teeth, did you see?"

"The reptiles are much smaller than us or our horses, and thus far they have not come close to us. If they do, I have my sword and my gift with which to defend us."

He'd been taught it was not sporting to freeze an opponent in battle, but when that opponent was a reptilian creature who might harm Rayne, he would have no doubts. Besides, after what he'd done to Segyn, did he have any honor left?

Rayne glimpsed to the western sky, and with great skepticism in her voice she asked, "Where will we sleep tonight?"

"I don't know," Lyr answered truthfully. "Perhaps on horseback. Perhaps we won't sleep at all until we exit this swampland." He glanced at her pale, frightened face, which was so beautiful. How had he ever believed her a traitor? Of course, he'd never seen Segyn as a traitor, either, and look where that misplaced trust had gotten him. "Then again, perhaps you can build us a treehouse of vines and we'll sleep there."

"Would we be any safer in the trees than we are on the ground?" She tipped her head back to look up, and her brow furrowed.

"I don't have any idea." Riding without stopping might be their only safe choice, but it would be hard on Rayne, who was not accustomed to such conditions. Just as he was about to decide that was their best bet, their only choice, Lyr caught a whiff of smoke.

Somewhere ahead was a fire burning in a fireplace. Somewhere ahead, there waited shelter.

LYR HAD TOLD HER THAT THEY WOULD COME ACROSS A house of sorts, and though she had doubted him and his nose, when she smelled the smoke herself, she felt a rush of relief. While she couldn't imagine anyone choosing to live here, at the moment she was very relieved. Surely whoever lived out here in the swampland would allow them to stay until morning.

She hadn't relished the idea of remaining on horseback when darkness fell and she could not see the water or the birds or the far bank where reptiles cavorted. What might come out at night in this place? She shuddered at the very thought. Every step she took away from the only home she'd known introduced her to something new. Love, violent death, pleasure, betrayal, friendship, fears such as she had never known . . .

Lyr, with his hawklike eyes, caught sight of the cabin before she did. He changed their direction of travel slightly, and soon enough she, too, saw the home they had been seeking. At least, she assumed it was someone's home. The small cabin was built of the sturdy wood which grew in the swampland, and the chimney which spat smoke was made of gray stone. One side rose out of the water, and a small barn of sorts sat crookedly, half in the water, half on the muddy bank. There was a sagging porch and steps which rose out of the water. A single rocking chair was sitting on that porch, and as Rayne watched, an unexpected breeze caught the rocker and made it move very slightly. A chill walked down her spine. Perhaps it was not a friendly house, but the home of an enemy.

The sky was growing gray, and on the opposite bank something entered the water with a splash. It sounded larger than what they'd been hearing all day, and in Rayne's mind it was much more ominous than the cabin and whatever waited inside.

Before they could dismount, the front door opened and a woman stepped onto the porch. She was middle-aged and slender, and her dark hair streaked with gray had been pulled back simply. Her colorful dress was unlike any Rayne had ever seen—not that she'd been exposed to worldly fashions in her lifetime. Gold bracelets hung from both wrists, and when the woman took another step, it was clear that she wore no shoes. Her feet were clean. For some reason, that simple fact made Rayne feel much better.

The woman did not seem surprised to see them. She moved onto the steps and lifted her face, focusing her attention on Lyr. "I thought you would not make it before dark. You'd best tie up the horses and get inside. Supper's waiting."

"How did you know we were coming?" Rayne asked, her heart turning over at the very idea that they'd been *expected*.

The woman smiled. "The two of you have been making quite a lot of noise, and the animals are all disturbed by your presence. They don't take to intruders well, and they speak to me of disorder in their swamp."

There had been a time when Rayne would've been quick to disbelieve that anyone could understand what the animals were saying, but no more. Anything was possible, for good or for ill, in this world she lived in.

Lyr dismounted and stepped into the shallow water, his tall boots keeping the murky swamp from his clothing and skin. He reached up to help Rayne, and she gladly allowed him to carry her to the porch before placing her on her feet. Up close, the swamp woman's age showed more clearly than it had from a distance. There were deep lines around her mouth, and her eyes were calculating. Still, there was no distrust or anger in those eyes, and Rayne took some comfort from that.

Lyr led the horses to the side of the cabin which was out of the swamp water. The small wooden enclosure there would protect the animals in the night, or so Rayne hoped. She would not wish anyone or anything to be unprotected in the darkness that was coming.

The swamp woman waited silently while Lyr saw to the animals, merely nodding at Rayne and smiling gently. The smile seemed real enough and was somewhat reassuring.

Rayne had been in the saddle so long she ached, and as she stood there, she stretched up onto her toes and circled her shoulders to remove the kinks in her body. It felt good to stand on solid ground, even if that ground was a less than sturdy porch in the middle of a desolate swampland. At least she was on her own two feet!

When Lyr returned, sloshing through the shallow water before marching onto the steps, their hostess smiled a touch wider. Even a woman of an older age would appreciate what a fine specimen of manhood Lyr was. His beard was coming in again and he had not had a bath in many days, and still . . . he was impressive.

And he was hers. Rayne felt that to the pit of her soul. Lyr was *hers*, and it had nothing to do with the sexual experiences they'd shared. She pushed down the jealousy that rose up strongly simply from watching the woman smile at the Prince of Swords.

"My name is Gwyneth," she said, "Gwyneth Ziven,

wife of Soren, mother of Borix, seer and keeper of the Blessed Swamp."

Lyr introduced himself and Rayne, and as he did so, Rayne began to smell a most delicious aroma which drifted from the cabin. Supper, Gwyneth had said. Rayne's heart hitched. She was starving, but having recently been exposed to food which was not all it seemed to be, she was also cautious. Would this seemingly innocent woman who smiled at Lyr poison them? Was she one of Ciro's soldiers in disguise? Had she aligned herself with the Isen Demon in some way? At the moment, Rayne trusted only Lyr. No one else was above suspicion.

At Gwyneth's invitation, they stepped into the cabin. It looked larger from inside than it had from the front. One large room contained a kitchen, where a kettle hung above a low fire; a long table and four chairs, all made of the same wood as the walls, floor, ceiling, and porch; two chairs, on the opposite side of the large room, each placed before another fireplace, which was currently cold. She'd expected to see a bed, but instead there were two doors off the main room. At least one of them, and possibly both, would lead to a bedchamber, Rayne supposed.

"I can see that you are hungry," Gwyneth said as they walked into the warm room. She grabbed one of three wooden bowls from a counter beside the fireplace, and with an iron ladle began to spoon a thick stew. One after another, she placed the bowls on the table, in no particular order. If she'd poisoned the stew, then she was willing to poison herself as well. It was Rayne who placed each of the bowls before a chair. When that was done, Gwyneth fetched large spoons, which were also made of wood. The mugs she placed on the table were of pewter, and the wine came from a large glass jar. Not everything in this cabin had been made by hand from what was found in the swamp. Most, perhaps, but not all.

They sat at the table, and once again Rayne eyed the stew. She had to eat something, and it didn't appear that this food was poisoned. The yettle berries had looked innocent, too, however, so how could she know with any certainty? Lyr studied his bowl with the same suspicion.

Gwyneth sighed and lifted her own spoon. "You two can contemplate your stew all evening if you'd like, but I'm hungry." She lifted a spoonful to her mouth and ate greedily.

Lyr followed, taking a small bite. "Very good," he said. "Nicely seasoned."

"I gather many herbs from the swamp and the forests beyond," Gwyneth said as she spooned up more and prepared to eat it.

As Lyr took another bite, obviously enjoying the taste, Rayne finally lifted her spoon. If he was willing to take a chance, so should she be.

The stew was delicious. There was meat of some sort and vegetables she did not recognize and those herbs Gwyneth spoke of. True, she was very hungry, but Rayne was sure she had never eaten a better meal. She soon forgot that she did not know or trust the woman who had prepared the stew, and she emptied her bowl and then reached for the wine, drinking greedily. Such simple pleasures were taken for granted until they were taken away. Food. Drink.

Love.

She looked at Lyr, who ate and drank as heartily as she. Love was not exactly simple, and yet it felt to her as essential as food and drink, as necessary as the air she breathed. What a horrible time to find love, when her future, the future of the very world, was at risk.

When their supper was finished, Gwyneth cleared the table quickly. "What of the world beyond the swamp?" she asked brightly. "It's been many years since I had news from beyond my home."

Lyr's face became solemn. "All is not well, I'm sad to say. A demon has taken control of many men, and they plot to take this land, to take all the lands, and turn all to darkness."

Gwyneth's chin lifted, and she looked at Lyr hard and long. "And you are fighting this darkness?"

"Yes."

She nodded, and then turned to saunter to the opposite side of the room, where she opened a squeaking drawer and removed a thick square wrapped in colorful silk. Gwyneth reclaimed her seat and unfolded the silk, revealing a deck of unusual cards. They were square, rather than rectangular like the playing cards Rayne had seen in the past, and as the seer and keeper of the swamp began to flip the cards over in a pattern of some sort, Rayne saw that the hand-painted pictures were of a different type than any she had ever seen. They were colorful and somehow twisted, as if the images there had been seen through broken or half-blinded eyes.

"Perhaps I can help you," Gwyneth said as she studied the cards she'd placed on the table. "Perhaps there will be guidance in the cards."

"This is witch's magic," Lyr said in a lowered voice.

Gwyneth's head snapped up, and her eyes flashed angrily. "Yes. Do you have something witty or degrading to say about that?"

Lyr smiled. "As my mother, two sisters, two aunts, and numerous cousins are witches, that would not be at all wise."

Gwyneth relaxed. "That explains the magic I see in your reading. Great magic." She allowed her hands to float above the cards as if she absorbed their energy. "And great sacrifice. You are important to this war of which you speak."

"Yes," Lyr whispered. "So I have been told."

"Before the first snows of winter fall, you will face your enemy."

"And the victor will be . . ." Lyr prompted.

"Unknown at this time," Gwyneth said simply. "Much must happen between now and then in order for you to win." She shook her head. "You must win, Prince of Swords," she added in a gruff whisper. "I cannot imagine the pain that will follow any other outcome." One finger came down and touched a particularly dark card. From where she sat, Rayne could barely see the picture there. It appeared to be a bird with wide, black wings, but the beak of the bird was crooked, and the wings were twisted. "You must throw off your heartache and be vigilant, Lyr Hern. You must not allow anyone, no matter how trusted, to keep you from what you must do."

Rayne imagined the seer spoke of Segyn, but Lyr looked at her as if he could not trust her, not even now. It hurt, just as it had hurt when he'd told her that for a short while he'd believed her capable of poisoning him.

"Can you read the cards for her?" Lyr asked, nodding his head at Rayne.

She wished to believe that he was concerned about the outcome of this war for her, but suspected he wanted more to know if he could trust her. Again, that hurt terribly.

"Of course." Gwyneth seemed happy to scoop up the cards and shuffle them, her attention shifting to another subject. She tried to smile, but the effort was weak. What the seer had seen in Lyr's reading had disturbed her. The uncertainty was not at all comforting, not for any of them.

Again, Gwyneth placed the cards on the table in a

seemingly random pattern. Before she was finished, the expression on her face changed many times. There was curiosity, worry, then astonishment, as she finished and placed the unused cards aside. "I see a child."

"Whose child?" Rayne snapped. Not Ciro's. By the heaven above, not Ciro's child.

"That I do not see. Perhaps like so many other things, that has not yet been determined."

Gwyneth moved on to another grouping of cards. "Your life has not been an easy one thus far, but if all goes well in weeks to come, your life will change." She cocked her head to one side. "Do you know that your father murdered your mother?"

Rayne gasped, shocked at the question and the cavalier way in which she had been asked. "He did not!"

Gwyneth barely listened to Rayne's protest. "He poisoned her. He made it look as if she contracted an illness, but in truth he simply grew tired of her." The seer shook her head. "Foolish man. He did not know who she was, what she could do." Gwyneth lifted her head and looked at Rayne squarely. "You are lucky that your father never discovered what you are capable of. It's no coincidence that your talents remained hidden until he was buried. Deep inside, where you cannot yet see, you knew he was a danger to you and so the gifts you have possessed since birth slept. Some of them continue to sleep, but as days go by, they will be discovered."

Rayne licked her lips. "Are you telling me that I'm a . . . a witch?" Even though Lyr happily claimed witches among his relations, to Rayne the word had an unsavory connotation. She did not wish to be a witch!

"You are not a witch," Gwyneth said gently.

Rayne sighed in relief, too soon.

"You are an Earth Goddess."

* * *

THEY'D BEEN IN THIS SPRAWLING COASTAL TOWN FOR
days, and still there was no sign of Liane. Isadora was getting frustrated. Even Juliet, who was usually so very helpful in such situations, could not point them in precisely the
right direction.

On this evening, she and her sisters rested in the inn
they had begun to call home. They'd taken the entire second floor for their extended stay, but spent most of their
hours in this sitting room. No one was getting much sleep
these days.

As much as Isadora enjoyed spending time with her
sisters, she was ready to go home. She missed her daughters, her home, her friends, her routine. And yet, until
they found Liane and her sons, she could not go home.
One of Sebestyen's sons would be emperor when Ciro
was defeated.

When, not *if*. She could not afford to think otherwise.

To take her mind off their recent failures, Isadora turned
to Juliet with a question she asked frequently. "How is Lyr
tonight?"

Juliet closed her eyes and reached for sensations from
her nephew. She took a few deep breaths. "Alive, distressed, determined." Juliet's hand lifted slowly. "I see
vines growing larger and twining together, but I don't
know what it means. I also see water and long-legged birds
and"—she shuddered—"snakes."

Isadora's heart skipped a beat. "Do the snakes symbol-
ize danger?"

Juliet shook her head. "No. These are actual snakes, not
symbolic at all. The birds are standing in muddy water, and
some of them are bright red. They have long, thin legs and
crooked beaks. I've never seen anything like it."

"Swamp," Sophie said gently. "The muddy water, the red birds, the snakes. Lyr must be traveling through the swamp."

"Why?" Isadora shouted. "Why on earth would Lyr leave a perfectly acceptable road and go into the swamp?" A horrible thought occurred to her. "Was he taken there against his will? Is he a prisoner?"

"No," Juliet said quickly. "He travels this way of his own accord, that much I can see. And he is protected by something or someone he does not entirely understand. I don't understand it myself."

"But he's all right?" At least for now.

"Yes," Juliet said. "Sad, confused, but well."

As any mother would be, Isadora was sad for her son. She did not know what had happened, but she wished to protect him. Even though he was a grown man, even though he was Prince of Swords, she wished to shelter him from all hurt. As if that were possible.

The knock at the door surprised them all. It was too soon for their husbands, who had gone to a nearby tavern to ask questions, to be back. Unless they'd found what they were looking for.

Isadora left her chair to rush to the locked door. They'd been nosing about the port town for days, offering rewards and describing the Liane they remembered from twenty-five years past. If Lucan and the others were not back with news, then perhaps someone had come to claim that reward. Someone who had the answers they sought.

As Isadora opened the door, Juliet sighed and said, "I should've known she would come to us."

The heavy wooden door opened on an older woman who had stark white hair pulled back into a tight bun. Familiar green eyes were sharp and intelligent and angry. There were lines around the eyes, and the dark clothing was not only simple but starkly plain and seemed to be made to disguise any figure that might lurk beneath.

But the face, the face had not changed. There was still a timeless beauty in the shape of the jaw and the high cheekbones and the perfectly shaped lips. There was also an unmistakable determination.

"You're stirring up too many questions with all your nosy inquiries, and they must stop. They must stop now. What do you want from me?" Liane asked sharply. "What the hell do you want?"

II

WHEN THEY'D FIRST ARRIVED, GWYNETH'S ATTENTION had been focused on Lyr. She'd obviously seen him as the most important of the two travelers, the man in charge, the man who possessed the most power. It was certainly possible that she'd focused on Lyr because she was a woman who lived very much alone. Was Gwyneth any different from the brightly colored women who'd offered their bodies to the warriors on a crowded street?

If that had been her intention, it was now forgotten. After reading their cards, Gwyneth turned her attention almost entirely to Rayne.

Rayne still didn't believe what the swamp witch had said. Earth Goddess? That wasn't possible. She only made things grow, that's all. That certainly didn't make her a *Goddess*, a supernatural being who was both human and more than human, a magical creature who walked with one foot in the world of mortals and the other in a magical world Rayne did not comprehend. An immortal spirit housed, for this lifetime, in a mortal body. A *Goddess* like the woman who had given birth to her. She also dismissed the woman's ridiculous assertion that her father had killed her mother. He had not been a good man, she knew that, but surely he wouldn't have taken his only child's mother away.

Deep down she knew it was possible, but she didn't want to believe. She had so few positive memories of her father, she didn't want to stain them with this horrid supposition. It was murder Gwyneth suggested. Cold-hearted murder.

When the cards had been put away, Gwyneth fetched clean water—rain water, Rayne supposed—for the Earth Goddess. She also offered a brightly colored skirt and a dark green loose-sleeved blouse which were plainly constructed but clean, and in better shape than the gown Rayne had been wearing for so many days.

The water and clothes were placed in one of the two bedchambers, a small room with a narrow bed which Gwyneth said was her son's. Not long after her husband's death, Borix had gone hunting and never returned. It had been many years, but she still held out hope that one day he would come home.

From Borix's bedchamber, which for tonight was Rayne's, a small, roughly fashioned window looked out over the swamp. Moonlight lit the stagnant water. Rayne looked through the window as she undressed and bathed, feeling safe in this cabin, feeling separated from the swamp and all its dangers. Tomorrow she and Lyr would travel in the swamp again, but for tonight, at least, they were safe.

She left the skirt and blouse Gwyneth had given her folded neatly on the single chair in the room, and crawled into the bed naked. A single candle burned. Lyr was feeding and brushing the horses, but she hoped he would join her before she fell asleep. Her body was aching and exhausted, but she did not want to sleep without holding Lyr. She didn't want to drift to dreams without hearing his voice.

But very shortly after crawling into the bed, she did sleep. She dreamed of thrusting her hands into the dirt and watching trees and flowers grow. She dreamed of moving rushing water aside with her very breath. She dreamed of calling down the rain and laughing as it washed over her.

When she awoke, the candle had burned down substantially, and Lyr was with her. He stood over the bed, uncertain and silent. She smiled at him and drew back the covers to invite him in.

After a moment, he shook his head. "I'll sleep on the floor."

Rayne sat up. "Why?"

"Because it is best. We have not been thinking, Rayne. A child, Gwyneth said. Is this the time to create a child? To lie together as if tomorrow is at all certain?"

She had thought of that, but she had also caught a more important thought. "I *will* have a child, according to Gwyneth. Should it be your baby I catch or Ciro's?"

A muscle in Lyr's jaw twitched. "I don't know if I'll survive the war that's coming. Of all the psychics and seers who have looked to the future for me, none has seen victory."

"Has one seen defeat?"

"No," he whispered.

She knew he was rushing toward the war that might claim him, which made this night all the more precious.

"We don't know what lies ahead, I understand that. But Lyr, if I have your child inside me, I can't carry Ciro's. If the worst happens, if you lose and Ciro captures me, he can't give me a child if I'm already carrying yours. I think any child Ciro and I create would be beyond terrible, beyond dark. Why else would he insist that I be the mother? He's a monster incapable of love, so there must be some dark reason. Maybe there's something among my newly discovered gifts which will be passed to the child, something which can be used for dark purposes. Would a child of mine and Ciro's be able to make things die as I make them grow? Would it be able to make the earth shake, and bring floods, and stop the rain?" She relaxed and lay back on the mattress.

"Besides, the simple answer is I want you to hold me. I want you to lie with me. I want you to make me forget all that might be and simply enjoy this moment." She gathered all her courage. "I love you, Lyr. Don't make me lie here without you. Don't make me feel horribly alone when you're so close."

It was the sensation of being truly alone that she feared most, and when Lyr held her, that sensation went away.

By the light of that one candle, Lyr removed his vest. He said nothing, but no words were necessary. In her heart she wished for a return of "I love you," but she didn't expect that from Lyr. Not now. Maybe later, if things worked out as they should, he would feel free to say the words, to mean them. Right now his trust had been damaged, and he likely did not wish to love anyone ever again.

He set his sword and knife aside and stepped out of his muddy boots, one and then the other, and then shucked off travel-weary trousers. In a matter of moments he was bare, but for the crystal dagger which was strapped to his thigh. An ordinary man would appear less powerful without his uniform and weapons, but not Lyr. His strength was in his heart and soul and body, not in the things he carried with him. Every muscle was perfectly crafted, and arguments aside, he *did* want her. Physically, at least.

For a moment he wasn't sure what to do with the crystal dagger he removed from his thigh. He briefly studied the weapon wrapped in velvet before lifting the mattress and slipping it beneath. Segyn had asked for that dagger, which meant Ciro and the demon knew of its existence and the threat it posed.

Completely bare, Lyr crawled into the narrow bed with her. His arms circled her, and he buried his head against her neck and kissed her there. His lips were gentle and then not so gentle. He kissed her throat, and her mouth, and the valley between her breasts.

And then he stopped to rise up and look down at her. "I have dreamed of this sight," he said in a lowered voice. "Until now you have been lost in darkness or shrouded by clothing. I have felt you, I have joined with you, but I have only dreamed of seeing you this way, by candlelight and moonlight." He touched her, and watched the movement of his hand against her skin. "You are more beautiful than I imagined any woman could be."

He spread her thighs and touched her with arousing fingers. He pushed the coverlet to the floor so no part of her bare body was hidden from him. There were many miles between "I love you" and "You're beautiful," but she gladly accepted anything which resembled sweet words from Lyr.

But that didn't mean she couldn't wish for whispers of love to go along with the power of his body aligning with hers. She wished for love to go along with the beauty of pleasure and his admiration for the physical, she wished for the fierceness of the heart to combine with the passion of raw release.

But Lyr's heart still stung, she knew, and she did not dare ask too much of him now.

With his hand and mouth arousing her so well, she soon forgot unspoken sweet words and bonds of the heart. Her body twitched and trembled and ached, until she wrapped one leg around his hips to draw him closer. He seemed determined to take his time, however, and did not give her what she wanted. She hurt with need, and exploring hands proved to her that Lyr was ready. He was hot and hard in her hands, and she stroked, urging him to come to her, trying to bring him to the place she had found, where nothing mattered but their bodies together. Still, he waited. He moved one hand over her sensitive nipples and sucked at her neck, which had proven to be surprisingly sensitive and erotic. She threw her head back to allow him full access to her throat, and stroked him harder. They were entangled like the vines she could speak to, twining and growing and reaching. Joined by the twist and weave of their bodies.

Again she tried to reach for him with her body, and again he held steady.

"Are you trying to drive me mad?" she whispered.

"Yes."

She heard the humor in Lyr's voice, and was glad of it. There had been little cause for humor in days past, and if this moment was the only respite he had from pain, then she was glad to be the one to offer it.

In a burst of joyful frustration she rolled atop Lyr and straddled him. He guided himself to her, into her, and with great relief she plunged down to take him inside her body. All of him, everything he had to give, inside her welcoming and needful body.

That done, she allowed her movements to slow. She rose and fell in a languid motion, and he moved his hips with hers. He reached up and twisted one hand in her hair, hair which fell loose and thick to touch his chest.

She'd never had what she'd call power in her life. Every day had been structured for her, every lesson well planned, every betrayal beyond her grasp. But as she and Lyr moved toward the pleasure of release, she felt true power. In her heart, in her soul, and in his. Making love was more than comfort or satisfaction or making babies, it was a great power all its own.

She moved faster as she felt release coming to her, but a part of her did not want this moment to end so she held back a little. She didn't move all the way down to take him fully into her body again. When she did, this moment of wonder would be over. Lyr's hands gripped her hips and he guided her down, all the way down, so that he was deeper than he'd ever been. Immediately she began to shudder, and then release came in forceful waves that brought intense pleasure from where they were joined to the top of her head. She saw stars; she saw the roots of life; and then she saw nothing. She felt Lyr's release as he shuddered and came into her body in yet another way.

Still joined, but much less frantic, she dropped down to take Lyr's face in her hands. His beard was rough beneath her hands, but she did not care. She kissed him deeply, holding his face so that he could not move away from the intimacy of mouth to mouth, so that he could not deny her what she wanted at this moment.

"I do so love you," she whispered against his fine, full lips. "I'm tired of war, Lyr, tired of what is asked of us. Give me a child, and take me to a place where no one will ever find us. We could hide there, far away from politics and war and responsibilities."

"It sounds tempting, but we can't hide forever."

"Why not?" she asked, but even though a part of her wished to escape, she knew he was right. They couldn't run, not from Ciro and not from what they knew had to be done.

"Because I am Prince of Swords and in possession of the only weapon that can kill the monster, and you, apparently, are a Goddess."

"I don't believe that," she said, so softly the words were almost lost.

"I do," Lyr said. "I very much believe."

"LEAVE MY SONS ALONE," LIANE INSISTED, NOT FOR THE first time. Hours had passed since she'd shown up at the room where the Fyne sisters, the Fyne witches, had waited. "You don't know their names, and you don't know where they are. You don't even know the name I have been using all these years!"

"Now that we have seen you, I suspect we can get that information, as well as the names of your children," Isadora said. She owed much to Liane, but she would not sacrifice an entire nation on her behalf.

"One of your sons fights for the rightful emperor," Juliet added calmly. "We know that much."

"Many fight," Liane said sharply, but she went a little pale. "He is only one. Foolish boy," she added in a whisper. "I told him to stay away, but did he listen to me?"

It was Sophie who sat before Liane and took her sister-in-law's hands in her own. "You know we would not come to you if there was another way. Placing your eldest son on the throne will save Columbyana from further war. Only the legitimate, rightful heir will be accepted by all when Ciro is defeated."

"If Ciro is defeated."

"When," Sophie said without anger, and then she took a deep breath. "Please tell us what you've been doing since you came here. Did Ferghus and Mahri stay with you?"

"For a while," Liane answered.

"Ferghus was in love with you," Juliet said as they left the questioning about Liane's sons behind for a moment. "Did you marry him?"

Liane shook her head. "No. He asked, many times, but Sebestyen never left me. I dreamed of him every night for years, and there were times when I was certain his spirit was with me. How could I marry another when I was still in love with my husband?"

Love was strange, that was sure, Isadora thought as she watched the angry woman clasp her hands tightly on her lap. There was no man less deserving of love than the former emperor Sebestyen Beckyt, and no woman less likely to remain faithful to a dead man than Liane Varden, former concubine and assassin, a decidedly cold woman.

Sophie nodded, as if she understood. "So you made your own way all these years."

"I'm not a bad seamstress," Liane said with a nod of her head. "And I remember how to put together a few useful potions. I looked over the shoulders of many a palace witch in my years as Sebestyen's slave and as his wife. Those talents were enough to provide for me and my children."

"It can't have been an easy life for you," Sophie said.

Isadora rolled her eyes and gently but firmly moved her youngest sister away. "Liane has never been a woman in need of coddling. It was one of the traits I most admired in our time together." She took Sophie's seat and looked Liane in the eye. After so many years those eyes were so achingly familiar. They brought back memories, horrible and wonderful. "You protected your children and I admire you for that. I would've done the same. But your sons are now grown men, and the eldest is emperor. Do you understand that, Liane? Your eldest child belongs in Arthes."

Liane's chin trembled. "I hate that palace," she whispered. "I do not want either of my sons to be trapped there."

The door opened, and the three men walked in bearing what they had planned to be a late supper for six. Liane's head snapped around. Kane instantly recognized his sister, even though it had been years since they'd seen one another. He swore, and then he smiled, and then Liane rose and they hugged one another tightly.

Isadora stepped back and watched, anxious to move on but willing to give the siblings a moment. Juliet sidled up beside her.

"We must get those names," she whispered.

"I know."

"No, you don't," Juliet snapped. "Sebestyen is coming for Liane very soon. If she doesn't tell us before that happens . . ."

"He's dead, and he's going to kill her?"

"No. Someone else is going to kill her, and Sebestyen will be waiting to greet her spirit."

"We will protect her," Isadora said insistently.

Juliet sighed tiredly. "That's a lovely idea, but I don't think we can."

RAYNE LOOKED VERY DIFFERENT IN HER BRIGHTLY COLored striped skirt and the green blouse which showed off more shoulder than her more proper traveling dress. Her hair was simpler, too, pulled simply to the top of her head and falling in tendrils around her face. She wore her mother's blue gem as usual, and it added yet more color.

Was there power in that gem which had once belonged to the woman who'd fashioned the crystal dagger? It was certainly as possible as the supposition that he'd awakened her gifts, or that somehow she'd been suppressing them until her father was no longer a threat to her.

Did he believe Rayne was a Goddess? Yes, he truly did. His life had been too enmeshed in magic to dismiss any possibility.

Last night she had told him more than once that she loved him, but he had not been able to say the words in return, even though he knew that was what she wanted. He would only offer her truth, and at the moment Lyr did not know what the truth was. He wanted her, he was dedicated to protecting her, he would die to keep her away from Ciro. Was that love? No. It was duty wrapped in physical attraction; it was honor mingled with the respite of sex. When this battle was over, would he still feel the same way about her? Would she feel anything at all for him?

Gwyneth had sent them on their way early in the morning, with the sun not yet over the horizon. She'd fed them breakfast and sent them into the swamp with one warning: Beware her sister Beatrisa, a spiteful witch who lived on the opposite edge of the swamp. She would be beautiful and sweet at first glance, but when one looked beyond the facade, she was rotten to the soul and filled with hate.

Rayne glanced down at the shallow water they passed through, suspicious even though Gwyneth had promised them that for at least the first few hours of their journey the creatures of the swamp would leave them be. Once they entered Beatrisa's domain, that would change, but for now they were in Gwyneth's territory, and the reptiles and birds kept their distance.

"Last night I dreamed I could make the water move," Rayne said, "but that can't be right, can it? No one can control the flow of water."

"I did not think anyone could make vines grow the way you do, so I cannot say it is impossible. Have you tried?"

"No."

"Why not? Afraid it won't work?"

Rayne turned her head to look at him, and he saw the

truth in her eyes. She was afraid it *would* work. The idea that she possessed such powers terrified her.

She turned her gaze to the front once again. "I wonder if I'm pregnant."

"If not, it's not for lack of trying," Lyr said lightly.

"Perhaps we can try again tonight, just in case we weren't successful at Gwyneth's cabin, or before. I'll feel much better when that is done."

"Even if you are with child, we won't know for a while," Lyr said.

"And so we must keep trying," she said, her voice almost calm. He heard the trill of anticipation, actually felt it somehow.

"So we must."

"If it's months before we see Ciro, perhaps he will be repulsed by my misshapen body and the knowledge that another man's child grows inside me and he'll send me away." She waved one hand casually.

Surely she knew that imagining was a fantasy. If Ciro was determined to plant his child in Rayne, he would not let another man's child stop him. That babe would not survive long at Ciro's hands, though Lyr would not put that theory to Rayne and spoil her good mood. Deep down, she surely knew she was speaking nonsense.

Ciro was not the kind of man who would send anyone away. Those around him would be servants and slaves, or else they'd be killed.

Lyr knew he had no choice. He had to kill Ciro in order to save not only Rayne but the country itself. The very world, parts known and unknown. And if he failed, he could not allow Rayne to fall into the monster's hands. The child of a demon and a Goddess would be too powerful, too dangerous, to allow to exist.

Lyr had known from the start that it was possible he'd

have to take Rayne's life before his duties were done. In his mind he saw her as she had been last night, lit by candlelight, swaying above him with uninhibited passion, writhing beneath him with need, smiling at him with a love she was not afraid to voice. For the first time in his life, Lyr wasn't sure he could do what had to be done, if it came to that.

For the first time in his life, Lyr was not certain he could accomplish the mission that had been entrusted to him.

PHELAN PLODDED TOWARD THE CABIN, EVERY STEP AN EFfort. He was on their trail, he knew it. He could smell Lyr and Ciro's bride, the traitorous bastards.

As he stepped onto the porch of the solid cabin, the front door opened and an attractive woman in a vividly colored dress greeted him. "I was told that you were coming," she said with a smile.

Phelan was instantly suspicious. "Told by whom?"

"The creatures of the swamp," she replied. "I'm sure that you are hungry. I have stew."

"I'm ravenous," he said.

"And you have been bitten many times by insects." The woman took his hand and led him into the house. Her hand was soft and gentle. He had not known such a gentle touch in many years. "I have a soothing balm which will help, if you'll allow it."

Phelan gave her his best, most charming, most Segyn-like smile. "I would be a fool not to allow such ministrations."

The woman introduced herself as Gwyneth and then she fed him well. When that was done and the dishes were cleared away, she insisted that he remove his filthy vest. When that was done, she bathed his chest and arms and neck and applied the balm, which was quite soothing. She even treated a few irritating bites on his bald head.

There was a sexual energy to her touch, an earthy connection neither of them could deny. She liked him. At least, she liked the man he pretended to be. Phelan had become adept at convincing others that he was someone other than himself, and he did so now. He charmed the attractive woman. He smiled at her and looked her squarely in the eye and touched her cheek when he felt it was appropriate to do so. She shuddered at his touch, in that way a needful woman might.

Gwyneth had been without a man for a long time, and Phelan was not one to turn away a pretty woman who wanted use of his body.

Since she'd introduced herself as a seer, he had been very careful. As he had in years past, he became Segyn, he *became*, for a while, a good man with nothing to hide. Phelan was buried deep, so deep she could not see him.

He knew very well how to seduce a woman, how to become someone he was not in order to get what he wanted. Gwyneth didn't need much in the way of seduction, but he smiled at her, he laughed with her, he touched her gently, and then he screwed her on the table where she'd fed him what he suspected was snake stew. Her half-clad body was not what he would call perfect, not like Ciro's bride. Her age showed here and there, but she was far from an old hag. There were nice muscles in her legs and her arms, and though her breasts were not firm with youth, neither did they sag.

It didn't take either of them long to find fulfillment. The woman screamed and wrapped her legs around him with an unexpected strength as her pleasure came. Her fingernails dug into his flesh, drawing blood, and he liked it. He liked it very much.

While Gwyneth was flushed and smiling and he was still inside her, limp and useless, Phelan traced the line of her jaw with one finger. "Have others been this way of late?"

Still breathless, she nodded once, though he could see the confusion in her eyes. Now was not the proper time for such questions, he supposed.

"Two, a man and a woman," Phelan said as he withdrew.

Suddenly she looked suspicious, rather than confused. "Yes. Do you know them?"

"They are dear friends. We were separated during our travels, and I fear they think me dead."

"You've only missed them by a few hours," Gwyneth said, reaching up to touch his face. "Pity," she whispered. "I suspect you will chase after them, and I was so hoping you would stay for a while. A long while."

"You would like that, eh?"

"Very much," she whispered.

The demon whispered to him, and Phelan listened.

"You are lonely here," he said when the demon had finishing speaking.

"I am."

"You need a man to see to your keeping."

"I do," she whispered. "A man and . . . a child. I do so want another baby. A child to raise and love and teach. Maybe a girl this time."

"A girl to replace the son you lost?"

Beneath him, Gwyneth's body jerked slightly.

"You wait for your son to return to you, but he's not coming back, lover. He's dead, long dead, bitten by a poisonous snake and left to die a long, painful death before slipping into the water to be eaten by crocs."

Her body stiffened, but he remained atop her so she could barely move. "I didn't tell you about my son."

"No, you did not."

"I would know if he was dead!"

"Long dead," Phelan whispered. "The animals who speak to you didn't tell you that, did they?"

"No."

"It was your sister's creatures who killed and ate him, that's why. Beatrisa knew. She's always known. Your son wandered into her part of the swamp, and she gleefully led the snake and the croc to him." Phelan leaned down and kissed Gwyneth's cheek and the tears there. "She laughed when she watched him die, she laughed at your foolish hopes that he would return, and right now she laughs at your pain."

If he had more time, he would stay for a while, but Lyr and Rayne were more important than this insignificant swamp witch. Those he sought were just a few hours ahead, Gwyneth said, and if he hurried, he could catch them.

Beatrisa would slow them down for him.

Phelan squeezed Gwyneth's pretty neck until she stopped breathing, and then he gathered a bit of food and one of her dead son's clean shirts before reentering the swamp.

12

SOMETHING HOWLED, SOMETHING *LARGE*, AND EVEN though the sound came from a distance, Rayne shivered. It was as though she had physically felt the exact moment they'd passed from Gwyneth's swamp into Beatrisa's. The sky had darkened, the creatures which had left them alone all day moved closer, and now there was that awful howl.

After a long day of travel, night approached. When the bank had appeared safe and dry, they'd stopped a few times during the day, but never for more than a few minutes. There was no decent place for them to camp. It seemed that they traveled more slowly than if they'd walked, since they had to plod along with great care when on horseback. Now and then, when the banks were high and fairly dry, they'd walked and led the horses so the animals could have a rest from the laborious plodding through the swamp water. Rayne wished to turn away from the swamp altogether, to turn north toward the forest and some semblance of civilization, but Lyr said that turning away from the swamp and making their way through the forest would cost them days of travel they did not have to spare.

This direct route through the swamp was the shortest course to the armies which fought against Ciro. According to Gwyneth, if they rode straight through without stopping, they'd reach a more hospitable meadowland by morning.

All they had to do was stay awake for the entire night, avoid the creatures which were determined to place themselves between the travelers and safety, and steer clear of Beatrisa.

It seemed that with every minute that passed, the snakes and crocs and unknown creatures beneath the water moved closer to the travelers. As they grew less afraid, as they grew more curious, they moved in. The soft splashes Rayne heard seemed to be nearer each time than they had the last. What was making those splashing sounds? Stars above, she did not want to know.

The faint cry that reached their ears was startling. But for Gwyneth, they had not seen or heard another human being in the swamplands. The call for help was most definitely human and female. Lyr pulled the reins to halt his horse and listened more closely, and Rayne did the same. There was much to be afraid of in this swamp. The witch, the crocs, the snakes, whatever splashed, whatever howled . . .

The call for help came again, and this time it was easy to note the direction whence it came. Lyr turned in that direction, and Rayne followed.

"Should we follow the cry?" Rayne asked. "Perhaps it's an animal which sounds like a human, or maybe it's Beatrisa herself and we're riding into a trap."

Lyr turned to look back at her all too briefly. "The cry for help could also come from one of the swamp witch's victims, or an innocent who wandered too far into the swamplands." He shook his head. "I can't ignore such a plea for help, Rayne."

Of course he could not. It was in Lyr's nature to run toward such uncertainties, not away from them. It was one of the traits she admired about him, but at the same time . . . she did so want to get out of this wet, dangerous swamp.

The spine-chilling howl was louder and closer when it came again. So was the call for help.

LIANE STEPPED BACK AND WATCHED HER BROTHER'S FAMily as they ignored her for a moment and argued among themselves about the best route to take in the morning. Those who had come looking for Liane and her sons had not let her out of their sight since she'd come to this sitting room last night. She'd been unable to rest since then, and while the others had gone to sleeping rooms down the hall for a couple hours of sleep, someone had always remained with her. It wasn't as if she hadn't enjoyed talking with her brother and hearing about his children and his farm, or reliving days long past with Isadora, but she wasn't blind to the fact that they'd been keeping a very close eye on her all the while.

They were all crowded in this rented sitting room at the moment, even though the party had taken the entire floor for their visit. Kane's wife, Sophie, and her sisters, as well as those sisters' husbands, argued without heat or rancor.

Liane felt a trill of envy as she watched them argue as only family can do. They had been blessed with lasting love, peace, and family. Her sons were her only blessings, her only family, and she would not allow them to be sacrificed for the greater good. She had given enough! She'd

promised Sebestyen, as he lay dying, that she would take
their sons away from the palace in Arthes and hide them
forever.

She and Sebestyen had never had the chance for the
normal love Kane's family shared. It was true that
Sebestyen had not always been a good man, but that was
not entirely his fault. He'd been manipulated and twisted
from childhood to be who he'd become. He'd been molded
into a heartless ruler who would do anything to assert his
authority and take what he wanted.

No, he had not been entirely heartless. In the end his
heart had won, but it hadn't been enough. He'd died anyway.

While the others discussed which route to take in the
morning, Liane, who had moments earlier grudgingly
agreed to travel with them, turned quickly and threw open
the door to the hallway. This was likely her only chance to
escape. If she ran fast enough, if she disappeared quickly,
they would not find her. She was very good at hiding, and
she knew this town in a way they did not.

She'd been hiding for more than twenty-five years now,
and she could make her way out of town and start over
somewhere else. When it was safe, she'd find the boys and
warn them . . . and in doing so she'd be forced to tell them
the truth of their heritage. How could she do that? Would
they ever forgive her for lying to them all these years?

Liane ran for the stairs, with Kane shouting behind her.
She didn't look back. If she did, she'd be lost, and she
would do anything for her sons.

A short, squat little man stood in the middle of the stairway. She cut to the right and tried to shoo him aside. He
would slow her progress if he didn't get out of the way, and
if Kane caught her, his vigilance wouldn't fail a second
time. No, they would keep a close eye on her from here on
out if they caught her. They could not catch her.

"Move!" she shouted as she hurried down the stairs as quickly as her old legs would carry her. Her knees always hurt these days, but still, she moved fairly well when she had to.

The man on the staircase did not get out of her way. He stood there, fat and grinning and sloppy, and when she reached him, intent on pushing her way past, he grabbed her arm. Liane tried to yank her arm away, but he held her fast, and then he whispered hoarsely:

"Emperor Ciro sends his regards."

She didn't feel the knife, not at first. It was very sharp, and slipped into her chest too easily. Once it was embedded, the pain hit her and began to spread. Her legs gave out, and the man dropped her to face Kane with his little knife. Foolish little man, Liane thought as she stared at the ceiling. Kane would kill Ciro's soldier, if not for murdering his sister then to keep him from reaching Sophie, his beloved wife.

The outraged shout and bloodcurdling scream that filled her ears and her head told her what had happened. The man who had killed her was himself dead.

Her knees didn't hurt anymore, she noticed. Her body felt light, as if she were floating on water. How odd, and how strangely and unexpectedly pleasant. Sebestyen appeared before her, misty and yet almost solid. He looked as if he could be solid if she squinted her eyes just right, and she was not surprised to see him.

"You're still young," she whispered as he knelt beside her.

"Tell them, love," he whispered as he took her hand in his. She felt him, more real than the stairs at her back, more real than the life she had built in this small coast town. "Tell them where to find the boys."

Liane shook her head. "I promised you I would protect them always, and I have, I truly have."

"I know." Sebestyen carried her hand to his lips and kissed her knuckles. It did not feel like a true kiss, but was like a breeze passing over her fingers. "But now it is time to let them go, to send them to their duty."

Liane narrowed her eyes to see Sebestyen more clearly. "Why are you here?"

"I have been waiting for you."

"Waiting to take me to hell, I imagine." Like him, her life had been filled with sin before leaving Arthes behind. Lust, murder, greed . . . hate. Surely she would be made to pay for all her sins in the afterlife.

Sebestyen smiled. He had not smiled much in life, and never like this. She saw the peace in that smile, and it warmed her. "No, love. We earned our way to the Land of the Dead with our sacrifice for the children."

"Then why aren't you there? It's been such a long time since you left me."

"I have been waiting. We'll go there together now, I promise."

All the dreams, all the times she'd sensed him with her . . . they had been real somehow. Suddenly she felt as if her body was light as a feather and was beginning to float above the stairs.

"Tell them," Sebestyen insisted. "Tell your brother where our children can be found."

It was only then that Liane realized Kane was standing over her, much as Sebestyen was. He tried to stop the bleeding by pressing his hands to the wound, and he shouted for Sophie to help him. Liane could tell by the stricken expression on her brother's face that he realized it was too late for help.

Liane focused on Kane's face and tried to stop the pull that threatened to lift her up and up and up. "Devlyn and Trystan, those are their names now. Devlyn and Trystan

Arndell. They don't know the truth, Kane. They think their father was a fisherman who was lost at sea."

Kane squeezed her hand. He tried to be brave but she saw the tears glistening in his eyes. "Where are they, Liane? Guide us to them."

"Trystan fights. Devlyn . . . Devlyn is too much like his father, I'm afraid. I'm not sure where he is."

"They are together, now," Sebestyen whispered. "Our sons have reunited, as is proper." Liane experienced a rush of relief. Her boys had found one another, and that gave her comfort.

Isadora was here, too, Liane realized. Always pragmatic, practical Isadora, who did not hold back her tears but cursed them as they fell. "Which is the eldest? We must know."

Sebestyen now looked more real than Kane and Isadora and all those who had gathered behind them, and Liane felt better than she had in years. She was young again. Energy rushed through her body, and her heart surged with love and peace. "The eldest keeps the ring," she said. "You know the ring of which I speak, Isadora. You know." The others faded and Sebestyen assisted her to her feet. He smiled at her, even as they stared down at the misty people who wept and mourned the old woman she had become, here in this shore town where she'd raised her children.

She looked up at her husband. "You waited for me."

"Of course I waited," Sebestyen said, with a touch of the arrogance which was so much a part of who he was, so much a part of the man he had been made by those who'd trained him to be emperor. "The land that awaits is not paradise without you, love, not for me."

"I love you still," she said as her husband led her away from the scene of her death.

"I know," he said as he lifted her hand and kissed it again. "I love you, too. Now, let's go home."

* * *

NIGHT HAD FALLEN, BUT THE CRIES FOR HELP PULLED LYR forward, as did the light from what appeared to be a fire. Fire, here in this wet place. Fire, burning in the darkness and leading him toward a woman's screams.

Rayne was right in suggesting that this could be a trap, and yet he could not ride by without being certain.

When the fire was close and he could see the figure of a woman tied to a barren tree trunk which rose out of the water, Lyr turned to Rayne, who followed closely and silently. "Wait here," he instructed.

"No," she said softly. "Whatever awaits ahead cannot be any worse than waiting here in the dark."

He heard the whisper and splash of a creature in the water not too far away, and nodded. "If it is a trap, I will hold off the enemy while you take your horse to the bank and then into the forest."

She did not answer, but he didn't have time to argue with her. With a powerful mother and two sisters, he had always known that women could be stubborn beyond belief. There were times when arguing with them was a waste of breath.

Fire burned on the water in a circle around the girl who'd been lashed to the tree. There must be some sort of fuel or magic there, he imagined, since he had never seen such a sight as fire dancing on water. Firelight and moonlight illuminated the girl's golden hair, which was loose and tangled and fell all around her like a curtain made of sunlight.

Again the captive screamed, calling for help. Her voice echoed in the deserted swamplands. Lyr approached cautiously, since it was possible this was a trap and the girl was bait. His sword was held ready, to strike at the enemy or to stop time, whichever might prove to be more prudent.

Apparently the golden-haired girl heard him. Her head snapped around as far as it would go, given her bonds. Her face was beautiful, young and smooth and frightened. "Did she send you?" she asked, her voice hoarse from screaming. "Are you here to finish me since the swamp witch's creature has not?"

A splash drew Lyr's attention to the creature she spoke of, a large, wide-mouthed reptile which seemed to be half-snake and half-croc. The creature swam just beyond the circle of fire. "Is the fire yours or hers?" Lyr asked as he came alongside the girl. From this vantage point, he discovered that she was unclothed. Large-breasted, firm and shapely, and completely naked.

"The fire is mine," she said, turning her head to look at him suspiciously. "So far the flames have kept the creature away, but it is becoming accustomed to them and draws closer."

"What creature are you that you control fire on water?"

"Some call me nymph, some call me fairy, some call me witch. In truth I am all three. I live in the forests beyond this swamp, and until now the swamp witch has left me alone."

Lyr's eyes reached beyond the circle to search for the witch, who had apparently used this forest nymph as bait to draw him and Rayne in.

"Allow the fire to dwindle and I will release you."

The nymph shook her head fiercely. "First you must destroy the creature. The witch Beatrisa has directed it to kill me, and as soon as the fire dies, it will move. I suspect the creature will move more quickly than you."

"Lyr?" Rayne's voice called to him, close and concerned and frightened.

He glanced back at her to find that she had not approached as he had. Apparently the swamp itself was not as frightening as the unnatural creature which stayed close to the bound nymph. "Move your horse to the bank," he ordered, and this time Rayne did not argue with him.

Lyr's horse refused to move any closer to the creature, so he was forced to dismount and send the animal with Rayne, to the relative safety of the marshy far bank. The shallow water did not come above his boots, but was murky and odorous and deep enough for the odd creature who popped up to show his teeth and then disappeared beneath the water once again.

The water swirled. There were other things beneath the surface, and Lyr could not tell exactly where the reptile had hidden itself. It could be inches away, for all he knew.

The bound nymph said the creature had been directed to her, so he moved toward her protective circle of fire. Sure enough, a furrow in the water indicated the movement of something larger than was normal moving toward the fire, then coming up out of the water inches from the flame. He swung his sword toward the slimy creature, but it dipped below the water once again, moving more swiftly than he'd thought possible.

"When the monster shows itself again, stop it," Rayne instructed, her voice near frantic and yet still strong as she yelled at him.

How long could it stay beneath the water? How far could it travel? Could it move as well on land as it did beneath the water? Would it turn on him, or worse, could it race to shore and attack Rayne's mount? He could imagine too well Rayne being thrown off her mare and into the dark unsafe water.

"You dreamed you could part the water with your breath," he shouted.

The nymph's head snapped around, and for the first time she gave Rayne her attention.

"It was just a dream," Rayne argued.

"Try," he said. "Look for an indication of movement beneath the water, and try. We have nothing to lose, and possibly everything to gain." Her powers were very new, and she did not know yet what she could and could not do. The nymph had control of fire. It was very possible that Rayne could move aside the waters which concealed the reptile.

Lyr saw, directly before the flame, a ripple on the water which was unlike any he had seen before. The creature or Rayne? He could not be sure, but he gave that small area his attention and held his sword ready, gripping it in both hands.

When the water moved again, he knew it was Rayne and not the reptile which caused the movement. A furrow appeared, as if a large finger ran across the water, parting it. The furrow grew deeper and longer, and as he heard Rayne expel a long, powerful breath, the swamp water split and rose up and peeled away from the muddy bottom, where a long and dangerous creature waited.

The thing turned its beady eyes to Lyr and leapt toward him, sensing the danger of the blade. Its coiled tail whipped into the air and its mouth opened wide. Such teeth . . .

Lyr swung his blade fast and hard, and cut the unnatural reptile in half. The two parts of the once dangerous body fell into the water, which quickly returned to its normal state.

As Lyr walked toward the nymph, he glanced toward Rayne on the shore. There was little light, and still he could see that she was stunned and pale. No, she did not yet know what she could do. Her education would take years.

The fire did not die entirely, but a doorway of sorts

opened and Lyr walked through. He sheathed his sword and drew a short knife with which to free the naked nymph.

"Thank you," she said breathlessly as he began to cut at her bonds. "What an impressive display of swordsmanship and magic. The two of you work together quite well." Her smile was wide and suggestive, and her eyes met his. They were blue; he could tell even in the odd light.

It was impossible to free her without touching her bare body, and as she was without the protection of footwear, he decided it would be best if he carried her to the shore. She did not hesitate to wrap her arms around his neck and even to lay her head on his shoulder. His progress to the shore was slow but steady.

"I owe you my thanks," the nymph whispered. "Do you know how a nymph shows gratitude to a champion? You have never known such pleasures as I can show you."

She was beautiful, bare, and seductive, but Lyr found he was not as tempted as he might've been even days ago. "What is your name?"

The nymph laughed. "No self-respecting nymph shares her name so easily, champion. There is power in a name, power I do not wish to give."

The nymph would offer her body but not her name. She was a magical creature not much different from the reptile he had just killed. Did she have a soul? A heart?

"We must be on guard for the witch," he said.

Again, the nymph laughed. "She is surely long gone by now. She cannot face the three of us and win. Together we have the power to stop her, and so she will hide like the coward she truly is."

"Perhaps."

When they reached the shore where Rayne waited, Lyr placed the nymph on her feet. Here, in front of another woman, she would likely be more circumspect.

The nymph walked toward Rayne and offered a hand, as if to assist her from her saddle. "Come," she said. "I have offered our champion my body as thanks, but he hesitates. Perhaps if you join us, he will agree." She closed her eyes and breathed deep. "I smell him in you, as I smell you on him. With the nastiness of the witch's creature behind us, we should enjoy the remainder of the night as men and women were meant to do."

"I . . . I . . ." Rayne said, ignoring the offered hand.

"Come now, you must share," the nymph said. "What are you, lady, that you can move water aside?"

A ribbon of warning crawled up Lyr's spine. This creature would not even reveal her name, and yet she asked prying questions.

Rayne opened her mouth but did not have time to speak before Lyr said, "Her father was a wizard. He taught her many tricks."

The nymph turned away from Rayne and looked at Lyr hard. For the first time, he saw something he did not like in her blue eyes. "Moving water is not a trick, my lord, it is magic. Real, powerful magic." She forgot Rayne and walked to him, her bare feet getting muddy on the sloppy banks of the swamp, her nipples tightening as she grinned at him. She pressed her body to Lyr's. "Come and take your lover from me, if you dare," she called. "None can resist a forest nymph, not even one as staunch and determined as this one. One touch and he is mine. You can watch, lady, or you can join us, but you cannot stop me from taking that which I want."

Lyr tried to set the nymph away, but she was as slippery as the reptilian creature he had killed and her arms snaked around him as she ground her body against his. She was unnaturally strong, her grip was solid, and she was as much a creature as the thing he had just killed. "Come, lover," she whispered. "Let us show your timid woman what sex can be when passion is unleashed."

He would freeze time and step away, but his arms were pinned down, and as long as the nymph was touching him, she would be unaffected by his magic. He had learned early on that whatever or whoever he touched when he called upon his gift moved with him as others were frozen in time. As he began to work free of the nymph's grasp, she slithered down his body and placed her open mouth against his penis. He wanted nothing to do with this unnatural creature, but his baser instincts responded. Beneath his trousers he grew hard, and she laughed with her mouth opening against the telling swell. A rush of lust, uncontrolled, leapt in his body, and in his mind he could see the nymph beneath him, he could feel himself inside her.

The vision in his mind was not his own, he realized, but was one she had somehow planted there.

The thing who was on her knees in the mud clasped one of his hands with her own, and her lips moved against him, but her grip was not as strong as it had once been. The nymph thought he was in her grasp in yet another way, that he would not dare move away. Lyr pushed away the visions she tried to force upon him, he stepped back quickly and waved his hand over her golden head, and everything stopped.

Rayne had dismounted, and she stood near the horses with an expression of dismay and petulance etched onto her face. Muddy and disheveled, she still managed to look like a proper lady, and all he could think of was how she'd wrapped her body around his last night. She was a real woman, with a fine soul and a big heart, and she was mightily annoyed with him.

The nymph remained on her knees in the muck, and he left her in that position as he fetched a bit of rope from his saddlebag and quickly bound her hands and ankles. He'd felt her strength and knew that she'd eventually be able to free herself, but by that time he and Rayne would be far away from this place. Maybe the witch would find her before then, but that was no longer his concern. She was not an innocent to be saved but a magical creature who would have to fend for herself for survival.

When the nymph was snuggly bound, Lyr waved his hand to set time into motion once again.

Rayne knew what he could do, she understood what had happened, and yet she still looked startled when time moved forward and the scene before her had changed.

"We should go before the witch decides to strike," Lyr said, moving toward Rayne and the horses.

Rayne snorted. Again, her expression was one of disgust.

The nymph screamed. "What have you done? Release me!"

Lyr ignored the naked and bound woman and gave Rayne his attention. "Seriously, this episode has cost us much time," he explained. "If the witch is nearby . . ."

"You are a dolt."

No doubt she was speaking of his brief encounter with the nymph. Perhaps she had seen his physical response and misinterpreted what it meant. "I stopped time and walked away," he said indignantly. "I don't know many men who would've done the same."

"Only anyone with a brain," she retorted.

"We had to save the nymph from the witch. There's no reason to be angry. In her own way she was only trying to . . ."

The nymph, still struggling, began to laugh harshly. He glanced at her to see that she was using her unnatural fire to burn away the rope he'd used to bind her.

"She is the witch," Rayne said sharply, "and the fact that

you can't see that for yourself means you are a simpleton or else she somehow blinded you to the obvious with a spell."

"And yet you can see," Lyr said, angry with himself for not even suspecting the possibility.

"I suspect a good portion of her magic only works on men." She followed that statement with a snort. "Those ropes won't hold her for very long, I suspect."

"Mind your own business," the nymph whispered as she tried to ignite a small flame on the knotted rope at her wrists.

"They'll hold her awhile longer," Lyr said. "Time enough for us to move on."

Rayne apparently did not trust his word, not where the witch was concerned. She glanced up, and with her newly discovered powers she called down the branches of a nearby willow tree. This time she did not need to thrust her hands into the mud or sing. She concentrated on the tree, and Lyr watched as those supple limbs wrapped tightly around Beatrisa's naked body.

"What magic is this?" the witch screamed. "How dare you turn my swamp against me?"

"Just in case," Rayne said as she turned away and climbed swiftly into the saddle.

Lyr remounted. Like Rayne, he ignored the curses and pleas of the witch Beatrisa. Only a few hours more, and they would be out of the swamp entirely. Taking this route had saved them many days so he could not be sorry for the choice, but he could not wait to drop his boots onto truly solid ground once again.

They reentered the water, which was tough to travel through but less treacherous than the sloping, slippery bank. The creatures, all of them no doubt at Beatrisa's command, had gone silent and still. Maybe they were called to her to help. Maybe she had her mind on other matters, like freeing herself. Whatever the reason, he was glad for the respite, such as it was.

As they slogged forward, he said to Rayne, "It seems no one can be trusted." Not Segyn, not a beautiful woman seemingly in distress . . . no one.

"I trust you," Rayne said simply and honestly. "Perhaps I can rely on no one else, not until this war is over, but I do trust you, Lyr."

His heart sank, and he felt more a traitor than he had when he'd gone hard with Beatrisa's mouth over his cock and her visions of lust in his head. "Don't," he said softly. "Don't trust even me." In the distance the howl which had haunted this night came again.

13

PHELAN CAME UPON THE WITCH WHEN THE SKY WAS touched with gray. He was close behind his prey, but the fact that they were horsed and he was not did not work in his favor. No matter how hard he tried, he could not catch them, and seeing the witch, bound unnaturally as she was, only angered him. He'd been running most of the night, splashing in muddy waters, fed and protected by the unnatural energy of the Isen Demon. And still, he had not caught them.

For hours he'd been oddly optimistic that at any moment he might come across the witch Beatrisa and two unconscious victims, but instead he found the witch trapped much as he had been, caught up in the limbs of a tree which served Ciro's bride.

Beatrisa had attempted to burn away the limbs and had been successful in some cases, but she'd also scorched herself here and there during the inexact process. The beautiful witch was clearly frustrated when Phelan found her caught in twisted limbs, covered with mud and spots of burned flesh and cursing more loudly and vividly than any Circle Warrior he had ever heard.

The witch instantly recognized Phelan as one of the demon's servants. "Release me," she commanded confidently.

Phelan stood a few feet away and studied her. "You worthless bitch, you've failed miserably at the one task you were given. Why should I waste my time freeing you?"

Her answer was to send a weak spit of fire his way, a bit of flame he easily sidestepped. The spark fell to damp ground and sputtered before extinguishing with a gentle pop. "How long have they been gone?"

"I don't know," she said as she struggled. "I almost had the man where I wanted him, and then the next thing I know, I am tightly bound and separated by several feet."

"He stopped time," Phelan explained. "You should've seen that trick coming, you pitiful hag."

"He should've been mine," she whispered.

"Perhaps you overestimated your charms," Phelan said as he examined her naked body beneath the twist of limbs.

Beatrisa's cold glare made clear what she thought of his statement, but then she ignored it and continued on. "It was the woman who called my own tree down to bind me with its limbs. I would've been free hours ago if not for that bit of magic. She parted the water with her breath, and called upon these limbs to bind me. What manner of witch is she?"

"I'm not sure," Phelan responded. A powerful one, one the Isen Demon wished to use for himself.

Beatrisa lifted her pretty blue eyes to him, beautiful eyes which concealed her age and her hate and her dark magic. Perhaps she didn't realize that through the demon which connected them, he knew her well. She'd used those eyes and her fine body to seduce many a man to his death, and she was foolish enough to think they would work on him. "Free me, and I will reward you well."

Phelan laughed loudly. "I have no need of your reward." He remembered Gwyneth and for a moment wished that he had not killed her. When he had his own army, he'd need women, too. He should've made her his slave instead of strangling her, and kept her for a while.

Beatrisa closed her eyes and took a deep breath. "I smell my sister on you. You should've waited for me, if your aging body only allows for one hard cock a month. I'm much more desirable than she. I'm prettier, I'm smoother, and I know tricks that would make poor Gwyneth blush to her toes."

She was trying to get a rise out of him . . . one way or another. "I killed your sister when I was done with her."

Beatrisa smiled. "All the more reason to free me and take me with you."

He didn't have time to worry about this pathetic, useless creature. He walked past the witch, following the path Lyr and the woman had taken. Eventually Beatrisa would manage to free herself. If not, she'd tire and the crocs would get her. "I haven't the time to waste on a miserable failure such as you."

She screamed as he walked away, and he found her reaction amusing. Phelan plodded through the swamp for a while and then he ran, splashing up the shallow water, his eyes focused straight ahead. He had been entrusted with a very important task, and unlike the witch he'd left behind, he would not fail.

Even the snakes kept their distance, as if they sensed that he was more dangerous than any of them.

RAYNE HAD NEVER BEEN SO HAPPY TO SEE SUNLIGHT AS she was when the sun rose over the last of the swamplands.

With the sun came hope. With light came promise. With this day came welcome solid ground.

She still had not forgiven Lyr, not entirely. He hadn't succumbed to the nymph's blatant attentions, but for a moment, a very long moment, there had been an expression on his face that she wished to be reserved only for her. It was an expression that spoke of need and promised pleasure, of burning desire and uncontrollable yearning. Of lust. She had seen that expression in his eyes before, and foolishly she had thought it meant more than a man's easy arousal.

If she had not been there, watching as the witch tried to seduce him, would he have succumbed to her wicked spell? Would he have lain with the nymph in the mud and muck, amid the decay of the swamp?

She could not answer that question with any authority, and that concerned her. Lyr said she could not trust even him. Was he right in that statement? Was she more alone than she imagined?

Rayne tried to push the disappointment out of her mind. With everything that had happened in the world of late, her apparent poor choice in love was of little consequence. It wasn't as if Lyr had promised her anything, it wasn't as if he'd sworn undying love to get what he wanted from her. Quite the opposite, in fact. He seemed determined to make her accept the fact that he did not care for her in any way other than the physical. Even more so since he'd been forced to kill Segyn.

His features seemed to ease a bit as they moved onto drier land. She suspected he would never know true ease again, that he had indeed been burned by the betrayal of his friend, but she was glad to see the hardness of his jaw diminish a bit, she was glad to see his fine mouth not so hard, at least for a while. She wanted to take his face in her hands and tell him again that she loved him, to see the expression of longing that was hers, and hers alone.

Rayne longed, so desperately, to know Lyr in a time when there was no war, no mission, no duty to drive him forward. She longed to hold him without feeling as if every moment they shared was stolen. She suspected that what she longed for was desperately and irrevocably out of her reach.

By midmorning they were leading their mounts across tall grasses, not sloppy marshlands or endless puddles of muddy water. No reptilian creatures would be hiding beneath the grass, not the way they hid in the water of the swamplands. Yes, she much preferred solid ground. The skirt Gwyneth had given her was muddy at the hem, but still in better condition than the blue traveling dress she'd stuffed into one saddle bag.

When Lyr indicated with a rise of his hand that it was time to stop to rest the horses, Rayne dismounted smoothly, dropped to her knees, bent forward, and kissed the ground. It was an impulse she gave into without question, and when the soft grass tickled her cheeks and the scent of dirt filled her nose, she was not sorry. She remained there, face against the ground. She didn't care how she might look to Lyr.

Earth Goddess, Gwyneth had said. She still didn't believe that could be true. Perhaps she did possess some magic, inherited through her father and perhaps even through her mother. She did have a special connection with the land and things which grew upon it. Maybe she would even admit that it was possible she was a natural-born witch of sorts, but Goddess? Goddesses were not of this earth, she was certain, so how was it possible?

A voice whispered to her, and though it had been years since she'd heard that voice, she knew it was her mother who spoke to her as she pressed her face to the ground.

"You are a keeper of the land, and very much of this earth."

Rayne held her breath and listened closely for more amid the long grass and sweetly scented soil. She needed sleep, her mind was spinning, and yet she knew that what she'd heard had not been her imagination or an illusion. After all these years, her mother spoke to her.

"You are *his* keeper, too," the voice whispered, and at that, Rayne lifted her head to watch as Lyr gave his attention to the horses. She had no doubt about the subject of her mother's insistence, but the Prince of Swords was a man who did not need or want a keeper.

"His heart needs a keeper, a healer."

Rayne sat up and watched Lyr, who gave the horses his full attention. He stroked their necks, checked their limbs, whispered to the animals words of thanks for leading them through the swamp. None could match him in battle, but there was more to life than swords and war. Even in war, life continued on. Perhaps he did need a keeper of sorts. Perhaps that keeper was her.

She knew the precise moment her mother's spirit left her. It was as if a physical presence departed. How many times over the years had her mother attempted to speak to her? Why had she never learned to listen? The dark energy of her father's house had interfered, perhaps, because here in the meadow so far away, wearing another woman's clothes and more than a little covered in mud, she heard very well.

Her fingers touched the gem at her chest, her mother's gem. If her father's pieces of gold jewelry held on to darkness, as Lyr had suggested, maybe this piece contained light.

Rayne sat on the soft ground, happy to be connected to the solid soil and glad to be surrounded by tall, soft

grasses. A yellow butterfly lighted on her hand, and she
smiled. Another followed, this one smaller and a bit
brighter in color than the first. In spite of all that was happening, she couldn't help but smile. Yes, life went on even
in the midst of war.

Lyr spun around quickly, drawing his sword smoothly
and moving toward her with haste. A heartbeat later than
he, Rayne heard what had alarmed him. A footstep and a
labored breath.

She glanced over her shoulder to see Segyn approaching, a drawn sword in one hand, a length of decaying wood
from the swamp in the other. His eyes were crazed, and he
smiled. Lyr ran toward her, and toward Segyn, but he was
too far away. She tried to rise from the ground but it was
too late.

"Not this time, bitch." With that, Segyn swung the
length of wood at her head.

HE WAS SO SHOCKED TO SEE SEGYN, HIS REACTION AL-
most came too late. Lyr called upon his magic and swung
his sword, and the sturdy limb his old friend had been
swinging stopped inches from meeting Rayne's head and
likely killing her. There was great force behind that attack.

Everything stopped. The butterflies which had flown
from Rayne's hand as she'd tried to rise, the grass which
was bent beneath the pull of her skirt, the horses which had
dropped their heads to eat. All stopped, all but him.

Lyr moved forward cautiously. He no longer trusted
anything, not even his own magic. Even though he had
been honing his craft for years, he could not always control
the amount of time all was frozen. Time sometimes moved
forward on its own, unbidden, but he usually had at least a
few minutes to do what had to be done.

He moved Rayne out of harm's way first, and breathed
a sigh of relief when Segyn's weapon was no longer upon
her. He placed her several feet away, in a position that
looked as if it would be comfortable enough when time
resumed its forward march. When that was done, he faced
Segyn, a man he had called friend for years, a warrior
who had taught him much of what he knew of battle, a
traitor who was not what he'd pretended to be. A man
he'd killed once.

There could be a quick end to this fight. A sword
through the heart while Segyn was immobile would end
it, but Lyr hesitated. He'd taken that route before, stab-
bing Segyn while the man had been helpless, and it had
tasted bitter for days. It tasted bitter still. There was no
honor in delivering such a death. Was that why the man
had come back from the dead? Was Lyr being punished
for delivering a less than honorable death to the once honorable warrior?

No, Segyn had never been honorable. He had only pretended, and though he had pretended very well, he was not,
nor had he ever been, a true and worthy warrior. Obviously
the wound Lyr had delivered had not been fatal as it had
appeared to be, and in his drugged state he had simply not
realized the fact.

No matter what the case, Lyr's own honor had been tarnished by offering such a death. It had seemed the only
way at the time, but now that he had the chance to face his
enemy in a fair fight, it was only right to take it.

Lyr did not need the wave of his sword to start time
again. That was the easiest way, it took the smallest amount
of energy, but he did not wish to move the point of his
sword away from the enemy. Segyn, the enemy. That combination of words still took some getting used to. They still
stung. Segyn, the enemy.

Lyr called upon his magic again, and with a brief flicker of his fingers, time resumed. Segyn's swing continued mightily, spinning the man around with great force, as the object of his weapon had been moved. Segyn spun wildly, lost his balance, and fell. He landed on his back as Rayne screamed briefly.

Segyn quickly realized what had happened and jumped to his feet, dropping the length of wood to grip his sword with both hands. He smiled, and that was when Lyr was certain there was nothing in this creature of the man he had once known.

"You should've killed me when you had the chance, boy. Killed me again, I should say."

"I will kill you again," Lyr said, realizing as he looked at the man before him that whatever he'd known as Segyn was gone. His old friend was a victim of the demon as surely as those they'd buried in that razed village days ago. He did not face a friend, but an enemy like any other.

"You can try." Segyn swung his sword with a battle cry, and Lyr stepped aside and brandished his own blade with more control and precision than his opponent had shown. Segyn was angry, striking out almost wildly. He had lost control, that was apparent. Segyn had taken quite a chance, attacking while Lyr was awake and able to stop time, going not for the deadliest threat first but for Rayne.

Segyn was fighting in a careless manner but that might not last. He'd always had great control in battle, and now that the fight had begun, he would call upon instinct and skill.

The older man had taught Lyr much of what he knew of swordplay, and that worked to neither's advantage. They knew one another's moves, they anticipated the next strike. For a few minutes they danced in the meadow, eyes locked and blades striking with force, steps carefully planned and precise. Segyn's wild anger faded, as Lyr had known it would. Rayne spoke, but Lyr did not listen. He couldn't afford to listen to her words, not when he needed all of his attention on the enemy before him.

He spoke to her only once, to order her to stay out of the fight. His fight. A fair fight. There were no vines about for her to manipulate, but in truth he had no idea what she might be able to do.

The battle was almost like sparring in the courtyard of the Circle of Bacwyr headquarters, but this was no practice session. This was life and death. Lyr was fast; he had always been fast. He was precise, thanks to years of practice. Segyn was strong and ruthless, and he knew Lyr's moves as well as he knew his own.

Soon perspiration ran down Lyr's face and his arms. His heart pounded. His eyes stung. So far no one had landed a blow against flesh, but as they tired, that would come. Segyn was possessed of an unnatural energy, so Lyr could not allow the older man to get the upper hand. He had to make a move Segyn did not expect, now, before his mind became incapable of anything but instinct.

Lyr dipped down, rolled to the side, and then struck out from an angle. His blade cut into Segyn's thigh, and the man was truly surprised. The injury didn't slow him down, though. In fact, Segyn laughed. That unnatural laughter sent chills down Lyr's spine.

It wasn't long before Lyr managed to dismiss the disturbing fact that his opponent was Segyn and simply fought through instinct, as he had been taught. He felt the blades, his own and the other, as much as he saw them. The sword he wielded felt a part of him, as much as an arm or a leg or the air he breathed. His heartbeat slowed, and all anxiety fell away. He no longer felt tired, and if he continued to sweat, he dismissed the nuisance. There was only the sword, and the sword was his.

Segyn stumbled, and again Lyr drew blood. The older man gasped but recovered quickly. "Lucky shot, boy," he said gruffly as he came around and swung hard.

Lyr deflected the blow, spun out of reach, and then moved in for another strike. There was no luck in swordplay which was not made by the man who gripped the weapon in his hands.

Again, Segyn gasped, but he also smiled. "You cannot kill me, boy. The demon brought me back from the dead after the last time you killed me. Do you think he'll allow me to die while the girl and the crystal dagger are within reach? No, they are mine, and you are nothing more than a soon-to-be-dead spoiled child . . ."

While Segyn taunted, Lyr kept his mind and his soul on the battle at hand. He did not listen, he did not take a single word to heart. It wasn't the man he had once known speaking, in any case. This opponent was the servant of a demon, a demon who wished to bring darkness and pain to the world, and most especially to Rayne.

Segyn's taunts were cut short when Lyr's blade pierced the place where his heart should be. For a moment Segyn was still, and then he dropped to his knees, oddly alive. He laid one hand against the blood that seeped from what should've been a killing wound. "I didn't teach you that move."

"No," Lyr said softly. "My father did."

The crystal dagger came alive, humming against the thigh where it was strapped, and as it had in the past, the thing spoke to him.

Take his head.

Lyr shook his head. "None of my warriors should die that way. It isn't fitting."

This vessel of darkness is no longer your warrior, and unless you take his head, he will return. The humming grew stronger. *He will go after her before you, as he did on this day. Give him the chance and he will use her against you.*

While Segyn studied his bloody hand and tried to make a firmer grip on the handle of his sword, Lyr stepped back, spun forward, and swung his weapon with strength and precision. Though he had never made such a move before, he knew it was not easy to take a man's head. Strength was called for, strength of arm and of heart.

It was an ugly sight, to see a man's head separated from his shoulders, to witness the moment when familiar eyes which had once been lively and laughing, which had once been dark and malevolent, went lifeless.

This time he defeated Segyn in a fair battle, and the man who had once been his friend was truly dead.

The humming against his thigh grew silent. Apparently the crystal dagger slept once again, now that the threat was past.

Lyr heard Rayne before he saw her. She ran toward him, her breath labored and uneven. He turned to face her, and she threw herself at him.

He caught her, which meant dropping his sword. Lyr never dropped his sword, but Rayne propelled herself at him so fiercely it was either let go of the weapon or take the chance that she'd fall. Her face was damp with tears, and her heart, pressed against his, beat too fast and hard.

"Why didn't you freeze time and finish him straight-away?" she asked, her face buried against his shoulder. "Why didn't you use your magic? Do you know how close his blade came to you? Do you realize what a risk you took in fighting him as you did? *Why*?"

"I'm not afraid to face any man fairly," he said, his voice oddly calm. No, he was not afraid of much at all, but when he thought of Rayne in Ciro's possession, he was truly terrified.

"Well, I was afraid," she said, a touch of petulance creeping into her voice.

"I would never have allowed him to hurt you."

Rayne loosened her grip and placed her feet on the ground. She backed away from him just a little, and let her hands fall to her sides. "I was not afraid for myself, I was afraid for you."

"You needn't have been."

Her chin came up a little, as if she didn't like that answer, and she changed the path of the questioning. "How far are we from the armies you seek?"

"Half a day or thereabouts, if General Merin is where he said they would be."

"Half a day," she repeated. "Our journey is almost done, then."

"Yes." Almost done. Just beginning.

The dagger against his thigh hummed.

WHEN THEY CAME ACROSS THE ARMIES OF THE RIGHTFUL emperor of Columbyana, Rayne felt a tugging at her heart. This was their destination, she was safe here, and yet she did not feel relief. Lyr would leave her now, and he would probably be glad to ride off without her to slow him down. After all, he didn't even think she had a right to be *worried* about him.

The sight of all the armed soldiers that spread before them should have been a comfort. The sprawling camp bustled. Ciro would not take this country and its people easily. There were many men who would fight to the death for what was right. Men like Lyr—though she suspected there was no other man precisely like Lyr Hern, Prince of Swords.

He slowed his pace as a soldier on guard came toward them. The young man in green was serious of nature and well armed. Lyr raised his hands so the soldier could see that he did not hold a weapon.

"You'll be fine now," Lyr said in a lowered voice so only Rayne could hear. "My cousin and her husband and the others will all gather round you and make sure Ciro does not come near you."

"Do you think it's really that simple?"

Lyr hesitated. "I don't know. I hope so." He nodded toward the army, a camp filled with soldiers ready to fight. "Getting past so many dedicated men will not be easy, not even for Ciro."

Rayne knew what Ciro had planned for her, and thanks to Gwyneth's claim that she was a Goddess of the Earth, she now understood why. Power. Ciro wanted to use whatever power she possessed to create a greater evil in the child he planned to give her.

Whether Lyr cared for her or not, she hoped with all her heart that his child was already growing inside her, that if Ciro did defeat Lyr and make his way past this army, she would not be suitable as a vessel for his child.

Not right away, of course. Not unless he waited or worse . . . harmed the child within her.

Rayne placed a hand over her flat belly. It was much too soon to know if there was a child or not, but if that was the case, she had not only herself to protect but the child as well.

The soldier recognized Lyr as he came closer. His face

relaxed, and his sword dropped. "M'lord," the soldier said. "Where are the others?"

Lyr's jaw tightened. "There are no others, I'm afraid."

The soldier nodded. "Ciro's Own has been at work in your part of the world as well as here, then."

"Here?" Lyr leaned forward in the saddle. "What happened?"

"The rightful emperor has been taken."

"Emperor Arik?"

The soldier shook his head. "Emperor Arik is dead. His son, Emperor Sian, has been kidnapped. We fear for his life."

True puzzlement crossed Lyr's face. "Emperor Sian?"

"Yes. Much has happened while you were away, m'lord. Sian Sayre Chamblyn, the wizard who is wed to our own Sister Ariana, is the illegitimate son of the late emperor and was named as his successor."

Lyr took a moment to allow the information to soak in. "Sian is emperor and he's been taken?"

"Yes, m'lord. He was taken last night."

"How do you know it was Ciro? Isn't it possible that Sian simply . . . wandered off?" As he asked the question, he knew that could not be. Sian was devoted to Ariana, and was not a man given to wandering.

The soldier shook his head. "A note was left." His face paled and his lips thinned. "It was written in blood, m'lord."

Lyr glanced toward Rayne, perhaps trying to judge her reaction to the news. "Sian's blood?"

"We don't know, m'lord."

Lyr nodded his head. "This is an unexpected turn of events. Good heavens, my cousin Ariana is—"

"Livid, m'lord," the soldier said. "She'll be glad to know that you've arrived. We're moving toward Arthes within the hour." The young man's eyebrows shot up. "Oh, yes, she's also empress apparently. Empress Ariana. That will take some getting used to."

Lyr turned again to study Rayne's face, and he saw the worry etched there. He'd been so certain that she would be safe here, that Ciro and his damned Own would not be able to touch her among these soldiers. But if the rightful emperor could be taken, was there any safe place in this world for her?

14

"You could've told me!" Lyr shouted.

"He didn't want anyone to know!" Ariana's voice was as loud and strident as his own.

"Obviously *someone* knew!" Lyr took a step forward, and General Merin, who stood behind Ariana, mirrored his step.

"You'll not speak to the empress in such a manner," the general said sternly, "even if you are Prince of Swords and a relation."

Empress. Ariana, with her wild hair and well-worn soldier's uniform, did not look like any empress Lyr had ever imagined. No, that was not entirely correct. There was a strength in her eyes, even now, that was downright imperial.

She dismissed her general's warning. Poor Merin might as well not have been in the vicinity for all the attention she showed him at this moment. "This discussion will have to wait. We're going after Sian now."

"Not in a panic you're not," Lyr said. "That's exactly what Ciro will expect and he'll be ready for you."

"I don't care."

"If he decimates this army . . ."

"I don't care!" Ariana shouted.

Lyr placed stilling hands on his cousin's shoulders. He understood too well what she was feeling. He had never before been torn between what he knew to be right and what he felt inside. Warriors did not take emotions into account when formulating a battle plan, but since meeting Rayne, he'd been turned inside out by the awakening of his own emotions. Killing her would put an end to a horrific possibility, but he couldn't do it. He couldn't even suggest such an action aloud, because Ariana's army was filled with capable men who, in the name of victory, would be glad to do what Lyr could not.

Rayne was presently under massive guard. If those men knew what Ciro intended, would they take her life rather than take the chance that she might give birth to a monster? Of course they would. They might shed a tear, they might regret the action for the rest of their days, they would not take on the task with any joy . . . but they would kill her.

The only solution was to succeed in his task and take Ciro's life with the crystal dagger.

He remained calm. "How many battles has this army fought against Ciro's Own?"

"Too many to count," Ariana answered tersely.

"They fight and they win, do they not?"

"Yes."

"And with each win you weaken the demon, with each soul you return to one of Ciro's Own, you keep the Isen Demon from the power it seeks."

"Yes, but we're talking about *Sian*!"

Could he reason with her? He wasn't sure. Ariana had sacrificed much to this war. Had she reached the breaking point? "If you lose this army with a rash move at the wrong time, Ciro wins. It will take years to build another like it, it will take a generation to construct an army capable of facing Ciro and the demon, and even then . . . no, the truth is if we don't defeat him now, we're lost, Ariana. Lost. Are you willing to sacrifice the world in order to save your husband?"

"Yes!" she answered quickly, and then tears filled her eyes. "It's not fair that you should even ask that question."

"These days nothing is fair." If someone as beautiful and good as Rayne had to be destroyed in order to save the world from the child she and Ciro might create, would that be fair? No. That meant he could not afford to lose. He could not allow Ciro to win in the days to come.

"I have a better plan," he said calmly.

"You can't expect me to sit back and—"

Lyr grasped his cousin's shoulders firmly. "Empress Ariana, please listen to me." He leaned in and repeated in a whisper, "I have a better plan."

LYR'S FAMILY WAS DECIDEDLY ODD, RAYNE DECIDED AS she watched and listened. For most of the day she'd been sequestered in a tent which offered the comforts she had been without during her travels. Pillows to rest upon, clean water for bathing and for drinking, tasty food—even a sweetcake! She'd eaten little, been unable to rest, and had cared only for washing the grime from her face. Throughout it all there had been a heavy guard outside the tent.

She'd been very much relieved when Lyr had arrived to collect her for supper, where he'd introduced her to his family. Ariana, leader of this army, healer, and empress. Queen Keelia, with her startling gold eyes and uncanny

powers. Joryn, Keelia's man. They ate at a roughly constructed table which was close to a large tent, Ariana's tent,
Rayne assumed. When they were finished with the meal,
they went inside the tent to resume a private conversation
which Rayne did not entirely understand. Apparently there
was a plan. Some of them thought it was a good one, others
did not. None of them bothered to tell her what this plan
entailed.

She waited for Lyr to escort her back to her tent, where
she'd be forced to spend the night alone, wondering if he
would ever come, wondering if he was gone for good, but
he did not. She remained silent as they argued about this
plan, and after a while it seemed that they had all forgotten
about her. She liked it that way. Forgotten, she could listen
and learn.

"It's a fair enough scheme," Ariana said, almost calm
even though her husband had been kidnapped. "But really,
Lyr, *Tonlin*? He's been a soldier for about two weeks. He's
much too young."

"I need someone young and small," Lyr insisted. "And
you're exaggerating his inexperience. He tells me he's
been fighting with you since spring."

Rayne had heard only a small part of the plot, which
somehow included Lyr riding off to face Ciro on his own,
rather than this entire army marching on Arthes. Her heart
did a dance at that very idea, even though she knew that it
was his destiny to face Ciro.

Ariana turned to her cousin Keelia, the Anwyn Queen,
as she had often during the evening. "Is he all right?"

They all knew she spoke of her husband, and as before,
Keelia's answer was unsatisfactory. "Sian is alive. That's
all I know."

Ariana's face turned red and her hands balled into fists.
"You're supposed to be able to see anything!"

"But not everything, cousin. Never everything," Keelia explained calmly. The Queen's man, Joryn, placed his arm around her in silent comfort.

Lyr glanced Rayne's way often, his hawk eyes hard and without emotion. He was riding off to face his destiny, a destiny not of his own choosing, and she didn't know if he would come back. He wasn't going to Arthes to face a normal enemy, but a monster. A demon.

Unable to remain silent any longer, Rayne asked, "Can't you just . . . stop time and kill him while he's unable to move? I know you speak of honor and fairness, but where demons are concerned, any advantage is fair."

Keelia shook her head. "No, no, the heart must be beating when the crystal dagger touches it. The body must be living and moving forward in time, otherwise it won't work."

A chill walked down Rayne's spine. "But—"

"That's as it must be," Lyr said.

Until now, he'd kept the dagger her mother had fashioned hidden against his thigh, but since coming to this camp, he'd moved the crystal dagger to a sheath at his waist. He gripped the handle and drew it, as all watched.

"It is alive," he said reverently as he held the dagger before him for all to see. "I cannot explain how, but this dagger lives."

The murky gray and white swirled within the crystal, moving slowly and with an unexpected beauty.

"I know what Keelia says is true not because she is a powerful seer but because the dagger itself tells me it is so."

"It is a thing," Rayne whispered. "It cannot speak."

"Your mother instilled this weapon with a powerful magic, Rayne, and it does speak to me."

At that moment, the gray and pink cast of the weapon disappeared, and Lyr held a crystal-clear dagger in his hand. The weapon was alive, as he'd said it was, and Rayne knew as she studied the crystal-clear stone that it was united with the Prince of Swords in the same way she was united with the earth.

Her mother had made it for him, no one else.

The gray and pink danced in the crystal once again, and Lyr returned the dagger to its sheath. He took Rayne's arm, and they left the others behind. As they exited the large tent, Ariana was still grumbling about using the young soldier in Lyr's attack, but he ignored her.

He held Rayne's arm snuggly and walked toward the tent she had been assigned. His body was rigid, his jaw taut. By the light of the fires that illuminated this camp, Lyr looked much older than she knew him to be.

He was scared.

The entire army had been prepared to march, but something Lyr had said to his cousin had stopped them. What? Why did he think he could do what an army could not, especially if he could not use his magic and stop time in order to fight Ciro?

"Let me help you," Rayne argued as Lyr walked with her into the tent, where she'd spent most of the day. How much time did they have before he left? She held on to his hand, afraid he might vanish at any moment if she didn't physically hold him here.

"You will help," he said.

"Let me go to Ciro and—"

He pulled her roughly against his body. "No! Not that, do you hear me? Never that."

"I would if it meant saving you."

His anger faded, and he caressed her face with one hand. "I know you would, but you were not built for war, Rayne. You were intended for better things. Nurturing, tending, growing, these are your gifts."

"What about love?" she asked. "Is love one of my gifts?"

"I believe it is."

Rayne did what she'd been longing to do all day, she took Lyr's face in her hands and drew it down. She kissed him, not with hunger or with desperation but with the love he confessed was one of her gifts. *His keeper*, her mother had said, and she felt the truth of that statement to her bones.

When she took her mouth from his, she asked, "When do you leave?" She knew better than to cry or try to convince him that he didn't have to do what needed to be done.

"Before first light."

"Then we have time."

She would not tell Lyr how to fight, and she would not cry. Not for herself or for him. That's not why she was here.

She pushed Lyr's purple vest off, allowing her fingers to trail against the muscles in his arms. She removed his sword from his belt, sheath and all, but when her hand moved near the crystal dagger, she hesitated. "May I?"

Lyr didn't move. "Yes."

Rayne touched the crystal dagger, and when she did, she knew that Lyr had been right when he'd said it was alive. It did not speak to her, as it did to him, but she felt a rush of energy as her fingers brushed against the grip. Faint firelight illuminated the tent, fighting through the fabric of the structure and through a small slit in the entrance. Though the amount of light was lesser even than moonlight on the night of the crescent moon, the crystal caught that light and held it for a moment.

Rayne set the extraordinary weapon aside. Tonight was not about war, not about death or a destiny of destruction. Tonight was just about the two of them and their destiny, whatever that might be.

When his weapons were set aside, she unfastened Lyr's trousers and slipped her hand inside to touch him. He shuddered in her grasp, this hard, hawk-eyed man who rarely shuddered. Lyr reached for her, but she danced just out of his reach and directed him to lie upon the pillows she had been unable to rest upon that afternoon. He obeyed, and when he was stretched out upon the pillows, she removed his boots and then his trousers, leaving him completely bare. She knelt beside him, and her hands gently traced his warm, hard skin. Their first time together she hadn't known entirely what to expect, and after that . . . after that, their encounters had been rushed or desperate.

She wanted neither tonight. She wanted to pretend that they'd run away to a safe place and had all the time in the world for this. For love.

Rayne lowered her head and kissed Lyr's taut belly as her hand gently gripped his penis. She could feel the tension in his body, she could taste the quiver. With a shifting of her head, she laid her lips against the shaft, tasting him, flicking her tongue against him as he buried his hands in her hair.

He liked it, so she continued. She licked him, she sucked gently, she teased until he grabbed her head and moved her away. She'd be concerned if he didn't laugh gently.

"Take off your clothes," he ordered gruffly, that laugh coloring the edges of his demanding words.

Rayne sat back and did as he asked. She pulled the peasant blouse Gwyneth had given her over her head, but left the blue stone and gold chain. Both were cool against her warm skin. She took off her boots and tossed them aside, then stood above Lyr to unfasten and drop her colorful skirt.

For a moment she stood there, watching him in the faint

light. Her blood pounded at the thought of what was to come next, her heart swelled with love. And when Lyr lifted his hand to her, she took it, and then she lay down beside him so they were skin to skin. Her breasts were pressed against him, one leg draped over his hip.

"If I asked something of you now, would you give it?" she asked.

"Anything," Lyr whispered.

"Let me be the keeper of your heart." She kissed his throat.

"You have my body, you have my undying allegiance, I swear, you have my. Is that not enough?"

"You said *anything*, and I want your heart."

His hand raked up her thigh and he touched her, much as she had touched him. His fingers aroused, they even slipped inside her so that she gasped and swayed against them. "I'm not sure I have one to give," he said. "What we have is enough, is it not?"

"No. I want all of you, Lyr Hern." Her voice was unsteady, and she felt a tremble in her body, a tremble that was much like his own.

"You have all that's worth having," he said. To make his point, he laid her against the pillows, spread her thighs farther, and took a nipple deep into his mouth while he caressed her. Her hips moved of their own volition, her breath was literally stolen away.

Rayne's eyes drifted closed. "This is so unfair," she whispered.

"What's unfair?"

"You have all of me, every shred of my heart and soul and body, and yet you will not allow me to keep that which I know is meant to be mine."

He moved above her, he lifted her legs so they were wrapped about his hips, and then he was there, inside her.

She could not think of anything else but the physical sensations as Lyr made love to her, she could not think of anything but how he felt inside her, how he touched her, how he made her body do strange and wonderful things. He robbed her of demands, of speech, of the ability to think.

Release came on waves, and she cried out as her body and his shuddered together. The pleasure was like none other and she wanted to scream, but the scream was caught in her throat. She felt Lyr's release, not only in her body but in some place deeper, in some place she had never thought any man could find.

She had taken his body, she had taken his soul. If necessary, she would steal his heart as well. He certainly had hers, so it was only fair.

"I love you," she said hoarsely. "I love you so much."

"You are unlike any woman I have ever known," Lyr responded. Perhaps that was as close to "I love you" as he dared to go.

Sleep was creeping upon her, but she did not dare to sleep until she had a promise from Lyr. "Do not leave without waking me."

"I won't."

She believed him. After all, Lyr did not lie. Much. "I wish you would let me help you, my love."

He twisted one hand in her tangled hair and held on tight. "You will." He leaned down and kissed her throat. "I promise, you will."

Lyr did not seem to be called by sleep, as she was. He was growing hard again, so soon. She felt it, she moved against it. She smiled.

There was no smile in Lyr's voice when he said, "I have only one instruction for you." He raised his head, and she saw a fire in his eyes unlike any other she had ever seen. "If I don't come back . . ."

"Don't say that."

He moved inside her gently, without haste but not without passion. "It's important, Rayne, and more than a little possible. If I don't come back, then I want you to run."

"Your family will protect me. You said they would."

"If my family knows what Ciro plans for you, and if they realize that he might win, then they will kill you. They won't like it, but they will do what has to be done to stop Ciro's plans."

The baby. The child Ciro had promised her. The child that could not be allowed to come into this world. "You could've killed me yourself when you learned of Ciro's plans."

"No, I could not."

It was then that she knew he loved her, whether he would say the words or not, and it was then that she knew the fear she saw in his eyes was not for what he was about to do, but for her.

The tension in his body increased, and he moved a little bit faster. Harder. Before turning his attentions entirely to pleasures of the body, he said, "If I don't return in four days, run."

DIELLA COULDN'T SLEEP, WHICH WAS ODD SINCE THE damned baby made sure she was exhausted all the time. She often slept too many hours at night, and then she napped during the day. Some nights were like this one, restless and uncomfortable. She ate and ate and ate and still lost weight, getting skinny everywhere but for her distended belly, and the sentinels no longer held any appeal for her. Sex had become too much trouble.

Once the child was born and out of her hands, all that would change. It couldn't happen soon enough to suit her.

Agitated and impatient to have this pregnancy done with, Diella roamed the palace that she had been so anxious to call home. Just as she was about to return to her chamber to attempt once again to sleep, a bit of late night excitement chased away her boredom.

The hallway should be deserted this time of night, but it was not. One soldier, one of Ciro's Own, escorted a bloodied and bruised man in black. Even though the prisoner's head was down, Diella recognized him. Instead of running away, she walked toward the prisoner, smiling at his obvious distress.

"Sian, dear, you look a bit the worse for wear."

The enchanter lifted his odd purple eyes, and at first glance he did not recognize her. When he did, his body jerked slightly, as he was startled by her appearance. Diella knew she looked haggard, but really, how bad mannered. She found the strength to draw back one foot and kick the rude man squarely in the shin. She did not have the power to aim any higher.

Diella walked away from Ciro's soldier and the unkind enchanter. "You're good as dead," she said casually. "Your woman is good as dead. Everything you love will soon be dead." The thought made her smile as she walked toward her bedchamber to claim a good night's sleep.

PROMISE OR NOT, LYR WOULD'VE SLIPPED AWAY WITHOUT waking Rayne if he didn't indeed need her help.

It was hours still until sunrise, and yet he and his small party were ready to ride. Ariana was anxious, and he could not blame her. She loved her husband very much and would do anything to save him. That much was obvious.

A part of him wanted to tell Rayne what she wished to hear, that he did indeed love her, that she did have his heart. How cruel that would be if he didn't return from his mission. What a burden that would be for her. If he didn't survive and she ran as she should, then she'd be able to make a life for herself somewhere else, somewhere far away. She could find another man, one who would care for her, one who would love and protect her.

It was best that she not know that he did believe he could love her. Maybe if grieving was necessary, that would make it easier.

He had everything he needed, and though there were those among them who did not like his plan, no one had any better suggestions.

Ariana called, "Let's go!"

"One minute," Lyr called.

"We do not have one minute to spare!" Ariana argued.

Lyr grabbed Rayne and pulled her against him, and then he waved his hand impatiently. He'd never before stopped time for a kiss.

Rayne glanced about. "What happened?"

"Don't let go," he said. "As long as you're touching me, you're where I am. As long as we're touching, time stops for everyone but us."

He kissed her, not knowing how long time would be frozen for the others, not wanting to miss a moment of this stolen time. A minute, two, three . . .

The kiss said good-bye, and it said much more. It said things he didn't dare voice aloud.

Rayne took her mouth from his, but she continued to hold on tight with one arm. With the other, she removed the blue gem that always lay against her chest. "Take this."

"I can't." After all, he couldn't guarantee that he'd be coming back.

"While I don't yet completely understand what my

mother was, I do know she possessed good magic. You
need all the light you can carry in order to face Ciro."

Lyr dipped his head and Rayne placed the chain over it.
It dropped heavily against his chest.

He kissed her again, and when he took his mouth from
hers, he said, "You're still beautiful."

She snorted.

Time restarted unbidden, and it seemed that no one
knew what had happened.

"Not even a minute!" Ariana said, thinking her tirade to
be unbroken.

Lyr stepped away from Rayne. "If you insist, your imperial highness."

"Stop calling me that!" Ariana snapped. "It's ridiculous," she added in a lowered voice.

Lyr mounted a new, fresher horse than the one he'd been
riding since setting out to recover the crystal dagger, and he
spared Rayne one last look. As he did, the stone he now
wore seemed to come alive as the crystal dagger did, pounding against his chest as if it had a heartbeat all its own.

15

IF LYR HAD HAD THE FREEDOM TO PLAN THIS MISSION without interference, there would be two travelers, not six. Interference was apparently his cousin's new middle name, and General Merin was not much better. As ardently as Ariana refused to remain behind, Merin refused to allow the empress to travel without a proper escort.

When it came time to approach the palace, Lyr *would* be in charge. There was no room for error in his plan, no room for interference.

If he'd been concerned only with the well-being of the soldiers, they would have ridden through without stopping. The horses, however, deserved better.

At one of their infrequent but necessary stops, his cousin approached. "I should've known that when you fell, you would fall hard."

"I don't fall," Lyr responded without emotion. "Ever."

"Sure you don't."

Ariana needed to have her mind taken off what was

happening to her husband as they rushed toward his rescue, but Lyr didn't think anything would accomplish that. If Rayne had been in Ciro's hands . . .

"Maybe I've fallen a little," he said. "Maybe not. It is hard to tell with everything else that's going on. When Ciro is dead and Sian is emperor and you're in the palace planning parties and I'm back in Tryfyn . . ."

"I am *not* going to spend the rest of my life planning parties. Mum and Aunt Isadora and Aunt Juliet will find Liane and Sebestyen's sons, and when the war is over, Sian and I will go to his home, a very nice, quiet house where we can have babies and sleep without constant guard and know peace and . . . and . . ."

"And what?" Lyr prompted. "This is my point exactly. Since I've known Rayne, we've been running from one threat to another. If I'm able to kill Ciro . . ."

"When," Ariana said sharply. "*When* you kill Ciro."

"Fine. When I kill Ciro, then what? Would Rayne and I have anything at all to talk about if we lived in a world where every day was like the next, where there was no danger, no prophesy to fulfill? If I had met her in the King's court, would I have looked at her twice? Would she have looked at me?"

"You're such a man," Ariana said with a sigh. It sounded oddly like an insult. "Why don't you just say what you mean?"

"I don't know what I mean."

"Of course you don't." Tonlin was leading the horses this way and Ariana headed toward them, ready to begin the journey once again. The young soldier offered Ariana her horse with a softly spoken:

"Your mount, sister."

And she took it.

"You want to know if Rayne will love you if you're not

the only thing standing between her and a demon. You want to know if you'll still love her if she's not your damsel in distress. You want to know if the sex will be as fantastic if you don't think every day might be your last."

"I'm pretty sure that's not exactly what I meant," Lyr grumbled.

Ariana stepped into her saddle with the ease of a woman who was accustomed to spending her days on horseback. "I think it is, and I also think there's only one way to find out." She waited while Lyr took his own saddle before finishing. "Kill the son of a bitch who's got my husband." With that, she turned her horse about and galloped toward the palace.

CIRO STOOD BACK AND STUDIED HIS BASTARD HALF brother with some amusement. Sian Sayre Chamblyn had not been treated well by the soldiers who had spirited him from his bed in the midst of the army which opposed them. They'd had the help of some magic, of course, the demon's dark magic. He imagined the armies of his Own were in a tizzy over the bold success. Such success would give them hope, and given their losses of late, they needed that hope.

If he'd had the strength to do so, he would've had his Own take them all. The witch, the soldiers . . . all who dared to defy him. But as the demon was not as strong as it should be, Ciro was forced to simplify his efforts. First he would remove the threat to his newly taken position, then he would worry about the others. Their time would come, and it would come in his way, in his time.

The trip from the enemy camp to this palace had taken two days, and Ciro's Own had taken some of their anger and glee out on the man whom some would call the rightful emperor. Chamblyn's face was cut on one cheek, and there were numerous bruises beneath the black shirt and trousers he wore. Ciro could not see all the bruises, but he felt them with his own surge of glee.

Chamblyn was on his knees, bound hand and foot, in this small room which had once been a chamber for a lowly servant. It had also been the last room the late Emperor Arik called home.

"So, your mother fucked my father some years ago."

Chamblyn remained calm. "So it would seem."

"When I was younger, I often wished for a brother," Ciro said thoughtfully. "Would you have been a good one?"

The wizard lifted his head with a touch of defiance. "Likely not," he responded with an unexpected arrogance.

Ciro stepped forward and let his hand fly. The back of his hand connected soundly with the wizard's cheek, sending the head snapping to one side and making the wizard gasp. While Chamblyn regained his breath, Ciro dropped to his haunches so they were face to face. In truth, they did not look like brothers. Ciro had his mother's fair coloring and blue eyes. Chamblyn was dark-haired and possessed unusual purple eyes. Ciro considered himself to be rather pretty. His half brother had a face of sharp lines, and a nose which was anything but pretty.

Since taking a turn a while back, Chamblyn's soul had become too white to take, too pure for Ciro to steal. He felt as if he grew stronger every day, and yet he was not yet all he could be. One day, one day soon . . .

That didn't mean he couldn't kill his bastard brother but it seemed a waste—especially since their father's soul had been lost. It wasn't as if the wizard would be going anywhere.

It would've been easy enough to have Chamblyn killed while he slept among Ariana's soldiers and thus end the possibility that some would view him as the rightful emperor. Ciro had considered that route at one point, but when he looked at the larger arena in which this war was being played, he saw advantage to holding the man alive—for a while. There were those who would rush foolishly forward in order to save Chamblyn, and that would be their undoing.

He most particularly wanted the blond healer who had cheated death once before, but now was not the time. When he was stronger and she was weakened by the loss of her enchanter. When he had the upper hand and she was not surrounded by men who would die for her. When he was certain he could kill her and she would not come back from the dead to harass him . . . then he would kill her again.

Ciro placed his hand on Chamblyn's throat and squeezed. Just because he had decided not to kill his brother just yet, that didn't mean the fear of death wouldn't feed him. Chamblyn didn't have to know that his death was not at hand. Ciro watched the purple eyes grow dark, and defiant, and finally frightened. His hand squeezed tighter, and an object smacked into his back. He glanced down to see a decorative vase lying on the floor beside him.

"Is that it? Is that how you defend yourself?" A heavy candlestick flew end over end and hit the back of Ciro's head, drawing a tiny bit of blood in his fair hair. The blow might've hurt another man, but not Ciro. "Too bad we're not near the kitchen. You could pelt me with pots and pans and perhaps a plate or two." He did not ease his grip until it appeared that his brother was about to lose consciousness. There was no amusement in studying an unconscious man while awaiting him to awake, so Ciro dropped his hand.

Before he could do more, there was a cursory knock at the door, and then it opened swiftly. A dark and ambitious priest, Cestmyr he was called, filled the doorway.

"You have a visitor," Father Cestmyr said petulantly. He was obviously annoyed at the menial task he'd been assigned.

"A visitor?"

"A woman. She says she is to be your bride." At this, Cestmyr pursed his lips. The fat priest didn't care much for women.

Ciro rose to his feet, the man before him forgotten. "Rayne? Rayne is here?"

"You sound like a smitten boy when you say her name," Cestmyr said boldly. "That sad infatuation is not befitting the powerful man I know you to be."

Ciro glared at the priest, who was in danger of losing his place of importance, and his very life.

Realizing he had gone too far, Cestmyr answered helpfully. "Yes, she gave her name as Rayne." The priest pointed toward the window. "She waits below."

"She came alone?"

"No, she arrived with one escort, a young green-clad soldier of Merin's army. The solider insisted that if he delivers your bride to you, you must release his sister's husband, the rightful emperor of Columbyana."

Ciro had no intention of releasing his half-brother, but he was determined to have Rayne with him, where she belonged. He strode to the window and looked down upon the walkway below. He could not see her well, not from this vantage point, but he recognized the dress Rayne wore as one she'd often chosen for cooler days at her father's house, though the blue had faded and the fabric was the worse for wear after days of travel. The fall of hair beneath a ridiculous hat was tangled, but unmistakably hers. He had dreamed of that dark silky hair spread across his pillow. Even though she had betrayed him, he continued to dream.

He shouted her name, and Rayne's head tilted back a little. With the sun positioned as it was, her wide-brimmed hat shadowed the top half of her face. A wrap she'd tossed over her shoulders crept up and covered a portion of her face, so that all he could see of her was one perfectly shaped feminine cheek.

All he could see of her soon-to-be-dead escort was a sentinel's green hat.

"Let them in," Ciro said. "Bring them to me so we can make the trade they seek."

"You're not seriously—" Cestmyr began.

Ciro turned to glare at him. "Do as you're told, or I'll suck your pitiful soul out of that pathetic body and then spit it out the window for the wild dogs to claim."

"Fine," the priest snapped, turning to leave the room as quickly as possible.

"I have a feeling you're not going to let me go," his half-brother said, his voice raspy and accepting.

"A man should always trust his gut instincts, eh?" Ciro responded.

It had to hurt to speak, but the wizard continued. "Tell me, before I die, is there anything of Prince Ciro left inside you or are you entirely Isen Demon now?"

That was a question Ciro had often asked himself, and he assumed that as long as he thought to ask, some of the man he had once been survived. "Why do you care?"

"As long as there is something of the man within you, perhaps there is a chance the world will go on. It doesn't need me to survive, it doesn't need any one person, but when the demon who possesses you is all-powerful, what will be left for the humans?"

"He'll need . . . we'll need some of them in order for life to go on." Slaves for menial tasks, women for breeding, gray souls, and blood for sustenance.

"Some," Chamblyn repeated.

"Yes, some." No soldiers, no magicians who did not do his bidding, no priests who did not know their rightful places at his feet, no children who were not his own.

"Does the little bit of the man inside you grieve for the world you're about to destroy?" Chamblyn asked. "Do you know any sorrow for what might've been?"

The question caused a ripple in Ciro's stomach. "If your soul was not so annoyingly white, I would take it now."

"When you are strong enough to take a white soul, there will be nothing left of you, Ciro. There will be only demon. Did he not tell you that yet? Did he not inform you that in a short while you will no longer be necessary? He needs your body, but that is all."

"I look forward to the day when I am entirely demon."

Chamblyn smiled, crookedly since his face was swollen. "When you are entirely demon, fuckwit, there will be nothing of *you* left."

Don't listen to him. He's dead to us.

Ciro stepped toward the oddly defiant man, who was bound and bleeding and bruised and who continued to annoy him. He raised his hand, but the sounds of footsteps in the hall stopped him. He hadn't seen Rayne in months, and he did not wish her to see him with blood on his hands. Not right away. She might not understand. In time she would be made to pay for her unfaithfulness, but not today.

The door opened, and a sentinel dressed in green stepped inside, his sword drawn as if he thought it might do him some good. Behind the soldier, the familiar swish of a skirt made Ciro smile. He'd waited so long for her, his reward, his bride.

"We will not proceed until I have ascertained that the Emperor Sian is well."

Ciro gave an uninterested wave of his hand, indicating the bound man. "See for yourself."

The sentinel walked crisply toward Chamblyn. It would be easy to kill the annoyance now, but Ciro had decided not to offer his delicate Rayne an unsavory welcome. There would be plenty of time for taking care of Chamblyn and the sentinel later.

The soldier placed a concerned hand on his emperor's head, and Rayne took a step into the room. She entered with her head down so that all he saw was that fall of wondrous dark hair.

His heart, what was left of it, was not unaffected by her presence. As long as he felt that swelling in his heart, there was something of him left in this body he shared with the demon. He did not have to sacrifice all to the Isen Demon who had given him so much. They could share this body, this power, and this woman.

"Rayne, my love," he said wistfully as she entered the room.

WITH HIS HAND ON SIAN'S SHOULDER, LYR WAVED HIS sword and time for all others stopped. Because he was touching Ariana's husband, Sian was not affected.

Sian lifted his face and glared. "Have you lost your mind?"

"Listen carefully, as I do not know how long my gift will affect one like Ciro. Your wife is about to enter the room. Ciro expects Rayne, and we are expecting that you can make him believe he sees his intended bride."

"You want me to make Ariana appear to be someone else to Ciro's eyes?"

"No, I want you to make *me* appear to be Rayne to Ciro's damned eyes so I can get close enough to kill him with this." Lyr drew the crystal dagger. It was no longer a murky gray and pink, but was brilliantly clear. It vibrated in his hand.

"Stab him now," Sian directed. "While he's frozen in time, stab him."

"I can't."

"Why not?"

"This weapon I am meant to wield will not work properly unless Ciro's heart is beating."

"How does it work?"

They both knew the blade was too short and insignificant to do harm to what Ciro had become. "I'm not sure. Can you do what I ask of you?" The man was not in the best physical shape, so it was possible his ability to create illusions had been damaged.

Sian nodded. "Yes, I think so."

"She should appear to be me, I should appear to be Rayne."

"I have never seen Rayne."

"Ciro has. You must make him see what he wishes to see."

"I'll do what I can, but don't take too long. You're asking for a complicated illusion in difficult circumstances, and I'm not sure the demon can be fooled. He does not see with eyes, as we do."

"Maybe when he's watching through Ciro's eyes, he sees only what Ciro sees."

"We can hope."

When Lyr took his hand from Sian, the emperor was stuck in time as the others were. Lyr collected Ariana, who wore Rayne's clothes as well as a woman's bonnet which had long strands of hair cut from Rayne's head sewn into it. She was heavy, but not so much so that he could not handle her quickly. He carefully placed Ariana where he'd been standing.

Lyr placed himself in Ariana's position, barely entering the room, and after taking a deep breath and hiding the crystal dagger behind his thigh, he waved his hand and time resumed.

HIS VISION SEEMED TO FLICKER, CAUSING CIRO TO BLINK hard a few times. Was seeing Rayne again so important that she affected him physically? In any case, the odd glimmer did not last.

Ciro had forgotten how beautiful Rayne was until she lifted her head and looked at him. He smiled at her, but she did not smile back. There was a sternness on her beautiful face. Of course, he had left her chained in the cellar of her home, and she might not have understood why he hadn't simply brought her with him. She had not yet forgiven him, but she was here and that's all that mattered.

She wore a blue gemstone he had never seen her wear before, and it caught his eye as she moved toward him.

Something is wrong.

No, everything is fine. Rayne is angry, but she'll get over it in time. She'll forgive me. She'll forgive us. Perhaps I will forgive her, for a while. We can be married tomorrow. Perhaps tonight.

She is not what she appears to be.

I know. There is strength in her that is not noticeable at first glance. She'll make a good mother to our son.

Rayne approached him quickly, not so much as sparing a glance for the prisoner and the sentinel on the other side of the room. Ciro spared no attention for them, either, but kept his eyes on Rayne's face.

The demon, who usually rose up only in times of great stress, attempted to come to the surface and take control, but for the first time in a very long time, Ciro fought.

Rayne had come for him, not the demon, and he did not wish for this moment to be tainted by the demon's control. Rayne would not understand if she looked into his eyes and saw the demon's darkness.

She had such a beautiful white soul. It shone around her, almost blinding him. Perhaps the day would come when he'd be forced to take that soul from her, but not today.

"Rayne, my love . . ."

Her hand came up swiftly, and he saw, too late, that she held something shiny in her hand. Not metal. If he had seen metal, he might've been forewarned, but this was simply a long and slender piece of stone that sparkled and shone bright, like Rayne's soul. Crystal. It was simply crystal.

With a force unexpected, she pushed the crystal into his heart. Ciro watched it enter his body, only then realizing that it was a weapon. A dagger.

The crystal dagger.

The demon screamed, and the sound all but burst Ciro's eardrums. It might've burst his heart, too, but for the dagger blade which was buried within it. He felt the demon leaving him, not of its own free will as it sometimes did, but by force. As the demon left Ciro's body, the dagger in Rayne's hand was filled with a smoky darkness, one swirling tendril at a time.

"Why?" he whispered.

Again, that odd glimmer affected his vision and he blinked hard. When that was done, it was not Rayne who stood before him, now-black dagger in hand, but the sentinel who had escorted her here.

"How . . ." His eyes cut to the wizard, the enchanter, and Ciro realized that he had been tricked. Another woman wore Rayne's clothes and even her hair, and when he saw that she was healing the damaged emperor, he knew who she was. The blond healer who had come back from the dead, the new empress of this palace, the woman who loved his brother the way Rayne was supposed to love him.

Why were none of his men rushing to save him? Why did they not fight? Even though the demon was all but gone, for a moment Ciro connected with his Own, his legion, his army. They were running away, fleeing him and the palace they had taken. They were soulless cowards unable to fight without the demon's strength to feed them. Most of them would be dead before nightfall. They would kill one another if his brother's armies did not do the deed for them. Even Diella ran, half-dead and desperate to save her child.

Our child.

Her child now.

Ciro dropped to his knees. He felt as if he'd been deflated. Sapped. There was no power left in his body or in what remained of his soul. He could barely lift his hand, and when he did, he saw that it was thin and childish, as it had been before the demon had shared its power.

"What have you done?" he asked.

The sentinel held the dagger in his hand. It was no longer crystal clear, as it had been, but was black as the demon's eyes, and when he saw that, he knew what had happened. The demon had been taken from him, taken and trapped, imprisoned in the dagger.

Ciro placed a hand on his chest, where he bled like any other man might when stabbed. He was no longer immortal, no longer immune to the wounds inflicted by such mortal weapons. Even the back of his head, where the candlestick had hit him, hurt horribly. He had forgotten pain, but pain returned for him.

Death was coming, too, and he was mightily afraid of what awaited him in the afterlife.

Ciro looked at the enchanter, who had been freed by his

wife. Sian Sayre Chamblyn, emperor, he supposed, was already somewhat healed, thanks to her ministrations. She loved him, he could tell. She'd come here for him when the odds had been against her; she'd come here at the risk of her own life.

Would he have ever known anything of the sort if he had not joined with the demon? Would any woman have loved him this way? He didn't know. He would never know.

"I had no choice," he said. "Fynnian tricked me. The demon seduced me with promises." But as he said the words, he knew there had been a time when he could've fought for his own soul and for others, and he had not. He had accepted all that the demon promised, not caring about the cost.

"I really did always wish for a brother," Ciro said, and then his world went black and he fell to the floor face first.

What came for him at death was as dark as the demon trapped in the crystal dagger. He tried to scream and beg for mercy, but could not.

16

RAYNE LOOKED TO THE WEST AND UNCONSCIOUSLY FIN-
gered her newly shortened hair. Lyr had said she was "still
beautiful" but she wasn't so sure. It was odd, to feel a
breeze upon the back of her bare neck.

If locks of her hair sewn into a bonnet helped to fool Ciro,
then she was not sorry. Her hair would grow back in time.

Some twit had suggested they use horsehair instead of
chopping off her long locks, but she'd been horrified to
think anyone would be fooled by such a ploy, and Lyr had
insisted that it would not be sufficient. They were taking
enough of a chance in trying to fool Ciro without that arti-
fice. Her hair, her dress, an incredible enchantment—if all
went well.

Would all go well? She hadn't slept since Lyr and the
others had left. Two days and a few hours, and she could
not even think of sleep until she knew. Had Lyr been successful, or was Ciro headed this way?

Queen Keelia, scantily dressed as usual and smiling

widely, approached with a quick step. There was joy in that smile, and Rayne felt the joy to her toes. Still she waited, breath held, for the words to come.

"He did it," Keelia said before she reached Rayne. "I felt a new light in the world the moment the demon was trapped and Ciro died."

"Ciro is dead?" Rayne asked. "Are you sure?"

"Yes." Keelia placed her hands on Rayne's shoulders, and those odd golden eyes locked on to hers. "A weight was lifted from us all, and a darkness which had hidden many secrets from me dissolved. There are still a few battles to be fought, but this war is almost over. We won."

The Queen released her grip on Raync and spun about, shouting to the nearest green-clad sentinel. "You!"

The young soldier jumped. "Yes, Majesty?"

"There are two brothers here. The Arndell brothers. Do you know them?"

"Yes, Majesty."

"Are they in camp?"

"They are preparing to ride with General Merin when word comes from the others."

Keelia shook her head, and long red hair danced. "No. They are to come to me immediately. If Merin gives you any trouble, tell him I insisted. He's welcome to argue with me himself if he cares to."

The sentinel nodded and rushed toward the other edge of camp to do as he'd been told.

Keelia said a darkness had been lifted and she could now see. There was so much Rayne wanted to know, and while they waited for the brothers to be fetched, she asked her questions. "Will Lyr be here tonight? Tomorrow? What happens next? For us, I mean, for me and Lyr. Am I carrying a child? Will he ever admit that he loves me?" Her heart caught in her throat. "What will become of me now?"

The Queen's face remained serene, but there was a touch of amusement in her eyes as she answered, "I can tell you everything you wish to know about your future, with enough time and concentration."

Rayne smiled herself and gave a soft sigh of relief.

"But I won't," Keelia finished, still serene.

"But . . ." Rayne began.

"Life is meant to be lived one moment at a time, not planned and set to the last detail."

"I just want to know what lies ahead."

Keelia shrugged her shoulders. "Life lies ahead. Life filled with surprise and heartache and laughter. It would spoil the coming if you knew what to expect."

"At least tell me that Lyr's all right," Rayne insisted.

Keelia nodded. "He is well."

"And tell me that he loves me," she added in a lowered voice.

Again, Keelia smiled. "Why should I bother to tell you that which you already know in your heart?"

The brothers Keelia had asked for arrived, ending the maddening conversation with an abruptness that left Rayne feeling dissatisfied.

The seer Queen studied the brothers from head to toe. Both were young and handsome, perhaps Lyr's age or a bit older. One was black-haired and green-eyed, solemn of face and precisely dressed. The other had streaks of blond in his dark brown hair, laughing blue eyes, and a half-smile on a wide mouth. He also wore a uniform, but his was sloppily fastened here and there, and his boots were muddy and had been for days.

"You wished to see us?" the black-haired Arndell asked.

Keelia took a deep breath. "Yes. I must travel south to meet my parents, and I am entrusting our guest into your hands. Watch her. Guard her." She glanced over her shoulder and caught Rayne's eye. "She is a very special woman, though she does not yet know *how* special."

Again, it was the black-haired brother who spoke. "Your Majesty, we are to ride out with General Merin perhaps as early as this afternoon. When we are called . . ."

"You have been called," Keelia said. "You have been called to guard over this woman with your very lives." She looked from one brother to another. "As you are both Arndell, I would have your given names as well."

"Trystan," the black-haired soldier responded.

His brother answered as well. "Devlyn."

Keelia nodded. "Trystan and Devlyn Arndell, do not leave M'lady Rayne's side until I return and relieve you of that duty."

Trystan nodded curtly, though he was evidently disappointed with his new assignment. Devlyn shrugged as if he did not care one way or another.

Keelia had a word with her husband and another with Merin, and then she did something which shocked Rayne to her very core.

The Queen sprouted wings. She put her head back and spread her arms, and then she sprouted wings like those of a large bird, or an angel. Her face changed subtly, feathers sprouted in her hair, and then she flapped those large wings and flew. Rayne stared, awestruck. The Arndell brothers stared. Everyone in the camp stared in awe, until the Queen was so far away they could no longer see her.

"How very odd she is," Trystan said softly.

"Yeah, but not at all bad-looking," Devlyn said. "I wouldn't kick her out of my bed if I happened to find her there."

Trystan sighed. "If her consort hears you say that, he will tear you apart and I will not lift a finger to stop him."

"Thanks, brother. It was just an observation. It's not as

if I'm actually likely to find a Queen in my bed. Shit, I don't even have a proper bed these days, thanks to you. How did I ever let you talk me into enlisting in this army?"

"You were drunk," Trystan responded.

"So I was."

Devlyn turned to Rayne. "How exactly are you so very special?" The question might've been a sarcastic and hurtful one, but his smile was sincere.

Rayne was not yet ready to introduce herself as an Earth Goddess, so she said, "I'm a very good gardener."

Instead of being put off by her answer, Devlyn said, "Excellent! I'd much prefer to stand guard over a pretty gardener than to clash swords against those nasty Ciro's Own fellows. They do *not* fight fairly."

"Neither do you," Trystan said as he joined them.

Devlyn studied Rayne's too-short hair with interest. "I knew a woman once who wore her hair just so."

"Really? On purpose?"

"Yes, very much on purpose. She would adorn her short locks with brightly colored flowers or jeweled clips, and it was ever so much easier to get to her neck." Devlyn leaned in as if he intended to demonstrate.

"Forgive my brother," Trystan said as he elbowed Devlyn aside. "He knows no boundaries and possesses no manners at all."

"We're twins, you know," Devlyn said, crossing his arms in a casual pose and ignoring her exposed neck.

"I never would've guessed," Rayne said. Though they did look somewhat alike, they were definitely not mirror images of one another. "Which one of you is older?"

"Dammit, Arndell!" General Merin's voice was sharp, and both Arndells turned to his call. Even Devlyn's spine straightened. "What the hell are you doing here? A small contingent of Ciro's Own has been spotted a short distance away, and we're riding out in minutes. I should not have to search the camp for those soldiers who are supposed to be ready to fight!"

"The Anwyn Queen ordered us not to leave M'lady Rayne's side until she returns, sir," Trystan explained.

Devlyn added a simple, "Yep. That's why we're here."

Merin sighed. "I have learned not to question that one. We'll miss your swords, but this will likely not be our fiercest fight." He glanced over his shoulder and smiled. It was the first time Rayne had ever seen his face in such a state. "They're not moving toward us in an organized fashion, they're running away."

They were running away because Ciro was dead. Rayne knew that but she wasn't sure how much Keelia had shared with the others before she'd flown off like a huge, graceful bird. Feeling it was not her secret to share, Rayne excused herself and said she wished to lie down in her tent. The brothers followed her, and as she entered the small tent which had become home for now, they settled themselves at the exit.

Rayne did lie down but she couldn't sleep. Her mind was spinning, and not all of her thoughts concerned her future at the moment. Why had Keelia asked those two to guard her? She wasn't even sure a guard was necessary, and if it was, then any soldier should do. Why them, and why had her eyes lit up so as she'd called for them? The brothers' voices drifted to her.

"I wouldn't kick M'lady Rayne out of my bed, if I had a bed," Devlyn said.

"Is there any woman alive you would kick out of your bed?" Trystan's voice was sharp.

"Of course. I can be somewhat discriminating. She has great tits, don't tell me you didn't notice."

In the privacy of her tent, Rayne's face grew warm. Trystan was right; his brother knew no boundaries!

"Keep your voice down," Trystan insisted. "Someone might hear you."

"I don't care."

"That's your problem," Trystan said sharply. "You don't care about anything or anyone."

"And you care too much," Devlyn countered.

Rayne shut her ears to the brothers' bantering and thought about Lyr. He was well, Keelia had said. For now, nothing mattered but that. He had succeeded, he had won, he had fulfilled his prophesy.

Now what? She didn't know what the future held and Keelia insisted that she didn't need to know. Her initial reaction to that refusal had been anger, but in the weeks since Lyr had led her away from home, she'd learned to enjoy what each day brought. Love had been a surprise, as it should be. What was to happen next was also yet to be written.

She closed her eyes, feeling safe with the odd Arndell brothers at her door. Keelia had been right about something else.

Rayne did know that Lyr loved her.

THE PALACE WAS MORE EMPTY THAN NOT, AS CIRO'S SER-vants had fled. Without the demon, they were cowards. Lyr was more than ready to return to the camp where he'd left Rayne waiting, but before he could depart, it was necessary that the new emperor and empress be settled in safely, with sufficient guards to prevent any attacks by dark soldiers who weren't content to flee. Sentinels had been called, but they were not yet at their posts.

Lyr could do nothing but wait. Wait and watch and listen, as his cousin and her husband tried to make sense of their new situation.

"This is ridiculous," Sian muttered. Thanks to Ariana's

enhanced healing powers, he was fully recovered from his ordeal. "For months I've managed to fight on my own, and now that I'm fucking emperor, I need an army of sentinels to stand between me and the rest of the world?"

"That language isn't befitting the new ruler of the country," Ariana said calmly.

Sian cast his wife a sharp glance. "You're enjoying this."

"I am not."

"Where are your mother and her blasted sisters?" Sian threw up a disgusted hand. "Where are those damn twins?"

"If they can't find Liane and the boys . . ." Ariana began.

"Then I'm it." Disgusted, Sian plopped down in the biggest chair in this room in which he'd been pacing.

The throne.

Ariana sat on his knee. "Whatever happens is meant to happen. Sebestyen's sons will be found or they won't. You will be emperor for many years or you won't. Whatever happens, I will be with you." She took his hand and led it to her stomach. "We will be with you."

Ariana had not said a word to Lyr about a baby, but it was now clear that she was carrying one. Smart woman. If she had revealed her condition to Lyr, he would've tied her up and left her behind—empress or not.

Sian stilled immediately as he contemplated his wife's belly. "I don't want my son to grow up like Ciro."

"No matter where we are, whether we're here or at your home in the mountains, he won't. I promise."

The guards Lyr had been waiting for finally arrived, and he said a quick good-bye. He'd told Rayne to run if he didn't return in four days, which meant he had a day and a half to get to her before she fled the camp. The countryside still wasn't safe for a woman alone. Too many of Ciro's Own survived.

Not for long.

* * *

RAYNE DID NOT PLAN TO RUN ANYWHERE, EVEN THOUGH
Lyr had told her to do so. Thanks to Keelia, she knew he'd
been successful and there was no reason to hide from Ciro
or those who would kill her to keep her from bearing his
son. And still, as morning and the deadline approached,
she could not sleep. If Lyr could be here, he would.

And yet she could not help but remember that while
Ciro was dead, his Own lived on, though their number was
less every day, and they were no longer fighting in an organized effort but in small and ineffective pockets of resistance. Would Lyr be so intent on reaching her that he'd
allow his vigilance to slip and fall into a trap?

No, his gift would aide him, if necessary.

She dressed in the clothes Gwyneth had given her, since
her traveling dress had gone to Arthes with Lyr and Ariana
and the others. Devlyn Arndell had told her a woman with
similarly short hair often adorned her locks with flowers,
but on this chilly morning there were no flowers to be had.
She knew Lyr would be here soon, and she wanted to be
beautiful to his eyes when he arrived.

And then?

She had no idea what would happen then. Keelia had
suggested that she did not need to know, but must take
every day as it came, good and bad, happy and sad. As long
as Lyr was in it, she could endure anything.

Devlyn Arndell was posted at the entrance to her tent, as
attentive as a man of his character could be. He and his
brother took turns sleeping for a few hours during the
night, and it was apparently Trystan's turn to rest. Since
they had been ordered not to leave her sight, the more
sober of the two Arndells slept on a bedroll a few feet away.

"You're up very early, m'lady." Devlyn kept his voice low, so as not to disturb his brother.

"I can't sleep," she said just as softly. "I'm expecting someone to arrive shortly."

"The Tryfynian fellow, I assume."

It wasn't unexpected that there had been talk about her and Lyr, since they'd arrived together and she had not gone to the trouble to hide her feelings. He'd even stopped time for a kiss, but of course no one but the two of them realized that.

"Yes, the Tryfynian fellow. Prince of Swords, to be precise."

Devlyn sighed. "So I have heard. Even so, I would fight him for you, if you'd like." The offer was playfully tendered, so Rayne did not take him seriously.

"No, thank you."

"Is this prince fellow worthy of a pretty and talented gardener such as yourself?" Devlyn asked.

"Most definitely," Rayne responded. She searched the immediate area for a plant which might flower if she commanded that it do so, but here in the center of the camp, all plants had been trampled or pulled from the ground to make way for soldiers. There would be no flower for her short hair, no adornment for Lyr's sake.

Now that the war was done, or almost done, perhaps there would be time for gardens, for vegetables and flowers and adornment. Perhaps she and Lyr might pass more than one night in a bed. Perhaps she would have a warm bath, and new clothes, and shoes which were not falling apart from constant abuse. Perhaps, perhaps, perhaps.

She heard Lyr coming almost precisely four days to the hour after he left. No, she didn't *hear* him exactly, she felt him moving nearer. She felt him in the wind, in the rumble of the earth beneath her feet, in the pit of her soul. Rayne stood with her feet firmly planted on the ground and her face lifted to the wind, and she felt him.

Moments later he was there, dismounting before his horse came to a full stop, not stopping to talk to any of the soldiers who hailed him for news or congratulations. He came directly toward Rayne, ignoring all others.

Lyr walked toward her quickly and strongly, and she could tell that he was uninjured. Ciro had not touched him. None of the Own had harmed him. He'd done what he was meant to do and he'd survived to return to her.

Devlyn placed himself between her and Lyr, adopting a protective pose. "If you wish to see the pretty gardener, you must come through me . . ."

Rayne blinked, and Lyr was directly before her. A bypassed Devlyn spun about. "Hey! How did you do that? When I said you had to come *through* me, I didn't mean literally."

"You've had your fun, Devlyn," Rayne said as she put her arms around Lyr's waist and held on tight.

"Not really, but I suppose I know when it's time to quit. Sure you don't want me to—"

"Positive," Rayne said before he could finish his question.

The commotion woke Trystan, who came off his bedroll with a grumble and a reach for his sword, before he realized who held his charge.

"Who are these annoying men?" Lyr asked.

"My bodyguards."

"They're dismissed."

"Only General Merin or Queen Keelia can dismiss us," Trystan responded.

Lyr turned and locked eyes with the soldier. "You've been relieved of your duties."

Trystan was ready to argue, but in this case it was his

brother who displayed the most common sense. "Come on, let's take a walk. I think our little gardener will be well protected in her present company."

"We were ordered . . ."

"We won't go far." Devlyn clapped a friendly arm across his twin's shoulder and they walked away from the tent.

Lyr removed the necklace she had given him for luck and placed it over her head so that the blue gem dropped against her chest. "Thank you," he said softly. "I believe this gem blinded Ciro for a moment. It was a moment I very much needed."

"I'm glad I could help," she whispered.

Lyr took her face in his hands and kissed her, much as he had before he'd left. One hand slipped to the back of her head and he held her there while he kissed her. He took her breath away with his mouth on hers. There was heart in the kiss, heart and soul and surrender.

And he said he had no heart to give.

When the kiss ended, he rested his forehead against hers. "The bastard will never touch you," Lyr whispered. "You're safe now."

Rayne sighed in relief. Thanks to Keelia, she'd known that Ciro was dead, but hearing the truth from Lyr's lips warmed her to the pit of her soul. "It's over."

Lyr's hand tightened at the back of her neck as he answered in a less than reassuring voice, "Almost."

17

Lyr led Rayne into her tent. It was best that no one else know what he possessed. He could trust Rayne with the secret, but until Keelia told him how to proceed, no one else could know.

Once they were inside the tent, he shrugged off the small leather rucksack he'd been carrying for so many miles and opened it. There was only one object inside, and he handled it with care. Rayne gasped when she saw it.

"Is that—"

"Yes," he answered before she could finish her question. "It's the crystal dagger."

The dagger was now as black as it had once been bright. The demon which had been sucked from Ciro's body was trapped inside the crystal. The dagger was not only black but heavier than it had been, and it made him uncomfortable to touch it, whereas before he felt as if the dagger fed his own magical energy. The weapon no longer spoke to him, now that its mission had been accomplished.

He could not wait to be rid of the blasted thing, but he was sure there had to be a specific way to dispose of the dagger so that the Isen Demon never escaped. He suspected simply tossing it into a deep river wouldn't be enough. Sian and Ariana hadn't had any clue how that could be accomplished.

"I'm hoping Keelia can tell me how to dispose of it," he explained as he returned the dagger to the rucksack. "As soon as it's light, I'll wake her."

"She's not here," Rayne said anxiously.

Not here? Impossible. "She was supposed to stay in camp!"

"She did, until she knew that you had won. She said it felt as if a weight had been lifted from the world, and then she got an odd and sudden urge to go see her mother." Rayne's nose wrinkled. "Lyr, she flew. She sprouted wings and took to the air like a gigantic bird."

"I'd heard that she's found new talents of late," Lyr said, disappointed to know that he could not immediately be rid of the dagger that was, until it was disposed of, his responsibility.

"And quite a talent it is. I did not know such a thing was possible. She does plan to return soon," Rayne explained. "She told the Arndell brothers to keep watch over me until she gets back."

"The Arndell brothers. Those two men who tried to keep me from you, I suppose."

"They're simply doing as they were told," she said, and then she smiled. It was a nice smile, one he had missed in his days away from her.

"What about you?" He reached out and touched her short hair. Cutting those long locks had been necessary, but he'd hated to ask her to make the sacrifice. "Have you discovered any new talents of your own? Have you tried?"

Rayne shook her head. "I thought about trying to produce a flower for my hair, but there wasn't a suitable plant in the vicinity. I didn't even think of exploring my abilities while you were away. I just thought of you and where you might be and what you might be facing."

Looking at her now, Lyr decided the shorter style suited her face. Her neck looked longer, her cheeks softer, her eyes larger. Even if her hair were as short as his, she'd still be the most beautiful woman in the world.

"While I am disappointed to know that Keelia is not in camp, I believe there are agreeable enough ways for us to pass the time until she returns."

Lyr placed the rucksack with the crystal dagger in it aside. When that was done, Rayne moved easily into his lap, and he kissed her again. Since leaving here to complete his mission, he had missed her so much. He had worried about her, he had craved her touch more than he dared to admit.

But now she was here, and there was no more need to worry. Ciro was dead, the demon was trapped, and Rayne was safe.

Ariana had boldly put forth the possibility that he might wonder if his sexual liaisons with Rayne would be as powerful if they did not face each day as if it were their last. In moments, he proved that concern to be invalid.

KEELIA RETURNED TO CAMP ON THE AFTERNOON OF Lyr's return, and she did not arrive alone. A woman traveled on Keelia's back, facedown as she hung on for dear life. Rayne and Lyr were at the center of the camp, the watchful Arndell brothers close behind, when the two women arrived. Lyr had been talking with General Merin about plans to track down and defeat what was left of

Ciro's Own, and Trystan Arndell had gladly joined that
discussion. They were all close enough to hear the mighty
swish of Keelia's wings, as well as the curses of the
woman on the Queen's back.

The dark-haired woman leapt off Keelia's winged back
as soon as she was able. She raked her hands through long,
dark hair which was touched with a few strands of gray,
and muttered a few curse words that made Rayne, for all
her lessons, blush.

Keelia stood tall and shook her wings, which at her
silent command retracted and then disappeared. Rayne
watched as the Queen's eyes became more human than
birdlike once again, as the feathers in her hair either fell or
retracted as the wings on her back had. Her gaze fell immediately on Rayne, then on the Arndell brothers, then on
Joryn, who rushed forward to greet her.

When the greeting was done, Keelia led the woman
she'd carried on her back toward Rayne. Was this the
Queen's mother, the woman she had left camp to seek?
There was no familial resemblance, if that was the case.
The wind-blown woman smiled warmly at Lyr, and he re-
turned her smile.

"It's good to see you well," she said. "Keelia told me it
was so, but such words are not enough for a mother when
her son is at war."

Mother! Rayne straightened her back. This woman was
Lyr's *mother*.

"It's good to see you, too," Lyr said casually.

Rayne expected that Lyr's mother and Keelia would
stop when they reached Lyr. Surely that's why they had returned on this day, when Lyr had himself just returned.
There was so much to be said, so many details to be taken
care of. Lyr had the matter of the crystal dagger to discuss
with his cousin, and since Keelia was a psychic, it was

more than possible that she knew about that important matter.

Rayne could not help but wonder what Lyr would say to his mother about her. Would he bother to say anything at all? Rayne held her breath, but Keelia and her companion walked right past her and Lyr, their eyes on Rayne's bodyguards.

"Aunt Isadora, these are the Arndell brothers, Devlyn"—Keelia indicated that twin with a wave of her hand—"and Trystan."

A wave of emotion crossed the older woman's face. "Stars above." She reached out to touch Trystan's face. "You look so much like your father."

With those words, she had the full attention of the sentinels.

"You knew our father?" Devlyn asked.

Keelia explained, as the woman she had carried to the camp seemed to be struck speechless. "Aunt Isadora knew your father and your mother well, and I have brought her here to tell you an incredible story."

Isadora recovered her composure and said, "We have more to do here than to rehash old times. Which of you possesses the ring?"

Neither of them wore a ring, Rayne knew, but that didn't mean they didn't possess one.

After a few moments passed, Trystan drew a chain from beneath his shirt. Dangling from that chain was a fat ring set with a blue stone.

Isadora smiled faintly. "Your mother told me that the eldest had the keeping of the ring." She curtseyed to Trystan. Curtseyed!

Trystan removed the chain from around his neck and passed it to his brother. "Devlyn is the eldest. I've been holding on to this family heirloom so he wouldn't gamble it away."

Devlyn held on to the chain, but did not place it around his neck. The ring dangled and swung, catching the afternoon light. "This is damned odd," he said without his usual easy smile. "Woman, do you care to explain yourself?"

Isadora curtseyed again, her attention on Devlyn this time. "Your brother has your father's looks, but lamentably, you have his manner." She looked up. "And his eyes."

"Our father has been dead many years."

"Yes, he has," Isadora said. "He was a horrible man. I hated him in a way I have never hated anyone else. He was truly despicable."

Trystan was shocked by her words, but Devlyn showed no emotion. "He was just a fisherman," the eldest said.

"No." Lyr's mother shook her head fiercely. "Your father was no fisherman. He was . . . This is difficult enough without interruption. If you will be so kind as to allow me to finish, it will be done soon enough."

Devlyn waved one hand. "Why not?"

"I despised your father," Isadora continued, "but your mother loved him very much. I saw only the bad in him, but Liane saw more and in the end she was right. He died saving her and the two of you."

"Liane?" Devlyn said. "You've made a mistake. Our mother's name is Bethlyn."

"Our father drowned when his boat went down in a storm," Trystan explained.

Isadora sighed. "No! Dammit, this is too complicated. Full explanations and the questions you will no doubt have must wait for another time." She turned her stern attention to the eldest. "Your name is not Devlyn. I was present when you were born. I saw you into this world, child."

Isadora took a deep breath, as if instilling herself with strength to continue. "You were tiny and wrinkled and you fought for your life. The name you were given at birth was Jahn, and you are the rightful emperor of Columbyana."

LEVEL THIRTEEN. KEELIA SAID THAT WAS THE SAFEST place in which to dispose of the crystal dagger. Lyr had no idea what or where his cousin was talking about but his mother had reacted fiercely to those two words. Level Thirteen.

Keelia admitted that some of the elder cousins had long ago overheard mention of the terrible place which so frightened the Fyne sisters, but Isadora had protected her children from the knowledge that the pit existed.

It had been a long and momentous day. His mother and her sisters had found what they'd sought, but at a price. Liane was dead. In the midst of everything else that was happening, she'd had to tell the twins about how their mother had died.

General Merin was quite distressed at the news that Devlyn Arndell was heir to the throne, and he'd asked more than once if it wasn't possible that the man he knew as Trystan Arndell was the eldest. Trystan, Merin was certain, would make a better emperor than his less responsible brother.

Lyr cared little for who ruled Columbyana. As soon as his duty was done, as soon as the crystal dagger was safe and the last of Ciro's Own had been defeated, he could return home to Tryfyn.

With Rayne? A part of him screamed *yes*, but in truth he was less than certain. Nothing about their relationship could be called normal. With the danger behind them, would she even care to stay with him? She'd said that she loved him, but perhaps she would think herself in love with any man who'd saved her from a demon's attentions. She was an Earth Goddess, after all, and surely she wanted more from life than warming his bed and giving him children.

Since the army had broken down their camp and taken to the road, with Arthes as their destination, Lyr had managed to avoid Rayne. He'd had long conversations with his mother, and he'd discussed battle plans with Merin. He and Keelia had discussed how best to dispose of the crystal dagger, once they reached Level Thirteen. When that was done, he'd gone to the head of the party and joined those who scouted ahead for trouble.

He did look back at Rayne on occasion. She rode with the Arndell brothers—the Beckyt brothers, more rightly—surrounded on all sides by sentinels whose only duty was to protect them from harm. The eldest, the one who was to be emperor, seemed almost amused by the turn of events. The other one did not seem at all amused. In any case, Rayne was safe. She was safer than she'd been in many years.

Riding far ahead of the others, his eyes peeled for trouble, Lyr was almost glad when two crazed swordsmen of Ciro's Own appeared. At the moment he welcomed the quick and easy fight.

IT WAS DARK BUT THE MOON WAS FULL AND THE PATH was wide and clear, so they rode onward. Rayne frowned as hours passed and Lyr did not join her even for a moment. He seemed to be well occupied, but surely he could spare her a word, or a smile.

Devlyn—Emperor Jahn—rode beside her. He'd been quiet and unusually thoughtful for most of the day, but now and then he spoke to her. They had become friends in days past. She hadn't had many friends in her life. She'd always been around servants who were kind to her, but until Lyr had come to rescue her, she hadn't known a single true friend.

In truth, Lyr had not come to rescue her at all. He'd come for the crystal dagger, and she'd been there.

Of the few friends she'd made since then, Til and Swaine had lost their lives in an act of unspeakable betrayal, and Segyn had turned out not to be any man's friend. That left Lyr, who was apparently avoiding her, and Devlyn, who was not actually Devlyn at all.

"Pretty girls should not look so glum," the new emperor said as they moved steadily forward.

"I'm not glum," she responded.

"Trust me, I am an expert on reading the expressions of beautiful women," he said with a touch of humor. "Your thoughts at this moment are not happy ones, I'd guess. I'd also guess those thoughts have something to do with a much-too-serious swordsman who has laid claim to you."

"Lyr has hardly laid claim to me," Rayne said softly.

"So I was right."

"Yes, you are right." She straightened her spine. "I'm being silly. There's much to be done in the waning days of war. Lyr will come to me when the time is right, when all is well and his duty is done—"

"For a man like Lyr, duty is never done," Devlyn interrupted. "For those like your Prince of Swords, there's always a fight, an injustice, a mission, a calling. Duty never dies, it just changes direction now and then."

While she wanted to argue with her friend, she knew he was right. "Where does that leave me?" she asked, her brow knitting in a frown.

Devlyn, Emperor Jahn, sighed. "It leaves you waiting until he decides he has the time for you. It leaves you alone for weeks and months at a time, while he makes himself a hero. It leaves you forever wondering when he'll come to you next, or if he'll come at all."

"But he loves me," Rayne protested without heat.

"Has he told you so?" the emperor asked. "Has he vowed his undying love and asked you to be his wife?"

Rayne hesitated, pursing her lips and then blowing out a bit of air. "No, not yet."

Devlyn rolled his eyes wildly. "Please tell me that you have not told the man that you love him."

"But I do love Lyr," Rayne said. "Of course I told him."

"More than once?" He sounded almost horrified.

"Yes."

Devlyn's sigh was one of pure disgust. "You have given him a mighty advantage, in laying your heart on the line as you have. Of course, being a woman, you can always take back your words. Women often do contradict themselves, and no one questions that fact."

"Why would I take the words back?" she asked. "I *do* love him."

"Do you want a man who will fight for you, my pretty gardener?"

"Lyr has fought for me."

Devlyn lifted his hand for emphasis. "No, he has fought for his destiny, he has fulfilled the prophesy, he has done what needed to be done in order to defeat an unimaginable threat to the world we live in. You, my pretty gardener, were no more than a pleasant reward for all his hard work."

"That isn't true!" she said, but her heart sank. She'd been the one to ask Lyr to lie with her. Hadn't she all but begged? He'd never had need to pursue her. She'd been the one to declare her love, again and again. She had all but thrown herself at Lyr over and over, and as any man likely would have, he'd simply caught her. "I'm an idiot," she said in a softer voice.

"No," Devlyn insisted. "You are no idiot. Naive, perhaps, but not an idiot. If you are content to sit back and wait for Lyr to come to you when and where he pleases, then by all means continue on as you have. I'm sure your time together is quite pleasurable. But if you want more . . ." He stopped and said in a slightly raised voice. "I'm a bit parched."

In moments a sentinel was there with a wineskin, which Devlyn took with a smile. "Being emperor is going to be excellent," he said when the sentinel had moved away. He took a long swig.

"If I want more?" Rayne prompted.

"Oh yes, now where was I?"

"If I want *more*," Rayne said again, her patience fading.

"Make him fight for *you*," Devlyn said. "Only for you. No demon, no prophesy, just the gardener and the Prince of Swords."

Her heart lurched. "I'm not sure I know how to make that happen."

"I do, so never fear on that front."

Rayne wondered if Lyr would fight for her, and that wondering made her realize that Devlyn was right. She had to know that she was more to Lyr than a pleasant convenience. Still . . . "What if he doesn't fight for me?"

Devlyn shrugged and took another swig of wine. When he was done, he wiped his mouth on his sleeve and said, "Then you haven't lost much at all, have you?"

SINCE THE NIGHTS WERE COOL BUT NOT HORRIBLY SO, when they stopped to rest no tents were pitched. Everyone, even the new emperor and his brother, even Lyr's mother, even Keelia and her man, even Rayne, slept beneath the stars. There were enough blankets to go around, two good fires, and plenty of food. The newly discovered heirs to the throne were well guarded throughout the night, but since they had run across only a handful of Ciro's Own in the past two days, the guard was just a precaution.

The palace which was their destination, the palace where Lyr had defeated the demon and where Ariana and Sian waited, rose in the distant moonlight. They would reach the palace tomorrow midday at their current rate of travel. There was much to happen after they arrived. A new emperor would be introduced, and there was a demon-filled dagger to be hidden in Level Thirteen.

And when that was done, Lyr could return home to Tryfyn.

He assumed that Rayne would come with him when that time came. She had no other place to go, after all. He couldn't imagine that she'd want to return to her father's house, and she had no family to turn to. He couldn't imagine deserting her. No, she was his responsibility as much as the dagger he carried with him.

It was true that his bride had been all but chosen for him, but if he returned to the Circle of Bacwyr with an Earth Goddess, surely he would be forgiven for not pursuing those plans.

He could not approach Rayne in the night, as she slept close to Keelia and Isadora and the well-guarded heirs. She had become friendly with both of the brothers, most particularly the one who was to be emperor. He should be glad that she was not alone while he did what had to be done, but something that could only be called jealousy tried to rise up within him. He stamped it back down. Rayne was entirely his, and he had no reason to be jealous.

When he rested in the night, it was near the edge of camp, where he could keep watch. If any danger approached, he could stop time and deal with the problem. It was unlikely that any who were left of Ciro's Own would approach such a large party, but it was not an impossibility.

All was quiet in the camp and beyond. All was well with the world once again.

There would be time to deal with the details of what was to come once he'd disposed of the dagger, and his mind wandered to those details. He would be returning to the Circle without those soldiers who had been closest to him. How would he explain away Segyn's betrayal? They had all been fooled. Even his mother had been shocked by the news that Lyr's second in command had been in league with the demon.

When the time came, perhaps it would be best to paint Segyn as yet another victim of the war with the Isen Demon, though Lyr suspected his most trusted warrior had been fooling him and many others for a long time before the demon had risen.

It was disheartening to know he could be fooled so easily and completely. Was nothing and no one ever as they appeared to be?

When Lyr slept in the early morning hours, he dreamt of Segyn and poisonous berries and traitorous swords, and then the dream turned more peaceful and Rayne was there. Naked, laughing, then turning away.

There were moments when he thought that he loved Rayne in a way he had never thought to love a woman, but did he know her at all?

There would be time to get to know her now that the war was done. There would be all the time in the world to make sure that they would be as compatible in a time of peace as they were in a time of conflict.

At sunrise the army moved toward the palace ahead. Lyr looked back only once to find Rayne in deep conversation with Devlyn Arndell . . . Emperor Jahn. There was that surge of jealousy again, though he knew he had no need to be jealous.

Lyr wasn't sure he cared much for the rightful heir. Like Merin, he suspected the more serious younger brother would've made a better ruler.

18

Since until a few weeks ago she'd lived in an iso-lated house far from the rest of the world, Rayne was un-derstandably awed by her first up-close glimpse of Arthes. Stone buildings of all sizes were crowded together, the streets which crossed this way and that swarmed with peo-ple who all seemed to be moving about with some purpose. In the center of it all the imperial palace rose ten stories into the sky.

The palace was an amazing construction. Balconies jut-ted out from the stone edifice here and there, and there were many, many windows which looked out over the city. The building itself spoke of power, and she could not imagine all that had taken place here, and would take place in years to come.

As they neared the palace, winding through the city streets, Lyr's mother shifted her horse in and out of the traveling party until she was near Rayne. Her presence, so close, made Rayne nervous. Isadora Hern was a commanding woman, a stern presence, a powerful witch . . . and most imposing of all, she was Lyr's mother. What had Lyr said to his mother about her? Which would be worse, the entire truth or nothing at all?

At first Rayne thought that perhaps the woman intended to speak to her about Lyr, to warn her away from her son, but then she decided it was more likely that Isadora Hern wanted to speak to the new emperor and his brother. Perhaps she was moving this way to apologize to them for speaking so harshly about their father.

Then again, she did not appear to be a lady who often apologized for anything.

Dark eyes settled on Rayne, and the uncertainty was ended. She herself was the intended destination, not the heirs. Rayne didn't know whether to be relieved or terrified.

"My son tells me you are an Earth Goddess," the lady said as she rode abreast of Rayne.

"So I have been told," Rayne said. "I'm not sure . . ."

"Never doubt your power," the woman said harshly. "Never deny who and what you are. Certainly never question what you have been sent to this earth to do."

Rayne had no idea what she'd seen sent to this earth to do. *To love Lyr* was her initial reaction, but at the moment she did not trust her heart or her mind. "I can only believe that what I am meant to do will be made clear to me in due time."

That response made Isadora smile. "Wise words for one so young." The friendly smile did not last long enough to suit Rayne. "Keelia tells me that you will be required to accompany my son into Level Thirteen in order to put the crystal dagger to rights."

Rayne twitched, startled by the news. "I don't know why I would be necessary for such a task."

"Neither do I, but as you said, the true path will be made

clear when the time is right." Her expression hardened. "I spent some time in Level Thirteen, and you should be warned that it is not a pleasant place. Many died there, many suffered there, and it is believed that it was in Level Thirteen that the Isen Demon was born. The thing which wished to destroy us all was born of damned souls who could not find their way to the light. Souls addicted to Panwyr and half starved and lost in darkness."

"Panwyr?" Rayne repeated.

"A very addictive and nasty drug. I'm glad to hear that it is unknown to you." She glanced back at the brothers, who were at this moment studying the palace much as Rayne did, in absolute amazement. "Their father tried to ruin me with that drug, many years ago. He forced it into my body and then threw me into a hole in the ground, where he expected me to suffer horribly and then die. He might've succeeded, if not for the diligence and care of loved ones who fought for me."

"If I may say so, m'lady, I would suggest that your strength of will certainly played a part in that victory."

"You do not know me well enough to be aware of my will, or lack of it."

"No, m'lady, but I know your son well enough, and I can see much of you in him."

"Lyr is somewhat like me," she said, "but he is more like his father. Heaven help us all," she added with a touch of humor.

"Perhaps, m'lady, but I suspect a man such as he cannot be born of a weak woman."

At this, Isadora smiled. "It doesn't seem right for a Goddess to call me 'm'lady.' Isadora will do just fine."

Though it was difficult to tell, Rayne suspected the invitation was an approval of sorts. "I would be happy to do so."

Isadora's expression as they neared the palace was less than happy. "I swore I would never set foot in this palace again. I almost died here." She shook off her melancholy. "I also met my husband here. Lucan courted me very well in this palace. I suppose I should attempt to remember the good times and forget the rest. It will likely be weeks before my husband and sisters arrive, since they do not have the advantage, or disadvantage, of Keelia's flight."

Rayne suspected it was easier said than done to dismiss such bad memories. "Did your husband court you diligently?"

"Very much so."

"He . . . he fought for you?"

"That he did," Isadora said warmly.

"Then you are a fortunate woman indeed," Rayne said. She looked to Lyr, who marched beside Merin with his attentions ahead, and then she glanced back at Devlyn, who bestowed upon her a wink and a grin. She supposed she would have to stop thinking of him as Devlyn and begin viewing him as Emperor Jahn, even though he looked and acted very little like the ruler of an entire country.

Isadora looked back, too, and she caught the tail end of the wink. "There are those who will welcome the twins because the blood of emperors flows through their veins, but there are others who will remember Sebestyen and not be so welcoming of his sons."

"Will any question that they are his blood?" She did not want to see the brothers pulled into yet another kind of war.

Isadora's laughter was harsh. "There will be no questioning their heritage. The boys both look like him in some way. The younger is his spitting image, and the emperor . . . but for the color of his hair, the new emperor could be Sebestyen made over if he does not receive the correct guidance."

"The new emperor is a good man." Rayne was quick to defend her friend. "He would not do any of the things you have told me his father did."

Isadora sighed tiredly. "I hope you're right, Rayne. I dearly do hope you're right."

THREE DAYS AFTER THEIR ARRIVAL, A SMALL ARMY OF sorts descended into Level Thirteen. Lyr, with the crystal dagger; Rayne, though Lyr was not yet certain why she was required; Sian, with his wizard's light; Keelia, with her knowledge of what was necessary to bury the demon once and for all.

Ariana and Isadora waited near the hatch in the floor as the others were lowered down by ropes in the hands of two strong sentinels, with Joryn's assistance. Lyr had never seen his mother so pale, but she refused to wait in a less harsh place in the palace until this deed was done. Sian refused to allow Ariana to visit the dark space beneath the palace again, and for once she listened to her husband.

Emperor Jahn, who'd been crowned that very morning, had insisted on being present for this endeavor, but he'd been left above with the women, as he was not necessary for what needed to be done here today.

Orbs of purple wizard's light glowed from Sian's palms, lighting the musty prison. Everyone was on edge, affected by the darkness and history of this place.

Everyone but Rayne, who stepped bravely forward. Sian had to walk directly behind her to make sure she didn't wander into darkness. Keelia followed Sian, and Lyr guarded the rear of the party.

"All is not entirely malevolent here," Rayne said. "What happened in this place was indeed terrible, but the stones are merely stones, and the dirt is merely dirt." She took a deep breath as she led them away from the open hatch high above. "Do you see the path which calls us forward? I see it, and it is quite lovely. There is peace here, peace lost in the darkness." Soon only Sian's magical light lit Level Thirteen, as Rayne led them down a narrowing path. Naturally formed stone walls curved on either side, and Rayne trailed one hand along the stone wall as if it were a comfort to her.

Earth Goddess, Lyr reminded himself. This was her domain, as much as her gardens or the swamp water she'd controlled with her breath.

He did not know her at all, and she did not know him. That was a truth he had ignored until now. What awaited her in future days, this Earth Goddess who was unafraid when wizards and seers trembled?

The path widened, and Lyr heard Keelia and Sian breathe easier once more. Soon the widening path opened onto a grotto, where an underground spring provided a gentle rush of water and fungus grew wild.

Rayne turned her head and smiled. "Here. The path ends here."

Keelia walked around Sian, who increased his wizard's light to illuminate the large space. "Yes," she said. "The dagger must be placed beneath. Beneath what?" Her brow furrowed slightly.

The Anwyn Queen did not see precisely what was needed, but Rayne did. She pointed at the stream of water and then turned her head to look directly at Lyr. For a moment he thought he saw pain in her eyes, but then the pain was gone. "Are you ready?" she asked.

He nodded and moved past the others to stand beside Rayne.

Rayne faced the water and exhaled gently, forcing a rush of breath across the surface of the water much as she had in the swamp. The water responded, parting a little bit at first and then separating, peeling away from the bottom to reveal smooth, hard rock. What appeared to be the same type of crystal which had once formed the dagger shot through the rock and sparkled in Sian's light.

Rayne blindly took Lyr's hand, but she did not look at him. All of her attention was on the rock which had once been beneath the water. She squeezed his hand tightly and took a deep breath, and at her silent command the rock began to split much as the water had.

Keelia gasped as the very walls of the grotto shook. Sian uttered what Lyr recognized as a curse word in the ancient tongue of wizards. Rayne did not respond to the shaking at all. She focused all of her attention on the rock, as it formed a chasm that grew deeper and deeper, and a little bit wider.

The opening of the rock and the vibration stopped, and Rayne glanced over her shoulder to Keelia. "Enough?"

Keelia shook her head. "Not quite."

Rayne squeezed Lyr's hand hard, and once again the rock cracked and split. How could such force be created by one so delicate and small? Rayne was small, but she was not without power. The sounds of the rock coming apart were deafening, as if the earth itself groaned and protested. Perhaps it did. Rayne continued to work at the rock until Keelia said softly:

"There."

Rayne released Lyr's hand reluctantly, her fingers trailing over his palm, and then she nodded at him. Now it was his turn. He took the blackened crystal dagger from the sack he always carried, as he could not bear to have the weapon against his skin. He peeled away the purple fabric in which he had found it wrapped so long ago, and held the weapon over the chasm Rayne had opened.

He hesitated. "Will the dagger break when it hits the rock below?"

"No," both Keelia and Rayne answered. They sounded very sure, and he had no choice but to trust these two extraordinary women.

Lyr held the dagger over the opening for a moment, and then he released it. He let the dagger drop into the chasm. He heard it fall, scraping against rock, pinging as crystal met stone, and then, finally falling silent.

That was it, or so he thought. Rayne stepped forward, removed the blue stone she had worn around her neck for so long, and dropped it in after the dagger, chain and all. The gem also hit against the stone, but the sound it made was lighter, as if it sang a song as it fell. The chain gave the occasional soft cling, until it was too far down for them to hear.

Rayne glanced up at him. "For keeping," she said softly.

That done, she closed the rock as easily as she had opened it. Again, the walls of the grotto shook. Small stones loosened from the walls and fell, some splashing into the water, others pinging sharply against the rock floor. Keelia began to back toward their exit.

"We need to go. Now."

"Not yet," Rayne said calmly. She saw the rock she'd opened firmly sealed, and then she allowed the water to rush over the dagger's burial place. She no longer moved the earth, but the damage had been done and larger rocks began to fall.

This time Keelia screamed. "Run!"

Lyr scooped Rayne up, his arm easily encircling her waist, and followed a fleeing Keelia and Sian. As they reached the exit, a large boulder came loose and fell directly behind him. He jumped into the hallway, Rayne in his arms, and hit the ground as the boulder all but sealed the grotto.

And then the shaking stopped. A few small pebbles continued to fall, but the danger was past.

Lyr sat up. It was finally done. Ciro was dead, the demon was buried deep in the earth, and at last count, most of Ciro's Own had been accounted for. The prophesy had been fulfilled, and Rayne was safe. In the dim purple light he caught her eye and held it.

"Can we get out of this place?" Sian suggested sharply when Lyr and Rayne did not immediately rise from the ground.

Lyr jumped up and offered Rayne a steadying hand as she stood. Everyone was anxious to leave this place and what was left of the Isen Demon behind, once and for all.

He heard his mother's relieved words first when Keelia appeared beneath the hatch. The others spoke also, in relief and congratulations. Ropes were lowered, and one at a time those who had ventured into Level Thirteen were pulled up into the light. The women first, then Sian, then Lyr.

When Lyr reached the top, Emperor Jahn peered into the darkness. "My father placed his enemies in this pit?"

"Yes." Isadora's voice shook as she answered.

The new ruler studied the hole in the ground for a moment and then lifted stern eyes to the sentinels who had done their duty in lowering and raising those who were forced to venture into Level Thirteen. "Fill it," he said simply.

"Pardon me, m'lord?" the elder of the two sentinels said.

"Fill. It."

"With what?" the sentinel asked, adding a belated, "M'lord."

"Rock, dirt, wood. I don't care what you use, but *fill* it."

"It will take years," Sian said wearily.

"I care not how long it takes," Jahn said tersely. "I want it done. I command it to be done." He tried a smile which was somewhat miserable. "My first command."

In a voice that continued to tremble, Isadora said, "You might make a decent emperor after all."

Jahn did manage a true smile then. "Only time will tell, m'lady."

Lyr could not wait to leave this palace. His mother had already said she would wait for her husband and the rest of their party to return before traveling back to Tryfyn, but Lyr was anxious to be on his way. Rayne would come with him, of course. He stepped around Keelia and Joryn, intent on speaking to Rayne about when they might leave, but the emperor cut into his path and offered his arm to her before Lyr could do so.

"Earth Goddess, I am told," he said, respect in his voice.

"So they say, m'lord."

The emperor and Rayne led the way, and all others followed.

"I believe it would be most excellent to have an Earth Goddess at my command."

Lyr waited for Rayne to tell this man who was supposedly her friend that she would never be at his command, but she did not respond at all. She did not look back at him either, though certainly she knew that he wished to speak with her about their travel plans.

"Celebration tonight!" the emperor shouted as he, with Rayne on his arm, sprinted up the stairs. "We have much reason to rejoice!"

Lyr hung back, moving slowly as the others did. He had never chased after a woman before, and he did not intend to start now.

The emperor and Rayne disappeared from view fairly quickly. Ariana and Sian, arm in arm, were not far behind them. Keelia and Joryn increased their step, anxious to be well away from today's chore. The sentinels stayed behind to contemplate the task of filling in Level Thirteen.

Lyr found himself plodding up the steps beside his mother.

"I did not believe I would ever be able to say that there's hope in this world for one of Sebestyen Beckyt's sons, but I'm beginning to think that boy might make a more than worthy leader."

"It's a bit soon to pass that judgment, isn't it?" Lyr asked, only a bit sour.

"He is very young," she said thoughtfully.

"He's older than I am," Lyr grumbled.

Lyr's mother took his arm. He wasn't sure if it was for moral support or for physically necessary assistance. There were lots of stairs between Level Twelve and ground level, Ten, and there would be more after that before they reached their quarters. "You've been horribly spoiled," she said without heat or emotion.

"Thank you, Mother," he responded with more than a little sarcasm.

"It's true. You've been gifted in so many ways, and everything you've ever wanted has always been given to you."

"I've earned my position."

"You were born to your position." She shrugged slightly. "You earned the worthiness and respect of that position. And still, nothing has been particularly difficult for you. Your talent for swords and your gift for time have always come easily. Yes, you work, but you do not toil. You do not *sweat*. Do you know the difference?"

"No."

"You have never had to work particularly hard for what you want. You ask, you reach, and it is yours." A smile tugged at her lips. "You might have to sweat for what you want this time."

"I have no idea what you're talking about."

His mother sighed. "I am not blind, Lyr. The girl you've

been avoiding for days? This woman you tell me is an Earth Goddess?"

By this time, all the others were out of sight. "I thought you wanted me to marry a Tryfynian princess."

"I do. I did," she amended. "All mothers want their children to be happy, above all else. I worry about you, Lyr, because you don't often seem truly happy."

"There was little happiness in what I was called to do."

"But you've done what you were called to do. You succeeded wonderfully. Now what?"

Now what? Good question. "I don't know."

"I do. Sweep the girl off her feet. Woo her. Court her. Get down on your knees and beg her to be yours."

Lyr twitched. "I do not get down on my knees for anyone."

"Brat," his mother said under her breath.

It was not the first time in his life that his mother had accused him of being spoiled, so he did not take the allegation to heart. "In truth I do not trust my own judgment at this time. Look at what happened to Segyn. He was in league with a demon, and I did not see the darkness in him. He killed two Circle Warriors, he almost killed me, he almost killed Rayne. And I never saw it coming."

"None of us did. He fooled many." No one could sigh quite like Isadora Hern. "Segyn betrayed you and that's terrible, but for heaven's sake, Lyr, let it go."

"Let it *go*?"

"Yes!" Her step slowed. He realized she was tiring so his step slowed, too. "If you want sympathy for all that has happened to you, wait for your Aunt Sophie to arrive. She'll coddle you if you wish it. She'll give you a hug and a pat on the cheek and she'll tell you what a horrible episode you've endured. And when that's done, nothing will have changed."

"What do you suggest?" Lyr asked sharply.

"Trust your heart," his mother responded quickly, a touch of warmth in her voice. "Trust your strength and your integrity and your mind as well, but most of all, you must trust your heart. It will guide you."

FOR MONTHS RAYNE HAD BEEN CHAINED IN THE CELLAR with no time for styling her hair and putting on pretty clothes. After Lyr had rescued her, they'd traveled almost constantly, with even the quickest bath a true luxury.

She'd been well cared for since coming to the palace, and on this evening the emperor had sent not one but three maids to assist her. As in days past, he had ordered her not to inquire as to Lyr's whereabouts, not to so much as mention his name. She was to be pampered, and she was not to give a moment's thought to any man. Easier said than done. For all she knew, Lyr had ridden away from the palace as soon as the dagger was buried!

Much as she hated that idea, she had grudgingly come to agree with Devlyn on that point. If Lyr rode away from her now, then he had never loved her and she'd lost nothing.

So why was her stomach currently lodged in her throat?

Her hair was washed and styled, and though she'd suggested that she could prompt a garden plant to flower, Devlyn had insisted that jewels were more appropriate for tonight's celebration. One of the maids had positioned a sparkling emerald adornment in her short hair. The bath was luxurious, warm and scented with rose oil. The dress they had provided was made of a fabric she had never seen before, one which sparkled green and gold at once, and which clung to her form in a way which revealed more than it disguised.

It even clung to her belly and surprisingly tender breasts in a way that told her it was not her imagination that a bulge was forming there. A child, the child Gwyneth had promised her, was already growing inside her. Lyr's child, though she did not wish to tell him of its existence until he had decided whether or not she was worth fighting for.

One of the maids applied cosmetics to her face, but not much. Rayne's eyes were lined, and a touch of color was added to her lips.

When they were finished with her, all the girls smiled widely, pleased with their efforts. Together they led Rayne to a mirror and posed her before it, and for a moment she did not recognize herself.

Her breasts looked too large in this dress, and she did not look entirely like herself with the dark liner beneath her eyes. The hairstyle . . . she found the new hairstyle oddly appealing, and the jewel there was eye-catching without being too ornate. She supposed it would do.

Rayne had already decided that she was not going to follow Devlyn's plan, not exactly. Lying did not come easily to her, and she could not bring herself to play games with the man she loved. But in many ways the new emperor was right in suggesting caution where Lyr was concerned.

Even if she was Fynnian's daughter, she deserved to spend her life with a man who loved her.

19

THE PROPHESY OF THE FIRSTBORN HAD BEEN FULFILLED, but the duties of those who had been called were not yet complete. Sian and Ariana had agreed to remain in the palace for a few months, in order to help the rediscovered twins Jahn and Alixandyr learn what was expected of them. The ministers and priests a new emperor might normally turn to for assistance had either escaped or been killed. Some would return, when news of the victory spread. Others would need to be replaced by those who had proven their worth in the war, but that rebuilding would take months.

Keelia and Joryn were anxious to return home to the Mountains of the North, but they had decided to remain in Arthes until Queen Mother Juliet and her husband Ryn—Keelia's parents—reached the capital city. Then they, along with those Anwyn soldiers who had joined in the fight, would return home to begin the rejoining of their people—Anwyn and Caradon.

The prison on Level Twelve was nearly filled to capacity with traitors, thieves, and a handful of Ciro's Own who had survived. It was thought inevitable that the few remaining soldiers of Ciro's army would have to be executed. There could be no redemption for the soulless.

One particularly important prisoner had been caught as she'd attempted to flee the capital city. Many people recognized her as one of Ciro's closest companions. Some days she referred to herself as Diella, but on other days she insisted her name was Lilia. There were a few in the palace who demanded that she be put to death immediately, but others were understandably squeamish about executing a woman who was with child—no matter what nature of child she might carry. The woman remained in Level Twelve, hysterical, perhaps mad, and oddly demanding for a prisoner.

Lyr was very glad the woman's fate was not in his hands.

There were those who expected bad blood between the brothers, those who expected a struggle for power. But while they had experienced or heard of Sebestyen and Arik's ways, they did not know the ways of these boys who had been taught to stand together. That's exactly what they did. Jahn and Alix—Devlyn and Trystan—they stood together as their mother had taught them.

Lyr had reluctantly agreed to remain in the palace and attend the emperor's coronation festivities before beginning the journey home. It seemed he would be making that journey alone. As much as his mother claimed to hate this palace, she insisted upon remaining until the traveling party from which Keelia had collected her in such an unusual, winged manner arrived in Arthes. She wished to say a proper farewell to her sisters, since it might be awhile before the Fyne family found the time for another reunion, and in a rare moment of vulnerability, Isadora Hern had confessed that she already missed her husband terribly and could not bear to travel toward home without him.

Though Lyr had accepted the invitation when it had come to him, in truth he had never cared much for formal celebrations of any type. He occasionally endured the festivities in the Tryfynian King's court because it was expected of him, as Prince of Swords, but he had never enjoyed meaningless chatter or shrill music, which always came with the expectation that he would dance.

But tonight he attended the emperor's celebration. He might've made excuses and waited until morning to present himself to Rayne and ask her about travel plans, but in truth he did not trust Emperor Jahn or the way the ruler looked at the Earth Goddess who so obviously impressed him.

As in Tryfyn, the women present had taken extra efforts to make themselves beautiful. Thanks to Ciro's gutting of the palace, there were few minister's wives or imperial relations to lend beauty to the relatively small gathering. Ariana and Keelia and Lyr's mother were present, as was the middle-aged wife of the Minister of Agriculture, a sturdy woman who had escaped the palace but had remained hidden in the city. She, her husband, and their daughter had returned soon after Ciro's death.

And then there was Rayne, who was too beautiful for words. Literally. For a while after arriving in the warm, music-filled ballroom Lyr did not even approach her. He did not know what to say. For the first time in his life, he was anxious. It was not a welcome feeling.

The women who attended Emperor Jahn's gala were all surrounded by attentive men. There were soldiers who had earned this celebration, the new emperor and his brother, as well as Sian, Joryn, and a handful of ministers who had rushed to the palace when it became known that Ciro had

been defeated. Many of the ministers were less than
thrilled to have Sebestyen's sons in residence, but the twins
were doing their best to charm them. One at a time. They
were succeeding. Even those who had hated Sebestyen realized that his sons were better suited to this palace than a
demon-possessed soul sucker.

Emperor Jahn also seemed intent on charming Rayne,
Lyr noticed from the wall he had propped himself against.
The man smiled too widely, winked too often, and touched
her as if he had the right. True, he only touched Rayne on
the elbow to guide her, or else he held her at a respectable
distance as they danced, but still . . . he touched her.

When the emperor leaned in close and whispered in
Rayne's ear, Lyr pushed himself away from the wall and
weaved past the revelers. It was time to get this over with,
one way or another. He had come to the celebration armed
as if he were going into battle. In truth he would feel naked
without his swords, and his position required him to be
prepared for battle at all times. At least he no longer carried the blasted crystal dagger. A long sword hung to one
side, a short sword to the other. A small dagger of steel
housed in a leather sheath was strapped to his thigh.

He was well armed, and yet he felt oddly unprotected.
Vulnerable in a way he had never experienced before.

As if she knew he was approaching, Rayne turned. She
smiled at him, and then her smile faded away. He supposed
his own expression did not invite grins or winks or flirta-
tious banter. If that was what Rayne wanted from a man,
then he would be leaving her here. His stomach flipped
over at the very idea.

"May I have a word?" he asked, his voice a touch too
sharp.

"Of course." With her short hair and the cosmetics
which had been sparsely and finely applied, Rayne's eyes

looked larger than ever. They looked deeper, darker, more magical. They were the kind of eyes that could suck a man in if he allowed it.

The emperor did not move away from Rayne's side, as one might expect in such a situation. Lyr gave the man a dismissive bow. The emperor ignored that broad hint. Was this new ruler a blind fool or an interfering scoundrel who had designs on a woman who did not belong to him?

Rayne turned to the emperor and placed a familiar hand on his arm. "It's all right. Lyr and I need to talk, I suppose."

"This is a celebration," Emperor Jahn responded. "Your friend does not look at all festive."

Rayne gave the man a smile which was too intimate for Lyr's liking. "Festive or not, I would like a moment. Please."

At the softly spoken please, the emperor nodded and turned away to offer his attentions to the woman he called Cousin Ariana.

"You look lovely," Lyr said to Rayne as Ariana and the emperor walked away. No, he did not flirt and woo, but that didn't mean he had to jump directly to the matter at hand. Besides, he spoke only the truth. She did look lovely, more lovely than he had imagined any woman could.

"Would you like to dance?" Rayne offered her hand, and Lyr knew he was supposed to take it. Soothing music filled the room, music without missed notes or the squeal of improperly played instruments.

"I don't dance. Sorry."

"Oh." Her arm lowered slowly, and he could tell by the slight pucker of her lips and the cut of her eyes that she was disappointed.

Instead of dwelling on her obvious disenchantment, he plowed forward. "I have come to ask you what plans you might have, now that Ciro is dead and the demon is no longer a danger."

"In truth, I have no plans."

It was an honest enough answer, one which thankfully left him the opportunity to issue an invitation. "You are welcome to travel with me to Tryfyn. The Circle of Bacwyr is home to many fine wizards who would be happy to instruct you and assist you in learning all your talents."

"That's very kind of you. Devlyn . . . I mean, Emperor Jahn, has made a similar offer."

Lyr's jaw went hard. His teeth clenched. What did Rayne expect of him? Was he supposed to get down on his knees and beg her to stay with him? Was he supposed to vie with an emperor for her attentions? Many women played games with the men in their lives, he knew from observation. He had never expected that Rayne was of that type.

"What do you want?" he asked simply.

She hesitated, and then she said, "Honestly, Lyr, I don't know."

There had been many occasions when she'd sworn that she loved him, but the situations had been different than the one they now found themselves in. They had not known how much time they had left on this earth, whether or not they would succeed, whether or not anyone had a future. They had barreled forward as if each day was their last, and in truth it might've been. Now there was no rush.

They had all the time in the world.

"I leave for Tryfyn in the morning," he said without emotion. "If you decide what you want before then, let me know." With that he turned away, and as he walked away from Rayne he knew his mother had been right. He'd never had to fight for anything, and he didn't know precisely *how*. Was Rayne worth fighting for? Of course she was. He had no need to worry or to rush. She was young. He was young. There was no longer any need for haste. If she did not ask if she could travel with him to Tryfyn, he would return to Arthes in the spring, and perhaps then . . .

Before Lyr reached the doorway, his feet grew heavy. So did his heart. Perhaps there was no need for haste, but months of waiting meant months of his life spent—wasted—without Rayne in it. He did not want to leave her here. He did not even want to spend another night without her beside him. The past few days had been torturous, and he was actually considering leaving her here until *spring*?

Yes, his mother had been right. Everything in life he cared about had come to him too easily, without sweat, without effort. His gift made defeat in battle all but impossible. That magical gift, combined with a lifetime of honing his skills as a swordsman, made failure almost impossible. Until now. Now, when it mattered more than ever before.

At the doorway Lyr stopped and turned to watch as Emperor Jahn moved once again to Rayne's side. He knew what he had to do . . . and he also knew his swords would not help him tonight.

RAYNE SMILED AT THE EMPEROR, BUT IT WASN'T EASY. "You were wrong, it seems."

"If you had followed my plan precisely, all would be as you wish it to be."

"I couldn't bring myself to lie to Lyr and tell him you'd asked me to be your . . . your . . ."

"Mistress, concubine, lover," Devlyn supplied when she stumbled. "If you had taken my advice, your Prince of Swords would not have walked away from you so easily."

"I don't want him with a lie," Rayne whispered.

She simply wanted to know that Lyr loved her, that he chose her . . . that he would fight for her if necessary. Not to save her life, but to claim her heart. It did not seem too much to ask for.

"You must've said something right," Devlyn said with a half-smile. "He's coming back."

Rayne began to turn to see if the emperor was telling the truth or not, but he stopped her with firm hands on her shoulders. "Do *not* turn to watch," he whispered. "Don't allow him to realize that you stand here impatiently awaiting his return."

Rayne smiled up at her friend and laid her hand on his arm. "I thank you for everything, but there will be no more false faces or less-than-honest words between me and the man I love. I know you mean well, but that cannot be my way."

Devlyn gave her a dismayed shake of the head as he released his hold. "You two are perfectly suited, you know? Noble to a fault, both of you."

"Thank you."

"It was not a compliment," the emperor muttered as Rayne turned about to see that Lyr was indeed striding toward her once again. The expression on his face was no more relaxed, no more filled with love or affection, than it had been when he'd left her standing here.

And then he moved close enough for her to see the fire in his eyes.

When he reached her, he did not so much as slow down or look at the emperor who stood so close. With grace and without any visible doubt, he dropped to one knee before her.

"Come with me," Lyr said, his voice even and strong. "I don't want to spend another minute of my life without you in it."

Rayne's heart caught in her throat, and she found herself surprised speechless. What had happened to bring about this change? A moment ago Lyr had very willingly walked away from her, and now . . .

"The Earth Goddess is going to remain here," Devlyn interjected. Rayne tried to subtly shoo her friend away, but he either didn't see the restrained motion or else he ignored her. She suspected the latter.

"No, she's not." Lyr caught her eye and held it. "Unless that's what she truly wants. All her life she's been told how to live, what to say and do, and even what to think. She'll have no more of that. I would never keep from her that which she most desires. The decision is hers, not mine and certainly not *yours*. What do you want, Rayne?"

"I told you minutes ago, I don't know," she said, and then she caught her breath and blurted. "But that's not entirely true. I know very well what I want, I just don't know if it's possible."

Lyr took her hand, and for a moment Rayne waited for the others in the room to go still, she waited for Lyr to use his gift to separate them from the rest of the world, to cut them off from all those who watched and listened. That didn't happen. "I know what I want," he said without hesitation. "I want you. It's that simple, Rayne."

She remembered her mother's words, as well as Lyr's assertion that he had no heart to give. "Will you give me the keeping of your heart?"

"You already have it."

Devlyn, blast him, had to interfere again. "If you think I will allow you to ride off to Tryfyn with my Earth Goddess . . ."

Very smoothly, Lyr drew a short bladed sword and pointed the tip at the emperor. He did not rise or take his eyes from her, even as sentinels moved in to protect their ruler. People who were close enough to see the threatening move gasped. Ariana uttered a disgusted, "Lyr!" The music stopped, inexpertly and with a screeching of a shrill wind instrument.

Devlyn held the soldiers off with a lift of his hand. "You dare to threaten me?" Rayne wondered if the others heard the hint of teasing in his voice.

"Yes," Lyr answered.

"Draw blood and there will be war."

"Then I suggest you back away and leave us be. This does not concern you."

Devlyn raised his eyebrows slightly. "Would you go to war over a woman, Prince of Swords?"

"If that woman is Rayne, yes," Lyr responded. "Yes, I would."

Out of the corner of her eye Rayne saw Lyr's cousins and their men headed this way. Ariana did not looked pleased, but a smile touched Keelia's golden eyes and the corners of her mouth. That good humor eased Rayne's fears. Judging by the Anwyn Queen's expression, all would be well tonight.

Devlyn backed away, a smug smile on his face. Others in the immediate vicinity looked concerned, but the new emperor dismissed what some might've considered a threat. Even the cousins, the other two warriors called by the Prophesy of the Firstborn, halted their rush to Lyr's side.

Lyr stood and sheathed his sword. "Tell me now, Rayne, what do you want?"

"I want all of you, heart and soul and body."

"That you have."

She wanted no more secrets between them. "I want the baby I carry inside me now, and in the years to come I want more."

For the first time on this long evening, Lyr smiled at her. "Baby?"

Rayne nodded her head.

She had forgotten that others were listening, until Lyr's mother said, "Stars above, I'm going to be a *grandmother*."

"Marry me," Lyr said, his voice lowered. He sounded so confident it was possible no one but her heard the uncertainty.

Rayne smiled. "Yes."

"Now."

She laughed. "Now?"

"Can't the emperor perform the ceremony?"

"You don't even like him," Rayne whispered.

"If he marries us, I will make myself like him well enough."

Devlyn looked to Sian for guidance. "Is it allowed?"

Sian nodded once, which was enough.

Devlyn raised his voice. "I admire this woman extraordinarily well, and I'm uncertain about handing her over to a Tryfynian cretin who would dare to threaten me with a sword, at my own party, no less."

"If I'd wanted to harm you, you wouldn't be speaking at this moment," Lyr said confidently.

"Yes, yes, I'm sure that's true," Devlyn said dismissively. "Still, I wouldn't be doing my duty if I handed one of my most precious subjects over to a foreigner who might not care for her properly. I must conduct a proper interrogation to assure myself that you are worthy."

"Interrogation?" Rayne tried to get the emperor's attention and call a halt to his foolishness, but she was ignored.

"Do you love her?" Devlyn asked.

"Madly," Lyr responded without hesitation.

"Will you treasure her as she was meant to be treasured?"

"Yes."

"Will you dance with her if she wishes it?"

"If she will teach me, yes."

"Will you . . ."

Lyr held onto Rayne tightly as he waved one hand to bring time for all others to a standstill. "I wanted to do this in front of everyone, to be open and honest and to put everything I am before you and all these people. But by my way of thinking, some things should be just for us," he said. "I love you. I can't imagine spending a single day of my life without you in it. Something good came out of this horrible war with Ciro, because it led me to you. I love you," he said again.

"I love you, too."

"Tell your friend to speed things up, if you don't mind. We have better things to do tonight than provide entertainment for his coronation festivities."

Time began again, and all continued on as if it had never been interrupted.

". . . see to her safety in all . . ." Devlyn continued.

"M'lord," Rayne said, interrupting the emperor in midsentence. "Lyr will care for me well, I assure you. Can the ceremony proceed?"

"Now?" Devlyn asked.

Rayne smiled at Lyr. "Yes, at this very moment, if you please."

"A wedding to mark new beginnings!" an unseen reveler said with glee, raising a sword high in the still ballroom.

"To peace," another said, raising yet another sword.

"To new life," Ariana said. To be in keeping with the others, she smoothly snatched a sword from a nearby sentinel, and with a grin she raised it into the air.

"To the new emperor!" a tipsy minister cried, raising a small dagger above his head. A few—including Devlyn himself—laughed at the pathetic blade which was lifted among the swords.

It seemed everyone had an idea of what should be celebrated here tonight, and one at a time they called out their hopes and dreams and joys. Peace, babies, family, loyalty . . . all were saluted in preface to her marriage.

Lyr drew his long sword and looked Rayne in the eye. "To love," he said, and though his words were loud enough for all to hear, she knew they were meant for her ears alone.

She drew the short sword Lyr wore at his side and raised it high, gently touching the blade against his. "To love."

Epilogue

NOT LONG AFTER EMPEROR JAHN TOOK HIS PLACE IN THE palace, a prisoner locked in a cell on Level Twelve gave birth to a little girl. Though the baby came early and was very small, she was extraordinarily pretty. Diella—or perhaps Lilia—died shortly after delivering her child into the world. Right before she passed, she named the little girl Ksana.

Knowing that Diella had been involved with Ciro and the Isen Demon, the parentage of the child came into question. Young as she was, the baby bore a striking resemblance to the deceased fair-haired prince. There were those who wished to do away with the baby girl, as it was possible she was not entirely human. But of course, it's difficult to see evil in a child, so Ksana was taken by a kind woman who could never see darkness in a newborn's face. Sophie Fyne Varden.

When Isadora revealed to her youngest sister that the Ksana flower which grew in Tryfyn was beautiful but deadly, Sophie insisted on changing the baby's name. She honored the mother's wish in naming the girl for a flower, but she chose one which was sweet and touched with good magic. Linara.

Sophie and Kane adopted Linara, knowing well that she might be very different from their own children. The years to come might not be easy, but Linara was Arik's granddaughter, and Sophie still had very fond memories of the former rebel and emperor. Besides, she believed with all her heart that love could conquer anything, even the blood of a demon.

She had expected to travel for home with no one but her husband and a wetnurse for company. That would've suited her just fine, but Isadora and her husband Lucan decided to travel to the Southern Province and visit for a short while. Sophie did not say so, but she knew her sister wanted to keep an eye on Linara to see that the baby grew and behaved as a baby should. It would be good to spend more time with Isadora, time when they did not have a curse or a prophesy or a momentous task at hand.

As she and her traveling party left the palace heading for home Sophie asked her husband—only once—"What if there are more like her?"

Kane did not respond, but she knew what he was thinking. Maybe there were more children like Linara, but that was a problem for another day.

This day was fine, and there was no room for borrowed troubles which might or might not come to pass. Sophie, Juliet, and Isadora would all become grandmothers in the coming year, and that was cause for celebration.

Yes, all was well. Ariana and Sian were settled in the palace, at least for now. Sebestyen's sons would need their assistance for a while longer. There had been a time when Sophie had hated the imperial palace, but the palace did not feel as dark as it once had, in spite of what had happened there in the past year. Love in abundance had returned light to a place which had once been dark. Ariana and Sian and their child would be happy there, until the time came for them to make their life elsewhere.

Keelia and Joryn were on their way back to the Mountains of the North, where they would marry in The City. They would work to bring their people together, and they'd have children who would be both Anwyn and Caradon. Joryn very much wished to find his friend Druson along the way, and Keelia assured him that they would. Or rather, Druson would find *them*. To bring Caradon and Anwyn together, they would need the man who was now called Grandfather, a man who possessed the knowledge of the ancients. Juliet and Ryn traveled in that direction, too, but as usual they had taken off alone. That was their way. It suited them.

Lyr and his bride, Rayne, traveled in a leisurely fashion toward his home—now her home, too—in Tryfyn. Wherever they passed, flowers bloomed. When the bride laughed, it was not at all unusual for a few sparkling snowflakes to fall. Just a few. Rayne had spent her entire life in isolation, and Lyr gladly shared his world with her. If they wished for fruits or vegetables that were not in season, those wishes came true at a whisper. If they wanted to stop for an entire day to enjoy a perfect view and make love with leisure, they did so. Now and then, time stopped for a kiss. Life was good.

The newly married couple loved often, laughed frequently, and argued with light hearts about names for their first child. They discussed the possibility of introducing Emperor Jahn and his brother Alix to one or two Tryfynian princesses.

And they stayed far, far away from anything resembling a swamp.

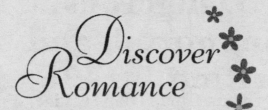